A LEARNING CURVE

D.M. ROSE

Published by New Generation Publishing in 2016

ISBN: 978-1-78719-147-1

www.newgeneration-publishing.com

Cover design by Jacqueline Abromeit
Cover photo by Anthony G. Miller

New Generation Publishing

AUTHOR'S NOTE

The Princess Victoria's Bounty and other charities and organizations, their clients and staff described in this book are fictional and not based on any current or former charities or organizations or individuals living or deceased. Any presumed likenesses are purely coincidental.

For good teachers everywhere, especially Miss Wells, Sister Anselm and Mr David Letchford. Their legacy lives on.

Other books by the author:

The Storyteller
Death of Eternity
Another country
Watching the World Go By
Fellow Travellers
On Reflection

CHAPTER ONE

Perry carefully finished laying out the agendas and note pads on the boardroom table. Normally, of course, his secretary would be doing this, but then he no longer had a real secretary. The Princess Victoria's Bounty didn't run to that kind of thing, even for its Administrative Officer. The little girl (thirty-four years old) on loan from Barwell's Bank as part of their campaign to improve their image in the public eye, was helpful, but had never been properly trained as a secretary. Still, Perry was a naturally cheerful and optimistic soul and, all things considered, he didn't mind these small inconveniences at all. Not when he thought about what he'd had to put up with in the last days and months of Barrett-Nyblum Ltd.

No, he wouldn't think about that. It was better not to. Not now, when things were going so well for him. Now was definitely not the time to be downcast, especially when he remembered what had happened to poor old Per, his former partner. When the crash had come, Per had simply climbed into his Jaguar and driven it at very high speed into the nearest brick wall. Perry had had a nervous breakdown, followed by a none too severe stroke. It was then, in his darkest days, he'd come across the PVB. His therapist had mentioned that she did some work for them. When, at the age of fifty-seven, Perry had begun to pull his life back together, one of his old friends from the building trade had mentioned that the PVB was on the look-out for an administrator. Not much of a salary, not for someone who'd been used to over fifty thousand a year, but he knew those days were behind him. He knew he'd never be able to start up again, not with those court judgements behind him. His friend was on the board of trustees of the PVB and had very kindly offered to push Perry for the vacancy. Now, three years later, his life was settled again. He had a small, modest house and a job and, strangely enough, was well content and satisfied with the work he was doing.

One by one the board members and paid officers of the charity began to arrive. Perry knew them all, except the middle-aged mousey-looking spinster who was the new fund-raising officer. Jack, Perry's friend, clapped him on the shoulder and enquired after his family.

"Fine, thanks; Simon's doing really well with that mobile phone company of his and Pam's got into the drama society again."

Jack guided him towards the newcomer: "Let me introduce you to our new fund-raiser. Perry Barrett, our administrator here, Joan Mayflower." Perry observed her closely as they shook hands. She was about fifty, he supposed, blonde-grey hair, no dye, very little make-up, but piercing blue eyes. Yes, her eyes were definitely disconcerting. For some reason Perry turned away from her. They settled down as the meeting was called to order.

Even when he'd had his own company, Perry had never enjoyed management meetings. There was always too much posturing and politicking. He always thought the thing to do was to get things done, not sit around yacking about them. Today was worse than usual. Fairbrother, a local Labour councillor, was at his worst, moaning on about government policy towards the adult disabled. There was nothing any of them could do about that, as Jack forcibly pointed out, but Fairbrother wouldn't give up. "It's scandalous, nothing short of scandalous. We treat the disabled worse than criminals." Despite his socialist leanings on the theory of crime and the treatment of criminals, Councillor Fairbrother was in hang 'em and flog 'em mode after his second break-in within three months.

"I don't think this is really a profitable speculation." Perry tried to change the subject and calm the troubled waters. It was no use.

"Look at what they're doing to the National Health Service. Now, I'm all in favour of efficiency. You've only got to look at the way I run the business to see that, but there are limits."

"It's the climate of the times," said Jack. "Efficiency, value for money, that's what the politicos tell us the public want."

It was then that Miss Mayflower spoke for the first time: "If I may say so, we should look to our own house before trying to put other people's houses in order. You expect me to raise, how much was it now?" She looked speculatively at her paperwork, as if not quite able to believe the outrageous nature of the task set her. "And we waste money hand over fist. It makes my job virtually impossible."

"That's not what you said when we interviewed you." Jack was beginning to lose his temper. Perry sighed. He really did not want this kind of row. He couldn't stand it any more.

"But then I didn't know how you run things here. Believe me, waste and inefficiency and highly paid officers are the kiss of death for a charity these days. The public simply will not stand for it. Believe me; I know. I spent twelve years collecting for the Martin Luther Missions."

"So you told us," remarked Councillor Fairbrother acidly.

"What exactly do you mean by waste and inefficiency, Miss Mayflower... er... Joan?" asked Perry quietly.

She simply goggled at him. Her blue eyes shone like marbles behind her reading glasses. "I would have thought you didn't need to be told that. Look at the hostel, the way it's run. It's over-staffed by people who can't really do the jobs, so that we have to go begging for help from businesses and financial institutions. And the patients live in the kind of luxury they could never afford in private life, even if they weren't disabled."

"Oh I say." "Now that's unfair." "You've only been here five minutes." "You leave the administration to us, you just bring in the money." Some of the shocked and distressed comments floated over Perry's head. He himself said nothing.

The meeting dissolved into acrimony and Perry took no further part in it. He had never thought of it before, but what she said was true. It wasn't only the patients, who lived in the hostel or outside and used the workshops to produce painted porcelain and leather goods, who were helped and supported by the PVB, it was the administrative staff too. People like him, who would otherwise never get another job. Why hadn't he seen it before? Because he hadn't wanted to. The administrator who'd been unable to manage his own business, kept carefully away from the fund-raising and just given a small budget to run the place with. He should have seen it. It was all around him: the notoriously inefficient switchboard, the post room which could never sort the mail correctly, the junior administrators, too frightened to ever make decisions for fear of doing the wrong thing and losing their financial life supports.

Perry pulled himself together; he'd missed most of what had been said during the last half hour. The meeting was breaking up. No doubt he'd be able to catch up on it by reading the minutes, assuming Sonya ever managed to produce them. He noticed she was still busily scribbling away on her note pad as they all filed out. Jack looked kindly at him and guided him towards his own office. When they were out of earshot of the others, he spoke: "Regular virago, that one, eh?"

"Oh yes," agreed Perry absently.

"I was against appointing her in the first place, but…" Jack shrugged. "But I suppose we have to make allowances; she hasn't had an easy life," he said confidentially. Perry raised his eyebrows in enquiry. "You know, I told you." Perry was sure Jack hadn't told him. "Well, I don't suppose you ever get over a thing like that." Perry clearly looked mystified, as Jack continued: "All that business about being a refugee from Yugoslavia. Mind you, she speaks jolly good English, eh?"

Perry didn't feel very well disposed towards Miss Mayflower. "So she should. She's been here long enough."

"Yes, still, we must be a bit tolerant and all that," suggested Jack. "It's probably just nerves, settling into a new job, you know. Anyway, must be going. See you Saturday."

"Same time as usual," replied Perry.

4

After Jack had gone, Perry made himself a cup of instant coffee. He would have liked to have asked Jack if it were true. Had they really taken him on out of sympathy, not because he was the best man for the job? But he'd been too frightened to ask. He looked down at the mug in his hands. It was one of their own, with a portrait of the princess on the side. It really was very well made. You could sell stuff of that quality in any chain store. But that wasn't the point; Perry had always felt himself apart from the patients, not dependent on the PVB like they were: able to pick himself up and start again, able to make his own way in the world. Now he had to face it: he wasn't. He was just like the patients sitting in their workshops, painting their porcelain.

Sonya came in. "Oh Mr Barrett, I'm sorry, but I simply couldn't keep up. I missed all that stuff about the campaign... Did you...?" She tailed off. It was always the same. She wanted to copy his notes of the meeting, but this time she was unlucky. He'd been too distracted to make any.

He looked up at her hopeful, friendly face: "I didn't get it either, I'm afraid. Just do the best you can. We can correct the minutes next time, if we need to."

Sonya said: "Oh," and hurried off to her computer. Suddenly Perry was angry. Very angry. What if it were true? If he and Sonya and the others were dependants of the charity they worked for. That's what it was there for, to help people like them and all the others. They were doing their best, after all, and no one else would work for the wages they got. It wasn't much to ask, a little bit of dignity. He'd worked and supported himself and his family all his life until he'd gone bust. And as for Joan Mayflower, she was as dependent on the PVB as the rest of them. Jack had made that plain enough. She had nothing to shout about.

CHAPTER TWO

During the course of the next few weeks Joan Mayflower made herself at home at Princess Victoria's. She was constantly bustling in and out of her tiny office and amassing a load of paperwork. The mound on her desk grew day by day. Perry was never sure what she was up to; she seemed to be into everything, poking about here and there, and asking endless questions. Still, there was no denying her success as a fund-raiser.

During her first week, she'd hauled in the regional fund-raising organizers for a very stringent pep-talk, and it had worked. The revenues were beginning to increase. Perry steered well clear of her. He couldn't explain why, but he felt afraid of her. Unfortunately, as surely as the money came in, so the walking wounded began to besiege him. Sonya was the first victim. Joan had exploded when she'd received her botched-up copy of the minutes. As Sonya tearfully explained: "I know I'm not very good at typing and shorthand, when the bank sent me on secondment, they never said anything about all that." Perry was too kind to ask her what else she imagined the post of secretary involved. He offered her a tissue to replace her own sodden one. "She said she'd complain to the bank. If she does that I'm finished. I couldn't go back there. Not after all that mess with the cash machine."

It transpired that Sonya's trembling hands had one day accidentally loosed a sheaf of banknotes destined for the cash machine into a grateful High Street full of shoppers. She'd broken the rules, unlocking the lobby door and rushing outside to prevent a toddler running into the road, and had dropped the newly unfastened bundles. She'd tried to catch the fluttering paper, but the passers-by had been too quick for her. The bank had lost a few hundred pounds and some

6

enterprising young man had photographed the distraught Sonya flailing her arms outside the bank. The local paper had gleefully printed the picture, together with a witty caption, on page two. The bank had been made a laughing stock.

Soon after, as part of their caring charity policy, Sonya had been dumped on the PVB. Perry couldn't bring himself to ask whether the bank had reclaimed their loss from her salary. Knowing banks as he did, he thought they probably had; with interest. The poor girl was probably still working off the debt. He reassured her: "Don't worry, Sonya, remember, you're my secretary, not Joan's, and I know you've never been trained as a secretary, and… er…." He plunged into a big lie. "I find your work perfectly fine, just fine. Don't worry. I wouldn't dream of letting the bank repossess you."

She smiled gratefully. "Oh thank you. I was so worried. Thank you. I'll get on with those memos," she said awkwardly, as she bowed herself out of his office.

Oh dear, he thought. Now I've done it. I'll never be able to get a replacement for her now. One more cross to bear.

CHAPTER THREE

After twice being cut off by the switchboard, the regional organizer for Mid-Kent managed to get through to Perry and invite him for lunch away from the office. Perry was by now glad of the offer of a pub lunch in the Duke Without a Head, so he cheerfully drove the twenty or so miles, and arrived to find Paul waiting for him in the car park. "Thanks for coming; I've got to see you. And it's best away from the office."

Perry didn't like the sound of that at all. He smiled cautiously at Paul. "That's OK. It does me good to get away from the office for a bit. Especially nowadays," he added with a sigh.

They ordered their pints and ploughman's and selected a quiet corner. "I thought I'd try to get you on your own, see if there's anything you can do." Paul sipped his pint thoughtfully, as if picking his words. "It's our new fund-raising officer." Perry sighed loudly. "She's not quite used to the way we do things." Paul paused. Perry clearly wished he wasn't hearing this. "You know, Perry, we've never been much on the street collections. It's just one of those things. Most of our supporters are older people; they just don't like standing for hours in the cold, they complain that with all the mugging there is these days, they don't feel safe. We've always done well enough with our summer fêtes and Christmas dinner dances and so on." Perry knew that, despite covering one of the richest areas of the country, Paul's group were often at the bottom of the league in fund-raising terms, but he was not disposed to argue. He and Paul munched their French breads.

Paul swallowed hard and continued: "Well, this new woman's been telling us we've got to meet targets, that she's going to be pulling the books in every month to see how we're

8

doing. She came over yesterday afternoon, called us all together and told us. She said she wasn't satisfied with our group, told us we'd have to pull our socks up. It caused a bit of an upset, I can tell you. After all, our people are only volunteers. They collect for us in their spare time. She tried to order them about as if they were kids. They won't stand for it. They enjoy their dances and their fêtes; they won't do it any other way."

Perry interrupted: "I know she has an unfortunate manner, but I'm sure she'll settle down. I understand she used to be a teacher at one time; she probably can't get out of the habit."

"I've had two resignations already this morning," moaned Paul. "And if she insists on street collections and targets, I won't have anyone left soon. Please talk to her; you know us. Make her see sense. Please."

Perry cut into his pickled onion. "I'll do my best, but she is in charge of the fund-raising, not me. We hired her to improve our finances; we can hardly stop her the first time she tries out an idea. Why not try to do the best you can? If you don't get volunteers for the street collections, you can't do 'em, can you? That would bring it home to her better than anything."

Paul drained his pint and fell silent. Perry sensed there was more to come. "I know you're right, and if that was all, I wouldn't bother you, but…" He trailed off. He seemed to be bracing himself for something. "She took the books, you know, yesterday, and, well, I've been a little short of ready cash lately. The car went phut and I can't manage without it. I needed £80, so when we got the money in from the dinner dance raffle, I just… er… borrowed it. I didn't pay it in. I should have done, I know, and I've never done anything like that before. It was only last week, and I can pay it back when I get paid. I always intended to do that. But now she's got the books, and when she finds out, I'm finished. She as good as said yesterday she thought it was my fault the area didn't raise more. She'll be looking for an excuse to get rid of me. Oh God, what am I going to do? If I lose this job…"

He didn't have to go on. Poor sod, thought Perry, unemployed for eighteen months, gets a fresh start, and then… He asked: "Haven't you got the money now?"

Paul shook his head. "I'd pay it in if I had and just say I hadn't got round to it, until her visit reminded me. All she's got to do is compare the cash receipts book with the bank statement, and I've had it. What am I going to do?"

"When we've drunk up here, we'll go down to my bank; they've got a branch in Tonbridge, and I can get the £80 with my debit card. We'll take it down to Eastman's and pay it into the charity's account. You can pay me back when you get paid."

"Thanks," Paul almost looked as if he would cry. "I'll pay you back, the minute I get paid, and I won't do anything like that again. You can count on that."

"I know," said Perry kindly. "And we won't mention any of this again. You just say you forgot to pay it in, like you suggested." Perry thought how ridiculous it was: £80 was nothing to him now. But once, not so long ago, it would have been everything. When he had been going bust, there had never been enough money. No money for the mortgage, no money for the car, no money to pay the suppliers, no money for food, even. It had been awful, unbelievably awful. He felt for Paul; he was a decent, if not very bright, soul, and he really did try. He'd learned his lesson, he'd never do it again. Perry was sure of that.

Perry's trust in Paul was fully vindicated. Two weeks after their conversation, Perry received a personal cheque and a covering letter from him in his office post. As far as Perry was concerned, the matter was closed. He was surprised, therefore, to see Jack in his office at the end of that week. He had no appointment, and claimed to be just popping in for a chat. It was unusual for Jack to turn up unexpectedly. He was very interested in the work of the PVB, but he had his own business to run, and hadn't got much spare time. Perry was even more surprised when Jack very pointedly closed the office door behind him. Sonya and her cups of coffee were

10

definitely excluded. Jack came straight to the point. "What's all this about Paul Russell?"

For one minute Perry was completely nonplussed, and then realization dawned. "How do you mean?"

"Didn't Joan tell you?"

"No. Tell me what?"

"You know Paul's group are never very good with the fund-raising, so she went down there and read them the riot act, told them to get themselves organized and that she'd be monitoring them." Perry passed his hand over his face. Jack continued: "Well the upshot is, we've only got about one third of the volunteers left. Most of them have simply upped sticks and gone over to the NSPCC or Cancer Research. Remember old Charles?" Perry did. Colonel Charles had been a well known war hero and explorer in his day, and had even written a few books about his journeys. Perry had met him through Jack at an Institute of Directors' dinner, when he had still had his business. "He wrote me a very stiff letter, said he objected to being treated like a recalcitrant squaddie. He offered to give me some advice about team work and organising volunteers." Perry could well imagine the kind of letter Colonel Charles would write on that subject. He looked at Jack, who made a disgusted face.

"It does seem as though Joan Mayflower is causing us problems," he said. "Perhaps it would be better all round if there was an amicable parting of the ways. I'm sure you could sort something out."

Jack groaned audibly, and carried on: "I never wanted her in the first place. I told you that, remember. Normally, I'd be only too glad to get shot of her. Pronto." He paused. "I even took the liberty of having a quiet word with her, suggested, you know, getting on with these old buffers wasn't perhaps her thing. After all, she's been a teacher most of her life. World of difference. I mentioned, as tactfully as possible, that it didn't do to upset the volunteers; we're entirely reliant on them. We don't use professional outside fund-raisers, couldn't afford to."

"What did she say?" asked Perry cautiously.

"She certainly didn't beat about the bush, anyway," replied Jack. "She came straight out with it. She said something like: "If you think you're going to get rid of me that way, you can think again.' And then she told me she'd checked the bank accounts for Paul's region against the cash receipts." Jack scrutinised Perry, who was beginning to feel distinctly uneasy.

"And…?"

"And it seems she found Paul hadn't always paid in everything he'd received. Oh, nothing much, just the odd fiver or tenner now and then; not very often, but, there it is."

Perry felt sick, this was just like the bad old days again, trying to get away with not putting all the money through the books, so as to keep enough to carry on living. Fortunately, the Inland Revenue hadn't pursued them; the amounts had been very small, and they were broke anyway. He stuttered: "Well, I know Paul was out of work for a long time before he came to us. I suppose he found it difficult to get on an even keel again. I know it's wrong, but if he repaid the money, we could give him a decent reference, at least for some job where he won't handle money."

"That would be my view too. We couldn't keep him on, but we are a charity. If we can't behave charitably, who can? But, unfortunately, that still leaves us with the problem of Joan Mayflower. We simply can't get rid of her. She told me straight out that if we try, she'll go straight to the press and plaster us and poor Paul all over the front pages."

"Oh God." Perry was despairing. "She'll lose us all the volunteers we've got and not just in Kent, but everywhere. What are we going to do?"

Jack fiddled with the papers on the low table in front of him. "She made her position very clear when I talked to her. Apparently, fund-raising is too much like hard work, and she agrees with me that she's not best suited to dealing with the types of people who are our supporters. 'Defective geriatrics' was the term she actually used, if I remember correctly."

Perry was horrified; how had they made such a mistake as to employ someone like that? "What does she want, then?" he enquired.

Jack looked him straight in the eye and said: "Your job."

"Well, she can't have it, I'm still using it." Perry tried to sound more confident than he actually felt.

"No, of course she can't. I know that. No one on the board would wear that. Not for one minute. If we were to put her in charge of this place, we might as well shut up shop altogether. The staff would be off within two months, and the patients would be up in arms. Can you imagine it? If that's the alternative, she might as well go to the press, it would come to the same thing in the end. There would be no charity left here anyway."

"So what are you going to do?" asked Perry with the alarm rising in his voice.

"There's more, I'm afraid. When she found out about Paul and the discrepancies, she went down there and gave him the third degree. She threatened him with public disgrace and all that. When she said she'd see to it he never got another job as long as he lived, he told her about you lending him £80 so he could put the books straight."

So that was it. The end. Back to square one again. Perry felt his heart beginning to churn in his chest, just like it used to. He felt faint. He should have known better. That was how the trouble had started when he'd had the business: he'd been too trusting of Per and the suppliers. He should have learned his lesson. But he hadn't, and now he was going to pay for it all over again. He looked helplessly at Jack.

Jack was a decent soul. "It's all right though, don't worry. Do you need one of your tablets?"

Perry reached in his pocket and struggled to undo the child-proof bottle. "What am I going to do, Jack? I just couldn't start all over again."

"Don't worry, you don't have to. There's no question of that. You've done good work here, very good work. The place is efficiently and happily run. It fulfils its functions very well under your administration. If we lost you, we'd never get another one as good; we know that. I've thought about this, and I think, if she makes an issue of it, your best bet is to tough it out. Let her prove you ever gave Paul that £80 and, even if you did, let her prove you knew what it was for. She's only got the verbal admission of someone who was in shock and frightened for his livelihood. She's got nothing in writing and no witnesses." Perry's heart began to beat a little more normally again. Jack continued: "I'll drive over and see Paul this afternoon, if you agree. I feel sorry for him and we need a store man over at the Erith Depot. There's no money involved and nothing he could sell if he stole it. Not that I think he would; he's basically an honest chap. I'll take him on, but in return he has to promise never to repeat what he said about you to Miss Mayflower, not even if she does go to the press. I'll make it clear to him that if he does, he'll be fired. And you just keep your mouth shut. Say nothing. What do you think?"

"Thanks, Jack, you really are a good friend. I'm sorry I've brought all this trouble on you, when you've done so much to help me. I know I should have reported it to the board straight away, but I felt so sorry for the guy. I've learned my lesson though. I won't be so stupid again."

"I know. The difficulty is that we've still got to deal with her job problem. I'm in favour of offering her some decently paid sop to get her away from fund-raising and keep her out of your job. I've no idea what, but we'll have to come up with something pretty quickly. Still, that's not your worry. And don't feel too bad about Paul, you were only trying to help him. I'd probably have done the same thing myself; I'm just glad I didn't."

By the end of the following week, Paul was safely ensconced as a deputy storeman and was duly contrite and relieved. Miss Mayflower had been a powerful adversary and had bullied him into admitting to more than he'd done. She had driven like a steamroller over his objections and explanations. He was glad to be away from her. Perry heartily wished he was away from her too. For some reason he couldn't fathom, she was haunting Sonya's office. She was always running in and out with letters and memos, and giving instructions for taking messages when she was out, even though Sonya wasn't really her secretary. Even if she was still coveting his job, Perry couldn't see why she was always hanging round Sonya. He thought he was going to be very glad when the next board meeting was safely out of the way and he could relax in his job again, and Joan would have her new post, whatever that might be.

CHAPTER FOUR

As usual, Perry did his rounds of the home and workshops. He made a point of going round and seeing the clients at least once a day. It was a time consuming and, perhaps, unnecessary exercise, but he thought it important to maintain personal contact with all the patients and non-resident workers. In an institution like the PVB there were always bound to be discordant personalities, and the difficulties of living and working together sometimes meant that goodwill was stretched to breaking point. A few well chosen words from him, after a sympathetic hearing, usually managed to smooth things out.

As he strolled through the pleasant grounds, with their gently sloping paths and flower beds, Perry realized how much he'd come to love the PVB. It really had become a home from home for him. It gave him genuine pleasure to watch the gardeners tending the grounds and working in the potting sheds and greenhouses, rearing the pot plants they sold to local florists and garden centres. They'd even got an office service going, supplying and maintaining greenery for local businesses. It was doing quite well.

Perry was walking up the central drive towards the construction site, where the new block with special accommodation for wheelchair bound patients was being built, when he saw Joan marching up the hill ahead of him. He instinctively slowed down. She was the last person he wanted to bump into. She'd apparently been in the big greenhouse. From that greenhouse, Perry saw Franjo appear in his wheelchair. He was shaking his fist at Joan behind her back and shouting something totally incomprehensible after her. Perry went up to him. "What was all that about, then?"

"Ask Madame," replied Franjo, in his heavily accented English. After so many years in England, Franjo still sounded very foreign.

"You don't seem too pleased with our fund-raiser."

Franjo turned in his wheelchair, looked up at Perry with his shrewd blue eyes, and said: "She is trouble that one. You get rid of her. She is trouble."

"What do you mean?"

"She is trouble. That is all. You ask her."

"Franjo, if you know anything that you think I should know, you should tell me. You shouldn't bottle it all up," encouraged Perry.

"You ask her," was all he got by way of a reply. It was quite clear he wasn't going to get anywhere with Franjo. He was not known to be loquacious at the best of times.

"Well anyway," said Perry with a smile, "it's a good job she couldn't understand whatever you were shouting after her."

"She understood all right." Franjo pointedly wheeled himself back into the greenhouse.

Sometimes Perry called in at the greenhouses and bought himself a pot plant, but today he didn't. Instead he walked slowly back to his office, wondering what Joan Mayflower had done to upset Franjo. Franjo had always been a bit of a problem. He'd been brought over to England when he was still relatively young, being in need of medical care he couldn't get in his own country. His family had eventually been able to join him and had made their home here. Franjo had lived in institutions all his life and had never received much continuous education. Eventually he'd wound up at the PVB, which had provided him with his first independent home, in the form of one of its flats on the outskirts of the complex, and a job he enjoyed and could do. But his personality had been marked by his traumatic and painful younger days, and he was not an easy person to get on with.

Back in his office, Perry mused that Franjo and Joan together were not a good combination. Neither of them had particularly appealing personalities. Franjo had his reasons, but then again, did Joan? After all, Jack had told him she had been a refugee herself. Because she was not physically disabled, it was difficult to feel the same sympathy for her, but perhaps she was, like himself, one of the walking wounded the PVB employed. It would explain a lot. Perry himself had had no say in the recruitment and selection of the chief fund-raiser. Recruitment was separate from his own function of running the hostel and workshop site. He had no access to Joan's personnel file or application, and really it was no concern of his, but he did wonder what was in her past. And that wasn't all; Franjo had shouted at her in his own language and had expected her to understand him. Perry made himself a cup of instant coffee in one of the new "Flowers of England" mugs produced by the PVB, and pondered a little further. If Franjo was right, it meant Joan must have come from the same country as Franjo. Perry thought it was the former Yugoslavia, but he couldn't really remember. Dropping another spoonful of sugar into his mug, so that the coffee was now far too sweet to drink, Perry had another thought. He didn't himself know where Joan had come from originally; how was it that Franjo did? Had he known her before she came to the PVB? Now that was an interesting speculation, one that might be well worth pursuing. Perry had the feeling that if Joan continued in the employment of the PVB, he was going to need all the information about her he could get.

CHAPTER FIVE

Draining his coffee and thinking he must stop taking sugar, Perry decided that there was one thing he could do immediately which might throw some light on the mystery. He told Sonya, who was tapping slowly away on her computer, that he would be in the design rooms, and set out to call Ben Farrell, who had designed the mugs in the "Flowers of England" series. In the course of his work he'd done a lot of research in and around the greenhouses, looking out for suitable species, and watching them developing throughout the season, so as to get the most attractive phases of their blooming and life cycles. He'd spent hours sketching and water colouring, and had managed to establish a grudging friendship with Franjo, who apparently admired a true craftsman when he saw one.

"How goes then, Ben?" asked Perry, as he pored over a sheet of tracing paper covered with designs in black ink.

"Not bad, some of these old churches had beautiful carvings and all that, but it's hard to translate them into something that suits the modern taste. Take this St. Anthony, for example." He shoved a coloured photograph in Perry's direction. "Beautifully carved, but not a face or posture sympathetic to the modern mind." Perry saw what he meant; not being religious, he didn't know whether or not St. Anthony had been martyred, but judging from the look of his statue, he had evidently expected to be. "All that wrestling with demons in caves," remarked Ben. "He was the founder of the monastic system, fasting and abstinence and all that." Perry thought that explained a lot.

He looked thoughtfully at Ben: how much he had changed in the two and a half years since he'd come to the PVB. At first he had been taciturn and withdrawn, and suicidal. Following a

19

minor accident, Ben had lost all confidence in his artistic abilities. His commissions for book illustrations had dried up, and his wife had left him. He'd twice tried and failed to commit suicide by taking handfuls of Paracetamol. With his confidence at rock bottom and his liver irreparably damaged, he'd come to rebuild what was left of his life at the PVB. Like the flowers he drew, he'd blossomed. Looking at him now, Perry thought it was likely he'd outlive them all. "What's on your mind?" asked Ben.

"Well, it may be something or nothing, but I saw Franjo earlier on, yelling at our new fund-raiser. You know what Franjo's like, he wouldn't tell me what it was all about, but I want to find out."

"Let's hope he gave Frau Hitler a good old mouthful; what did he say, by the way?"

"That's just it. He was yelling in his own language, so I don't know what he said and he wouldn't tell me. If there's any internal friction, I want to know about it and get it put to rest. So I thought you might be the best person to have a chat with Franjo about it. I'd be very grateful."

"Yeh, sure I'll try," offered Ben. "But you know what he's like, so I don't guarantee anything. At least if he was yelling at her in Serbo-Croat, she wouldn't have understood him either. Perhaps that's a good thing in the circumstances."

Perry was rummaging appreciatively through beautifully drawn sheets depicting St. Francis and St. Cecilia, and others. "No St. Christopher these days, I suppose?"

"No, he's gone, more's the pity. He'd have been a good seller."

Perry continued his previous theme. "That's the funny thing, though; when I asked Franjo what he'd said, he told me to ask Miss Mayflower; he said that she would understand what he'd said."

"Curiouser and curiouser." Ben's interest was quickening. "Whatever it was, I'm sure it was justified. She's a real rat-bag, you know." Perry knew that already, but thought his knowledge was about to be expanded. "She came trouncing in here, wanting illustrations for the new brochure, you know, the anniversary one, with the gold lettering on the front?" Perry said he didn't know much about the details of the new promotion. Ben continued: "We agreed to do the illustrations all right, after all, it's what I do, but she just came in, no discussion, said she wanted this or that, by next Monday. She'd got no idea of what size she wanted or even what kind of illustrations she wanted, but she expected me to produce perfect illustrations in ten days, on top of all the other stuff I've got to do. I told her it couldn't be done, particularly if she was thinking of having full colour. I didn't have anything to work from. Most people would sit down and discuss what they want, toss a few ideas around, before settling on a format for the preliminary sketches. But not her. She expected me to read her mind and told me I was an idiot, when I said I couldn't do it."

"Oh, I'm sorry." Perry was sorry. He knew Ben couldn't stand pressure of any kind. That was why he'd never left the PVB hostel even though he wasn't physically disabled. The stress of living in his own flat and fending for himself would be too much.

"It's not your fault, Perry. I know you didn't employ her. I can't think what the board was doing, taking on someone like that."

Perry sighed. "She certainly seems to be putting people's backs up, left, right and centre. That's one of the reasons why I want to get to the bottom of this business with Franjo. If she's upsetting our clients, that's a serious matter. I didn't know she'd had a run in with you, but I'm glad you've told me. What's happening about the brochure now?"

"Nothing. I can't do anything until she behaves sensibly. I'm not a mind reader."

"Well, see what you can dig out and let me know." Perry patted Ben on the shoulder and ambled back to his office.

CHAPTER SIX

The following day was the last one to be got through before the board meeting, and Perry was busy for most of the morning preparing his notes and carrying out his regular duties. He didn't hear anything from Ben and was just settling down for an afternoon of checking designs for furniture in the new block, when Sonya crept in with the agenda. She seemed reluctant to go when she'd given Perry his copy. "Is there anything you want, Sonya?"

She looked very miserable and pushed the door to behind her. She was fiddling with her customary tissue. "I don't know whether I should tell you. I don't want to make any more trouble."

"Sit down and tell me all about it, Sonya. Now you've started, you may as well tell it all." Perry tried to produce his uncle-father smile, the reassuring one.

"Well, it's Miss Mayflower."

Somehow, that hadn't come as a surprise. "What about her?" he asked cautiously.

"You know she's been hanging about the office?"

"I had noticed," he replied drily. "She's not trying to palm off some of her paperwork on you, is she, because, if so—?"

"No, it's not that," interrupted Sonya. "It's, well, she wanted to know about that letter you got from Paul, you know, the one with the cheque for £80 in it." Perry could remember that letter all too well. He wished he didn't. "I never told her, honestly, I didn't. I said it was none of her business," she protested.

"Thank you, Sonya, that was an entirely proper course of action on your part. If Joan wants to discuss the contents of my post, she can do so with me directly. I'm sorry you've had all this unpleasantness."

She looked a little relieved, but not enough. "You know I wouldn't ever tell anyone about that." She soldiered on loyally: "but Barry on the switchboard overheard Paul asking you out for lunch that day, just before, you know. I'm sure he didn't mean to listen in, it's probably just that he hasn't got the hang of things, but he told Miss Mayflower you'd been meeting Paul."

He would, thought Perry. Barry was just the kind of little toad who would bite the hand that fed him. As always when he was angry, Perry was getting his metaphors mixed. He had to hand it to Joan though; armed with that small piece of information from Barry and her knowledge from comparing the books and bank statements for Paul's region, she had reached the conclusion that a broke Paul had suddenly acquired £80 on the afternoon of the day he'd met Perry for lunch. A visit to Paul had confirmed her suspicions.

"I didn't tell her what was in the letter, I didn't even tell her you'd got a letter from Paul." Sonya was feeling braver now. "She kept on at me, she said she'd get me the sack if I was 'party to anything dishonest concerning the handling of the charity's funds,' that was the way she put it. 'Party to anything dishonest.'"

Perry took her hands in his. "But you weren't, Sonya, you weren't. You merely opened my post, organized it, and passed it on to me, like any good secretary should. You can't possibly be expected to remember what's in every letter I receive."

She smiled. She was like a little girl when she smiled. "Then I found her one day going through your correspondence file in the filing cabinet. She said she was looking for a memo you'd sent her that she'd lost, but I don't think she was."

The devious cow, thought Perry.

"She didn't find it; the letter I mean. I'd put it in my handbag," said Sonya proudly. "After she first asked, I took it out of the file and hid it. Here it is." She handed Perry the letter.

"Clever girl." Perry really did admire her. He thought she might be a lousy typist, but she had definitely got hidden talents. "So are you happy now?" he asked.

She radiated pride and happiness. "Yes thanks, fine."

With that problem solved, Perry returned to his catalogues and estimates. He'd have to watch that Barry in future, and he'd definitely have to watch Joan. He'd underestimated her by a long way. She wasn't only rude and devious, she was daring too, and if she'd got a friend in Barry, that could be a lethal combination.

Just before he was due to go home, Jack called in on Perry. Sonya had already tidied her office and left for the day. "I just thought I'd let you know what we've come up with for Madam Mayflower," he said. "In view of the damage she can do to us, all of us, and the work of the PVB charity, we've decided to offer her the post of education officer."

"But we don't have an education officer, whatever that is," objected Perry.

"We do now," replied Jack. "Thirty a year; that's more than she's getting now, but it's cheap at the price. We don't anticipate it will last for ever. Give it a couple of months or so and, with any luck, she'll be wanting something better; but if not, we can tell her she's surplus to requirements and let her go. She won't have been with us long enough in any capacity to qualify for a redundancy package. By then all this business with Paul will be water under the bridge, stale news. No one will be interested."

Much as he wanted to keep his own job, Perry wasn't too sure about this. She would still have a hold on them over Paul. "What do you envisage the education officer will do exactly?"

"She'll prepare factual material for public consumption, concerning our work and history, for the anniversary, and about the effects of various disabilities on the sufferers, and safety items about avoiding injuries due to accidents at home and at work and so on. From time to time, she'll be part of a team giving public lectures and displays, but not on her own. The job's a bit of a hotch-potch, but, after all, she used to be a teacher, and it's easier work than she's doing now, and more money."

"Will she go for it, though?" asked Perry anxiously. "What she really wants is my job; she wants power, not just money."

"It will be made clear to her in the most uncertain terms that no matter what she does, that is simply not on the cards. I've talked to the others, except Palmer, who's on holiday, and they're behind me on that, so there's nothing for you to worry about."

"I hope not," ventured Perry, "but you know she's been giving Sonya the treatment, and she's been nosing around trying to find the letter Paul sent when he paid me back. Sonya hid it, and now she's given it back to me. I never wrote back to him, so there's nothing more in the correspondence file."

"I've always thought Sonya was a good sort, and not so daft either. But how did our friend get on to all that business with Paul in the first place? That's what puzzles me."

Perry explained: "Barry on the exchange listened in to the call when Paul asked me out to lunch. He told Joan, and she put two and two together. She was also cute enough to realize that he'd have to pay me back and, as we haven't arranged to meet since I gave him the money, and since he would be unlikely to have my home address, the cheque would come here."

"Clever." Jack sounded almost appreciative. "But she still can't prove anything without the letter; all she's got is the word of someone who was earwigging on the exchange that you went out to lunch with Paul. That's nothing. Even with Paul's verbal admissions, she still has no proof. Keep quiet and deny everything, like we agreed. You've got nothing to worry about."

"Yes, I agree, but I thought I'd better tell you, so you know how it stands."

Jack was still thinking. "This really isn't the right kind of place for Barry. I know you were reluctant to take him on in the first place, and it looks as though you were right. It doesn't matter what's wrong with him, if he can't fit in with other people, there's no point in trying to settle him in to a structure like ours. It'll never work. Perhaps it would be better for all concerned if we tried to get his local authority to take him back again."

"And in the meantime I'll take him off the switchboard," said Perry firmly. "If he listened to my conversation with Paul, ten to one he listens to everyone's, and that's not on."

"Especially if he's relaying the information to Joan Mayflower."

"I could put him in the leather-craft workshop. That should be well within his capabilities, I should think and, after all, no one could say he does a good job on the switchboard. Everyone complains."

"Right-o then," agreed Jack. "See you tomorrow." With a wave of the hand, he was gone.

Driving home, Perry thought about young Barry. He'd been in constant trouble with the law from the age of about thirteen. He came from a decent family; both his parents were bus drivers, and his brothers and sisters all seemed to have grown up reasonably well, got jobs, got married and settled down. But Barry, the youngest, had been different. He'd truanted at school, and at one time had been sent to a special school for children with behavioural problems. He'd never had a job after leaving school, but had taken to buying and repairing old cars and motorcycles in his parents' front garden. The neighbours had complained about the noise and pollution, and he'd thrown concrete blocks at the old lady next door. His parents had disclaimed all responsibility for him and the police had become involved. He'd got away with that and with the few minor motoring offences which had followed over the next couple of years. Then it had all gone horribly wrong.

Barry's sidelines and his benefit payments had together enabled him to cut quite a dash on the club scene. Following a good night out, and fortified by a suitable quantity of ecstasy tablets, Barry had decided to go for a drive in the country, so he'd simply taken the keys and driven off in the coach his father had parked outside their home in readiness for an early morning charter. He'd not got very far before he crashed into a car, killing the three young people in it. Barry himself, although not killed, had been pitched violently sideways and had broken his back. Now he was a resident at the PVB; his thin, mean frame wheeling itself around and his spotty face, topped by the lavatory brush haircut, defiantly staring up at anyone who dared to talk to him. Without doubt, it wasn't going to be as easy to get rid of Barry as it had been to acquire him.

Perry could only hope that his local authority would relent and take him into one of their few homes when the heat had died down a bit. For heat there had certainly been, not least from the parents of the three students Barry had killed. One father had even threatened his life, and it was for this reason that the PVB had been approached to take him. Barry's parents had been subjected to abusive phone calls and had bricks thrown through their windows. It had been generally felt that they hadn't done enough to control him. Eventually they had got divorced, sold up, and left the district. Both of them had made it plain they wouldn't have Barry back home at any price.

CHAPTER SEVEN

On the morning of the board meeting Jack was in early and made a bee-line for Joan Mayflower's poky office. As the other members of the board and other senior paid officers of the charity made their way upstairs to attend the meeting, they could hear raised voices issuing through the closed door. They all knew Jack had been entrusted with the delicate task of persuading Miss Mayflower to accept the newly created post of education officer. They all surmised he wasn't making too good a job of it. Both Jack and Miss Mayflower emerged red faced from their confrontation. They were the last to join the group in the board room.

Councillor Fairbrother, acting for Palmer, the absent chairman, called the meeting to order and asked if it was their pleasure he sign the minutes of the last meeting. It was not. Joan Mayflower complained that they did not accurately reflect the content of the last meeting. Sonya dropped her notepad and exclaimed: "I did my best, but you were all talking so fast and all at once." Joan Mayflower smirked.

The acting chairman was ready for this and was not prepared to accept any insubordination. "I should perhaps point out to our new fund-raising officer that these meetings are not board meetings in the normal sense of the term; they are liaison meetings between senior members of staff and representatives of the board of trustees." He spoke slowly and deliberately, so Sonya could catch every word. "To this extent, verbatim minutes are neither necessary nor asked for." He beamed at Sonya. "We merely require a written memo of the main points raised in discussion and a clear statement of any decisions reached."

"I hardly think——" began the fund-raiser.

"That's your bloody trouble, woman, you don't seem to think at all." Councillor Fairbrother had dropped into blunt north countryman mode. Perry was grateful he'd got over hang 'em and flog 'em. "And you don't need to write that down, Sonya," he added. "And now, shall we take it that it is the pleasure of you all that I sign the notes from last time? Good." He signed them while Joan Mayflower was still opening her mouth to speak.

Having negotiated that hurdle, the acting chairman felt relieved and inadvertently plunged headlong into another row. He was so ill-advised as to enquire about the progress of the anniversary brochures. Joan Mayflower patiently explained to him that when one was forced to rely on an educationally subnormal artist, one couldn't expect a great deal of progress.

"Now that's really unfair, Joan," began Perry. "Ben's a really good artist, and he's always been very co-operative and helpful. None of us have ever had any trouble with him before."

"None whatsoever," chipped in Jack.

"Well, then, he'd better have it made clear to him that it's his duty to co-operate with me." She sounded icy.

Perry was ready for that one. "Perhaps you could explain to us exactly what it is you want him to do?" It transpired that she couldn't. At the end of a rambling five minutes of vague descriptions and self-justification, the board members sat staring at their blotters. No one spoke, but it was obvious that their new fund-raiser hadn't given more than two minutes thought to their anniversary brochure.

Councillor Fairbrother looked pointedly at Jack. Jack continued to say nothing. Perry couldn't decide what the outcome of the meeting between Jack and Joan was likely to have been. Had she accepted the new post? Judging by her determination to make trouble for Sonya and Ben in the present meeting, Perry thought it more likely that she was fighting on. Slowly, the acting chairman began to speak, picking his words carefully. "Sonya, perhaps you would be so kind as to make us all some coffee and biscuits; there's no rush." Sonya took the hint and scuttled out of the board room. He continued: "Joan, I know Jack has had a little chat with you before this meeting, to er… well, outline what might be a better use of your undoubted talents than your present position with us. I think we'd all like to know how you feel about the post of education officer. It's challenging, of course, but new and er… exciting." He sounded more hopeful than expectant. Perry's heart started to churn again; he felt in his pocket for his pills. Jack looked miserable.

"Before we do that, there is an outstanding fund-raising matter I wish to draw to the Board's attention." Joan Mayflower sounded cool and complacent; she'd obviously rehearsed that little speech. Perry managed to get the top off the bottle and swallowed a tablet. "As you may know, I discovered massive mismanagement of funds and theft in the Mid-Kent Region, as a result of which, Paul Russell has now resigned."

"I don't think the term 'massive mismanagement and theft' is applicable." Jack was clearly cross. "The total sum involved was less than £130, and it has all been repaid by Mr Russell, who, as you say, no longer works for us."

"Unfortunately, it isn't as simple as that," she continued slowly. "I have evidence that Mr Barrett was also involved in this fraud." Mr Patel gasped. Perry thought he was going to collapse. He had to get some water. He stood up and, with a brief word, put his head round the door to ask Sonya to fetch some. She wasn't there and he managed to stagger back to his seat again. He just couldn't think what to say. It had always been like this. Well-laid plans about what to say to the bank manager or tax inspector had always fallen apart when he'd tried to implement them. He'd always left that kind of thing to Per.

This time Jack came to his rescue. "Prove it."

"I have—" she began.

"Well," snapped Councillor Fairbrother. "Have you any proof of wrong doing on the part of Mr Barrett here? If you haven't, you should keep your mouth shut."

"I have proof Mr Barrett met Paul Russell for lunch on the day Mr Russell repaid £80 of the money he'd recently stolen from us. A strange coincidence, wouldn't you say?"

"No, I would not say," shouted Jack.

"Good God, woman, is that it? What are you trying to suggest here?" Councillor Fairbrother was purple with rage.

Mr Patel interjected: "I think Mr Barrett's personal life is no concern of ours. If he met Mr Russell out of the office for social reasons, or if he still meets him, it is none of our business."

Miss Mayflower persisted, even though she must have realized it was doing her no good. "I want to know what Mr Barrett and Mr Russell discussed that day and I want to know where Mr Russell so conveniently found that £80 before pay day."

The acting chairman spoke formally: "I understand Mr Russell repaid that money from his own resources and since he no longer works for us, I should have thought that was the end of the matter."

Mr Patel concluded: "You know I'm not even sure he really stole that £80; he might have stolen the other smaller sums, I don't know, but I, for one, would be quite prepared to believe he'd simply forgotten to pay that money in."

Miss Mayflower was exasperated. "He confessed, damn it."

"Only after you'd had a go at him." Jack's interruption raised laughs and sniggers round the table. Even Mr Patel smiled.

Councillor Fairbrother was nothing if not firm. He continued: "Now we've got that out of the way, the question still remains. Miss Mayflower, what do you intend to do?"

"I'll consider the matter and let you have my decision by the end of the week," she replied coolly.

Perry wondered if he dare risk taking another pill. At this point the acting chairman moved that the meeting be closed and re-convened when a decision had been made about Miss Mayflower's future. With relief, they all agreed. As they started to file out, they came face to face with Sonya, carrying a tray of coffee mugs and a plate of biscuits. "You won't be wanting the coffee, then?" she asked plaintively.

"No thank you, Sonya," replied Jack kindly.

"What shall I do about the minutes?" she asked him.

"Never mind them for today. I think we'll just say today was an informal discussion."

Perry was still sitting at the board room table and he called out: "I'll have a cup, Sonya. I'm thirsty."

She brought him two and the plate of biscuits. "Are you all right?" She looked very concerned.

"Oh, yes, thank you. Just the old heart problem. It crops up now and again."

"If there is anything I could help you with, I would, you know," she offered.

"That's very kind of you, Sonya, but it's all right. There's nothing you can do."

"Oh, by the way, there were a couple of calls for you: Ben Farrell and Wendy Jackson."

"Thanks, I'll call them back as soon as I can." That was one good thing; with Barry off the switchboard at least the telephone calls got through.

When he got back to his office Perry found Sonya eating her sandwiches. "I thought I'd have an early lunch, you know, with the coffee being made and all that."

"Quite right," he smiled. He called Ben first.

Ben reported the results of his detective work with Franjo: "Apparently, she's just had a conservatory built on to her lounge and she expected the greenhouse staff to stock it free of charge. Franjo refused and she started to call him a defective; he lost his temper and started slanging her. In the end she beat a hasty retreat, with him shouting after her. I tried to ask him about whether or not she could understand him. All he would say was that he knew she would. He wouldn't say how he knew. Is that any good to you?"

"Yes, Ben, I'm sure it's going to be very useful. Thanks a lot."

"You've got to say one thing for her though: she's got a bloody cheek. She seems to think she can get away with anything."

Perry thanked Ben again and thought about the information he'd been given. On the face of it, it was a simple enough row, but Ben was right. Joan Mayflower seemed confident of her ability to do exactly as she pleased within the PVB and get away with it, and not only as regards the acquisition of house plants.

Wendy Jackson proved to be very upset when Perry returned her call. This time the source of the problem was not Joan, but her protégé, Barry. Wendy was one of the independent therapists who gave their time to the PVB in addition to their normal NHS duties. "He actually threatened me with a leather-craft knife," she protested.

"Are you all right? Did he hurt you?"

"Yes, I'm all right; he didn't hurt me, he couldn't get near enough. Alec belted him on the arm with one of the wooden battens and he dropped the knife. But I'm not having him here a second longer. He's dangerous."

"No, no. I understand," soothed Perry. "I'll be over directly. Where is he now?"

"I've no idea. I don't know and I don't want to know. He wheeled himself out and I don't know where he went."

"Close the doors, Wendy, put the catches down for a few minutes, until I get there. That'll keep him out if he tries to get back in again."

Perry ran, rather than walked, over to the craft complex. He waved to Ben as he passed his window and was with Wendy in a few minutes. She undid the door catches to let him in and then re-fastened them. The patients gathered round Perry. Josie said: "I saw it all, he just went mad, yelling and shouting. He said he didn't want to do poxy leather-craft. And what's wrong with it? It's good enough for the rest of us, why not for him?"

Wendy herself was more composed by now. "It was such a shock, I couldn't believe it."

"I'm glad he didn't hurt you," said Perry sincerely, "and of course I won't let him come back here, but it's very difficult to know what to do with him. I can't put him back on the switchboard."

Wendy said: "At least he couldn't cause any mischief there."

Perry replied quietly: "You'd be surprised. It's out of the question for him to go back there, I'm afraid. It wasn't just that he was inefficient... but be assured, he won't come here again. Are the rest of you all right?" he asked.

They agreed that they were, but Alec voiced a common concern. "It's not just here, Perry, we do other crafts and things, and some of us have to live near him in the hostel."

"You mean you wouldn't feel safe anywhere near him?"

Freddie piped up: "Not after today. He really meant it, you know. And it's not only this: I live next door to him and he's always playing that CD player of his at top volume. It gets on my nerves. The same stuff over and over again, late at night. You know me, I don't like to make a fuss, so a couple of times I've just had a quiet word with him, asked him to turn the volume down. He just told me to fuck off."

"I wish you'd told me before, Freddie. It's what I'm here for, to see things run smoothly and that everyone here is as satisfied as possible."

"That's all very well, but we are dealing with an attempted assault with a deadly weapon here" Cedric had been a military policeman in his time. "If he hadn't been in a wheelchair, God knows what he would have done, and if next time he loses his rag with someone more disabled than himself, where will it end?"

He was right, of course; Perry knew he was, but it seemed too grotesque to report a boy in a wheelchair to the police. "It's up to you, Wendy; you were the one who was threatened and you have witnesses; do you want me to call in the police? I will support you if you want to. It's your decision."

"No, it's all right," she said heavily. "I'll let it go."

34

"Don't do that; file a formal report of the incident with me, and get everyone here who saw anything to add their observations and signatures. And Freddie, you write a formal complaint about the noise. It will help me decide what to do with Barry. In the meantime, he won't be working anywhere, least of all here."

They all agreed to do as Perry asked them, but Wendy said she would have to write her report later because she had to set off for her afternoon clinic at the local hospital. After putting on her coat and collecting her bag, she walked back down the drive with Perry. "I can't say how sorry I am that this should have happened to you, Wendy. I really am."

"Thanks, but I suppose I'm lucky it hasn't happened before. I was the union rep. up at the hospital for a while, and these days it's nothing for the patients and their relatives to assault the staff. Just because someone winds up in a wheelchair, it doesn't make them a saint."

"Especially not that young man," agreed Perry with feeling.

They passed Joan Mayflower on her way to the cafeteria. "Good morning, Miss Mayflower," called Wendy.

"Wendy," she replied curtly.

"I didn't know you knew our fund-raiser."

"She used to teach me at school and a right tartar she was." Perry could well believe that. Wendy was still speaking: "She used to pick on me something rotten, and the worst of it was that I had to have special lessons from her. My parents wanted me to do Serbo-Croat. It was their own language and they asked the headmistress to allow me to join the class she did for the other kids of Yugoslavian origin, so they wouldn't lose their culture. It was ghastly; I could never get the hang of it, all those unpronounceable words and that double alphabet." She laughed happily.

"You sound very English to me, if I may say so without giving offence."

"I am. I was born here; my parents had come here to escape Tito. My name was Lalovic before I married. There were quite a few Yugoslavian refugees around here then. I

35

suppose they tended to huddle together in a strange country. Anyway, I'll let you have that report tomorrow. Bye."

"Bye," said Perry thoughtfully.

CHAPTER EIGHT

Perry decided he would treat himself to a pub lunch and, feeling in need of company, asked Sonya to join him. She'd already eaten her sandwiches, but said she could put away a small ploughman's. "Where shall we go then?" he asked as he drove slowly down the driveway.

"What about the Printers over at Swale Vale?" So the Printers it was. Sonya then remarked that her choice was ironic: she'd had to call Barber's again; the computer wasn't working.

"Oh dear." Perry didn't like to say more, not after all the kindness Sonya had shown him, but she was like the kiss of death to that equipment. It was always breaking down under her tender ministrations.

Rather to Perry's surprise, Sonya proved to have sophisticated tastes: she selected a wurst-based ploughman's and sipped her dry white wine with the appreciation of a connoisseur. "Of course, I don't know much about wine myself, I'm strictly a beer man these days," he remarked.

Sonya was very knowledgeable and spoke of vacations spent touring the wine growing valleys of France and Germany. She even proved *au fait* with the German language in so far as to be able to specify, with a good accent, her choice to the publican, who completely failed to understand what she was asking for. Perry was sure this was a mark of sophistication. "Where did you learn?" he asked.

"At school and later at college. Then I lived out there for about nine months, working as an *au pair* and doing a bit of translation and so on. I just went for the experience, you know." This threw yet another new and interesting light on Sonya. It was difficult to imagine her as a carefree young student boldly travelling throughout Europe. The fire of youth looked to be long departed. Now she was creeping into mousey middle age. Perry wondered what had brought about this premature change.

She was chattering on about the Meuse Valley and Perry let the monologue wash over him. He was only giving her half his attention, but he found her voice very soothing. "At least that's one thing I've got to thank Miss Mayflower for, if nothing else."

"Eh?" Perry jerked into attention.

"Didn't you know she used to teach me? She taught German."

"I'd no idea. Do you know Wendy Jackson then, the therapist?"

"No, I don't think so. I don't recall the name."

"She was Wendy Lalovic before she married." He pronounced the name carefully.

Sonya looked dumbstruck. "Wendy, Wendy Lalovic," she repeated. "I'd no idea she worked at the PVB. I suppose I must have seen her around, but I didn't recognise her. Of course it was years ago. I don't suppose she'd recognise me now."

"I was talking to her about Barry before we came out. He'd threatened her with a craft knife and she was naturally very upset."

"My   God,   that's   awful.   Is   she   OK?" "Oh yes, she's fine, but of course Barry will have to be transferred away from the workshops. It's difficult to know what to do with him." Perry sighed; he'd have to try to get the local authority to take charge of Barry. The PVB really wasn't the place for violent people, no matter how disabled they were.

Sonya was still musing. "Fancy Wendy turning up here after all these years; and she's married? Still, I'm glad things worked out for her. She had a rotten time at school. She wasn't in my class, but we all knew about it. When she left, it all came out." Perry was mystified and looked it. Sonya sipped her wine and offered to get him a refill. He accepted, even though he knew he shouldn't drink too much, particularly at lunch time and especially after taking his tablets.

As she threaded her way to the bar, he called after her: "Better just make that a half." She managed to get the half back to their table without spilling any. Perry's curiosity had been roused, but he didn't want to pry into Wendy's private life, particularly for something so long in the past. On the other hand, if it was anything to do with Joan, it might well be another source of conflict, and perhaps it would be better if he did know about it. He ventured: "She did say she had some difficulties with Miss Mayflower's lessons."

"Yes, I remember; her parents made her join the Serbo-Croat classes she ran. That just made things worse really, isolated her, you know, set her apart as a foreigner. Not that she was, but bullies will pick on anything."

Perry thought: So that was it, nothing to do with Joan, just simple bullying. That in itself was serious enough, but at least Wendy appeared to have overcome the obstacles put in her way and to have suffered no lasting damage. That problem, at least, could not be laid at Joan's door.

"Of course, it was Miss Mayflower's fault really," continued Sonya. "She was her form mistress and she should have done something about it when she found out, but she just turned a blind eye."

She would, thought Perry. That woman has a way of making enemies that must be without parallel. "What happened to her? You said she left the school?"

"She went to a private Catholic school, I think," replied Sonya. "Her parents weren't badly off and they were Catholics anyway."

"It must have been pretty traumatic for her, being bullied and then having to pick up sticks and go to another school like that. Still, as you say, she seems to have come out of it all right."

"I'm glad. Next time she's in, I'll go and have a chat with her."

Perry looked at his watch. "We'd better be getting back to see what the afternoon brings."

CHAPTER NINE

The afternoon brought the fire brigade, followed by the police. Perry and Sonya saw a small fire tender parked by the residents' complex as they drove in after lunch. Perry stopped by the administration block to let Sonya out, and then drove straight up to the fire tender. He introduced himself to the first fireman he saw and was given a run-down of the situation by the officer in charge. Someone had, it appeared, started a small fire in one of the residents' rooms. It had not spread out of that one room and had been easily extinguished. The fire brigade had been called when another resident, on their way back from lunch, had heard the alarm and seen smoke in the room. The fire crew were currently examining the room. No one had been injured and the young man whose room it was had even managed to rescue his CD player.

The mention of a CD player alerted Perry. "Which room was it?"

"143," replied the officer.

"Barry, oh no."

"He's over there, behind the tender." They walked over to the rear of the tender, to find Barry sitting in his wheelchair, wearing a blanket, and surrounded by firemen and inmates. There appeared to be an expensive CD player in his lap.

"Are you all right, Barry?" asked Perry. "We should get Dr Anderson to look you over in a few minutes."

"I called him about ten minutes ago," said one of the residents clustered around Barry.

"Thank you, Janice. Then he should be here any minute now. You showed great presence of mind." She blushed modestly at the compliment.

"I don't want no poxy doctor and I don't want no fucking leather-craft." Barry had finally erupted into speech.

"Well, just to be on the safe side," said Perry with great forbearance. "And I think you may safely assume you'll never set foot in any of the workshops again."

Barry eyed him suspiciously. "What's that fucking cow been saying, then?"

Of all those present, it was the fire officer who looked shocked. One of his men beckoned him away. "Excuse me," he said, leaving Barry alone with Perry and Janice. The rest of the residents were drifting back to their own concerns.

"If you mean Mrs Jackson, she informed me that you threatened her with a craft knife this morning. Is that true, Barry?"

"Oh Barry, you never did, did you?" asked Janice.

"Sod off, you nosy bitch." Janice was only too grateful to do so.

"Well, Barry?" repeated Perry.

"What if I did. She was ordering me about. I don't take that from no one."

The fire officer called Perry over, and he left Barry to join the small group of firemen. "I'm afraid it looks as though the fire was started deliberately, sir."

One of the firemen elaborated: "There were separate fires started in two or three places in the room. We found a cigarette lighter on the floor. Some paper had been set alight in the waste paper basket and two separate heaps of bedding had been set on fire. Whoever it was wasn't taking any chances. Any ideas as to who might be responsible, sir?"

"Apart from Barry himself, I'm afraid not. The rooms all have individual keys so that the residents can protect their privacy, just as they would in their own homes. A set of master keys is kept in the admin. block for maintenance and emergency purposes, but it's unlikely Barry would have left his door open, especially with that expensive sound system he's got in there. Most of the residents are careful about locking up; even though the blocks have locks on the external doors to prevent access by outsiders, there have been cases where some of the residents have proved to be less than scrupulous as regards their neighbours' goods."

The fire officer agreed: "I'd be inclined to go along with that view, sir, particularly as the young man was on hand, so to speak, and managed to rescue his own CD player. I doubt whether he could have done that and emerged unscathed once the fire was under way. Logically, he gathered up the player before he started the fire."

"But why?" asked one of the firemen. "It looks to me as if you do the patients pretty well here. Much better than they would get on the NHS."

"He'd been involved in an incident this morning in which he threatened one of the therapists. I'm not sure what's behind it all. He claims not to like craft work, but I'm sure it must be more than that."

Dr Anderson drew up in his modest car. "Hello, Perry, got a fire, then?"

"Good of you to come; could you look at Barry? He was involved. It was only a small fire and he looks all right, but I'd be grateful if you could look him over." As he talked, Perry was walking with Dr Anderson towards Barry. "I don't think he was actually caught up in the fire, but it's best to be on the safe side."

"Hello, Barry, I'm Dr Anderson."

"Bugger off," replied Barry. Jerking his wheelchair into action, he propelled himself down the driveway towards the main road.

"Stop him," called the doctor sharply. "I think he's going to wheel himself into the road." Two of the firemen ran after Barry and brought his wheelchair to a halt. Dr Anderson caught up with them. Perry and the officer in charge looked on as he bent over the wheelchair and tried to talk to Barry. Within a few minutes, whether willingly or not, he was being wheeled by the doctor and one fireman towards the clinic which had been established on the site.

"Well, that's it then, we'll send you our report as soon as we can," said the fire officer. "You'll have to get in touch with your insurers and I would advise you to call the police straight away. In a case like this we shall notify them anyway. Sorry about all the mess, but you'll soon be able to get it cleared up. It's not as bad as it looks, and it's safe to go in. Once the insurance loss adjuster has been round, and given you the all clear, you can get it tidied up. Don't use any of the electrics in the building until the wiring has been checked over and made safe."

By way of goodbye, Perry thanked the fire officer for dealing with the fire so promptly and efficiently. He added: "I'm only sorry one of our patients has caused you so much trouble."

After the fire crew had departed, Perry walked swiftly back to his office and called Councillor Fairbrother, in his capacity as acting chairman of the board of trustees, and gave him a summary of the day's events. "Isn't he that boy who killed those youngsters while he was all drugged up?"

"Yes, I'm afraid so."

"You weren't keen to take him on in the first place, if I remember, and quite right too. These young people, they run wild. They've got no sense of responsibility." He was back to hang 'em and flog 'em. "What the hell did he think he was up to? I suppose we can only be grateful if Mrs Jackson doesn't sue us. The board should have listened to you in the first place. Still, no one was injured, that's the main thing. Hopefully, the insurance will cover us, even though it is arson, and by one of our own residents too. That's out of our hands now. You go ahead and call the police and the insurers, and we'll have to go from there. One thing's for sure though; that young man will have to go. There's no way we can keep him. God alone knows what he'll do next."

"I'll have a word with Dr Anderson," volunteered Perry. "He's always been very helpful in the past. I'll see what he can come up with."

"Good idea. I know we can rely on you. Let me know as soon as you hear any more."

44

Perry called the police and told them about both the fire and the attempted assault, and then he called the PVB's insurers who, in view of the unique nature of the situation, offered to try and get a loss adjuster round to inspect the damage that same afternoon. While he was waiting, Perry received an internal call from the doctor. An ambulance would be taking Barry to hospital. On inspection, the reason for his manic behaviour earlier on had become clear; he wasn't suffering from burns or smoke inhalation; he was high as a kite. Dr Anderson hadn't been able to find out from Barry what he'd taken, but it was possible it was more than one kind of drug. At least Barry wasn't belligerent now; he was comatose, hence the need for the ambulance. Dr Anderson asked Perry if it would be possible to venture into his room to see if there were any pills, bottles or syringes. Perry volunteered to go, and the doctor said he would remain with Barry and accompany him in the ambulance.

Perry started out again for the residence and was overtaken on his way there by the ambulance and the police. He signalled the ambulance towards the clinic and the police towards the hostel. When he caught up with them there, he gave them a brief account of the day's excitements and explained that it was necessary to search the room to see if they could find any traces of drugs. "The fire brigade said it's safe to go in, but it's a bit of a mess."

"We'll come and have a look with you, sir, see if we can't find out what he took, and we can make notes about the damage at the same time. There's not much else we can do, with the lad himself being out of it, unless we get a statement from Mrs Jackson."

The one room flatlet was an appalling sight: black and sodden. Perry had never seen a fire-damaged property before, and had no idea how bad it would look. He hadn't counted on the effects of the water used to extinguish the fire; it was everywhere, making the room wet and cold. "I'd better get on to the other residents either side and above, in case they need to be moved. Fortunately, he was on the ground floor, being in a wheelchair. Otherwise, I suppose the water would have flooded down the stairs and through the ceiling into the rooms below."

The two young constables poked about in the mess, but none of them could find any traces of drugs or syringes. "And you've no idea, sir, what he was taking or how he got hold of it?"

"None at all, I'm afraid. Dr Anderson said he thought he might have taken more than one thing, but he couldn't say what. As to how he got hold of the stuff, I suppose in the same way they all do. He wasn't a prisoner here, he could go out. All he'd got to do was wheel himself down the road or ride the patients' bus into town when it went in. We try to encourage our residents to be independent and expand their lives away from the PVB. There's no reason why they shouldn't develop friendships outside and have visitors, and most of them do. We don't check up on them."

The older of the two constables asked: "How did he get here in the first place, sir?"

Perry replied: "He had a motor accident, driving his father's bus while under the influence of drugs. He killed three people. When we agreed to take him for physical rehabilitation and to help him rebuild his life again, the hospital and probation service assured us he was no longer dependent on drugs. We wouldn't have taken him otherwise."

"They never really get over it, not really, sir. You see, there's always that little temptation, that need to feel good on a bad day, that need to be among the crowd again." The younger constable sounded cynically worldly wise for his years. "I don't think there's much more we can do here, sir. We'll notify the hospital we couldn't find anything, and we'll be in touch when we've got some news for you."

"Thank you both, I'll let you know if anything fresh crops up here, and I'll talk to Mrs Jackson about making a statement."

They parted company, and that only left the loss adjuster and the other residents to be seen before Perry went home.

Strangely enough, his heart hadn't troubled him at all that afternoon. It was anxiety that did for him, not physical exertion or management. It was worry that was so bad for him. He resolved to stop worrying.

The loss adjuster, when he arrived, looked more like a run-to-seed army officer than Perry's idea of an insurance agent. He had a remarkably sallow complexion and complained about the cold. Together they inspected the ruin. As far as could be ascertained at such short notice, the PVB was thought to be insured against that kind of damage. Presumably some prudent trustee in the past had understood that not all disabled people were angels. The loss adjuster was very helpful and informed Perry he would phone the insurers directly to get an agreement to arrange an electrical wiring inspection, structural examination, and boarding-up of the window and door, so that the room was secure. He would try to get his full report to the insurers by the following morning.

On returning to his office, Perry made arrangements for the residents of that block to receive all their meals free of charge in the cafeteria and for a television set to be sent over there from the admin. block, so they could watch in the evenings. All the residents were in for an inconvenient time until the electrical wiring had either been repaired or pronounced safe, and some of them would have to be moved to other rooms until the structure was certified sound. Sonya typed a notice informing all the residents of the temporary arrangements which had been made for them and requesting that any difficulties be notified to Perry or the night security staff.

Perry phoned their office to prepare them for the new situation and, as usual, found them very helpful. Initially, he had been against the introduction of a private company to provide night security for the PVB complex, but it had rapidly become obvious that petty thieves and vandals regarded the residents of the PVB as sitting ducks, particularly at night, and that the police simply couldn't provide the required degree of protection. Nite-Safe, a local company, had therefore been engaged to provide security at night, and they had proved to be unexpectedly sympathetic, helpful and efficient. An attempted stabbing, arson, and the prospect of a load of disgruntled residents didn't seem to worry them at all.

After one last phone call to Councillor Fairbrother, a long day was over for Perry. Sonya had loyally stayed behind, and Perry offered her a lift home. Tomorrow was another day; surely it couldn't be as bad as today.

In fact, the following morning proved to be one of those beautiful mid-summer mornings when the sun shone in the almost clear blue sky and the scent of the blooms in the flower beds filled the air. When Perry drove into work, Sonya was already there, fielding telephone calls from the trustees, local fund-raisers and the press. All in all, she was coping very well by the simple expedient of saying that all enquiries should be addressed to the Administrator, who was currently engaged.

However, there soon entered one problem Sonya couldn't cope with. Joan Mayflower marched into Perry's office and demanded in a loud voice: "What's all this I hear about Barry, then? Is it true he's in hospital?"

"I'm afraid so, Joan; after setting fire to his room, he became comatose from the effects of drugs."

"I can't believe it. Why wasn't I told? Why did he do it?"

Perry patiently explained that no one really knew why he'd set fire to his room or threatened Wendy with a craft knife. "Maybe it was just the effects of all the drugs he'd taken. I'm afraid there were a lot of people we didn't have time to notify yesterday, and it's not really something that affects you in fund-raising. We were rather busy yesterday," he said deprecatingly, "but we'll get a memo out today for the paid officers and trustees, and another for the rest of the patients and workers."

She clearly hadn't been listening to the last part of Perry's explanation and instead fastened on the incident with Wendy. "What do you mean, he threatened her?"

"Just that, Joan. He tried to stab her with a knife."

"Rubbish," she said forcefully. "I know Wendy Jackson of old; I taught her at school. She was always making trouble then, trying to make out the other girls were bullying her. She was always trying to get attention. It doesn't seem to me that she's grown up yet."

It was early in the day, but Perry had already had enough of Joan Mayflower. He said firmly, raising his voice a little: "I'm not in the least interested in Mrs Jackson's school days, and most particularly I'm not interested in your assessment of her character. I'm only interested in the happy and efficient running of this complex. As far as I can see, Mrs Jackson behaved very well over the incident; she didn't even want to involve the police, although she had plenty of witnesses to support her. Since I have now placed both matters in the hands of the police, I suggest you leave it to them."

She turned on her heel and marched out of Perry's office as abruptly as she had arrived.

Sonya put her head round the door. "Board meeting at two-thirty this afternoon for those who can attend, to discuss the fire and the situation with Barry."

"Right-o."

"Specifically not Miss Mayflower; the acting chairman instructed me not to notify her." Sonya seemed inordinately pleased.

Perry walked over to see if he could persuade Wendy to make an official statement to the police, and to inform her of the involvement of the police in the investigation of the fire. Miss Mayflower had got there before him. As he walked towards the workshop, he could see her through the window. She was pacing up and down in front of a very hurt-looking Wendy. Perry reached the door just in time to ask the first patients to arrive to wait outside for a few minutes. He entered and quietly closed the door behind him. Miss Mayflower was in full flow: "You always were the same, Wendy Lalovic; you always were a trouble maker. What did you do to Barry to upset him? I want to know. Now."

Wendy looked close to tears and Perry was about to intervene, but she found voice, a little uncertainly at first, but then with growing confidence. "I'm not at school now. You're not my teacher. You can't use bullies to intimidate me because it suits your purpose any more. All that is over. And in any case, what exactly is your interest in Barry?"

Joan Mayflower was not accustomed to insubordination and she didn't know how to handle it. Perry stepped forward, with a smile of approval for Wendy and said: "I thought I'd made it clear to you that this is not a matter for your concern, Joan. Please return to your fund-raising duties." For the second time that morning, she retreated. Perry thought he was beginning to get the measure of the woman. She was nothing more or less than a bully herself, albeit one who would get other people to do her dirty work for her, if she could.

He opened the doors to admit the patients and spoke to them all together. He satisfied their curiosity concerning the fire and explained the involvement of the police and the need to talk to them when they arrived.

Wendy agreed to make the complaint official and asked: "What will happen to Barry?"

"I don't really know," admitted Perry, "but I shouldn't think it would be possible for him to come back here in view of his actions and his drug problem. We're having a board meeting this afternoon, and I shall recommend his transfer back into the care of his local authority." The patients and Wendy looked very relieved.

For the rest of the morning Perry was busy attending to the aftermath of the fire. By the afternoon the builders and electricians had moved in. With any luck, the residents of the hostel would have their usual accommodation and comforts restored by the evening of the next day at the latest.

The board meeting was brief and to the point. Eric Palmer, the chairman, had returned from holiday and moved the meeting along briskly. Perry was praised for having done a wonderful job in difficult circumstances, and it was resolved to have Barry prosecuted for both the arson and the attempted assault, distasteful as such action might be. What happened to him after that was not the concern of the PVB. Under no circumstances was he to be allowed to darken their doors again. Until the trial, he would have to remain the responsibility of the health service and his local authority. Presumably, they might make another attempt to rid him of his habit. None of the trustees had any expectations of such an attempt being successful.

Much to Perry's relief, the chairman was also pleased to announce that Miss Mayflower had written to him accepting the post of education officer. They were therefore free to find another fund-raiser. Several members of the board sighed with relief. Perry wondered what had persuaded Joan to accept the post, but it really didn't matter. What mattered was that she'd given up trying to oust him. He was safe. Jack was smiling at him, as the chairman closed the meeting. Even Sonya looked happy; for once she'd managed to keep up with the minutes.

Dr Anderson called later in the afternoon. Barry had regained consciousness and had the police with him now. At last, Perry had a few minutes to himself. He brewed a coffee and sat thinking about the events of the past few days. Even for someone on drugs, Barry's behaviour had been bizarre. He just couldn't understand it, but then he supposed that was what drugs did to people. Even more incomprehensible was Joan's clumsy attempt to extricate Barry from trouble by trying to imply that Wendy had exaggerated the knife attack. It was ridiculous, as was her second attempt to save him, by badgering her, Why had she behaved so strangely?

A really ugly thought entered Perry's head. Barry had to get his drugs from somewhere. Supposing someone at the PVB had been supplying him? One of the more mobile patients, or a member of staff perhaps? Despite what he had said on the previous day, would it really have been that easy for Barry to go out and get his own supplies? The idea of someone in a wheelchair hanging around dark street corners to make a connection now struck him as grotesque. Perry realized at this point that he was hopelessly out of his depth concerning the "drug culture", as he believed it was called.

Letting his thoughts run on, it occurred to him that Joan's concern for Barry might be rooted in his drug problem. He couldn't envisage her supplying him with drugs, but he could envisage her supplying him with the money to buy them. Payment for services rendered on the switchboard. And when Barry had no longer been able to provide the service, he knew the payments would dry up. Perry wondered if that might explain the outburst of the previous day. It would certainly explain why Joan didn't want Barry to fall into the hands of the law.

By the following Monday Barry and the problems he had brought in his wake were almost history. The builders and electricians had completely refurbished his old room, and it was now ready for a new inhabitant. It only remained to replace the soft furnishings from the supply the PVB held, until new ones could be purchased with the insurance money.

The police had almost finished their enquiries. Barry had admitted both the assault and the arson, and was now in the secure wing of a hospital on the outskirts of London, awaiting recovery and reports. If he were to continue to plead guilty at the trial, it was unlikely that Wendy or any of the other witnesses would have to appear in court. As to the question of motive, the police were as mystified as anyone else. Apparently, he didn't have one.

However, the police had discovered the source of his supplies. If Barry had been reluctant to talk about himself, he was more than ready to drop other people in it. He had not lost touch with many of his friends from the old days, and he had phoned them up when he had been working alone on the exchange. They had been only too happy to deliver, for a price. The police were curious as to how Barry had acquired sufficient funds to support his habit, but Perry didn't offer them the benefits of his speculations.

CHAPTER TEN

During his morning rounds Perry called on Ben. "That bloody woman's been in again." Perry braced himself for another onslaught. "She came to tell me that, and I quote: 'what little work', I'd done for the new brochure would be wasted, because she's changing jobs. She reckons I'll have to pull my socks up and start all over again when the new fund-raiser comes."

"It is true she has accepted the post of education officer," replied Perry evenly. The advertisement for a new fund-raiser has already gone out, I believe. Joan will finish in her present post at the end of the month."

"Well, thank God for that," said Ben. Then he added: "Education officer? That wouldn't involve literature and lectures and posters and visual aids, by any chance, would it?" Before Perry could break the bad news, Ben continued: "Because if so, I can tell you right now that wherever she gets them from, she won't get them from here."

"We'll have to see how it goes; I wouldn't worry about it now." Perry was concerned. Ben looked to be getting worked-up, like he used to just after he came to the PVB. Perry thought that, after all, Miss Mayflower was going to continue to be a problem wherever she worked in the PVB. The sooner they could get shot of her altogether, the better. Unfortunately, there was nothing he could do about that.

After leaving Ben, Perry went to the leather-craft workshop to give Wendy and the others the latest news about Barry. They were all relieved to learn they probably wouldn't have to give evidence in court.

That lunch time Perry and Eric Palmer had arranged to meet the local fund-raisers in the board room to give them the news about Miss Mayflower and to repair some of the damage she'd done. "A bit of PR And a bit of bridge building," as the chairman had put it.

Some of the fund-raisers, were unable to attend, but those who did were treated to a buffet lunch, a glass of wine (as recommended by Sonya) and some good tidings. Not one of them appeared to regret the passing of Joan Mayflower as fund-raiser. They all congratulated Perry and the chairman for getting rid of her so quickly, although not a few doubted the wisdom of installing her as an education officer. Janet Thompson, from Sevenoaks, did point out that, whatever her personality defects, Miss Mayflower had been a teacher, and was therefore presumably competent in that field. Some of the other fund-raisers doubted even that, and Fred Solas, from Brighton, thought that it seemed pointless to employ, in any capacity, someone who was so out of sympathy with the work of the charity. Colonel Charles, who had relented of his previous hastiness, and had now "taken Mid-Kent in hand" after Paul's departure, agreed with him. "Ghastly woman. Can't think why she was ever appointed in the first place." That thought found a chord in Perry. He resolved to find out at the first opportunity who on the board had voted for her.

After their lunch the local fund-raisers were treated to a tour of the complex. They'd all been there before, but there were always new things to see, and they were pleased with the progress on the new block. The problems caused by Barry were tactfully minimized; although several of the fund-raisers had heard the news about his drug addiction, none of them appeared to want to talk about it. Their main concern was that it should be kept from the press as far as possible, especially when he came to trial. The last thing they wanted was to have it appear that the PVB was a home for drug addicts.

As they sauntered through the grounds, several of the fund-raisers remarked on their immaculate condition, much to the pleasure of the gardeners, whom they warmly congratulated.

Even Franjo smiled, offering hints and tips to those who were having problems with their own gardens or house plants.

Perry waited patiently for them to finish. He knew these meetings were as important to the workers as they were to the fund-raisers. He was not disposed to hurry them. He found himself standing beside Eric Palmer and Colonel Charles, who either didn't have a garden or, more probably, knew how to keep it in order. He was staring fixedly at Franjo, who seemed not to have noticed him. "Of course, of course," he muttered. "After all these years. I'd no idea, but of course."

"Pardon?" asked Perry.

"That gardener, Franjo, Franjo Mihailovic, I'd no idea he was here."

"Franjo's been with us a few years now," replied Perry. "Do you know him, then?"

The colonel shrugged. "I haven't seen him for years, but I did know him. We were both much younger then, but I never forget a face. Especially one with those eyes. I don't suppose we've got anything in common now, but Maggie knew him, and so does your former fund-raiser."

"Oh?" Perry was intrigued.

"Oh yes, didn't she tell you? She's his sister."

Perry was genuinely amazed. He'd never thought of Joan Mayflower as having any family, although he'd known Franjo's family had settled in England. "I'd no idea," he said. "She never said anything. Nor did Franjo, come to that."

"I wouldn't have thought about it myself, but having seen her at close quarters that day she came down and lectured us all, I thought she looked familiar. Then, seeing Franjo here today, I remembered her. She must have changed her name, but they've got the same intense blue eyes. Just you look next time you see her."

Perry had already noticed her eyes; even behind reading glasses they were very remarkable. "We always thought Franjo was on his own, that he had no one who could look after him; if he has an unmarried sister, there's no reason why he should have spent most of his life in institutions. Even now, with a bit of care, he could live away from here. I wonder why Joan didn't take more of an interest in him?"

The chairman was fidgeting, as if he were cold despite the heat of the afternoon. With a brief "Excuse me," he wandered over to the group gathered around the rose bushes.

The colonel looked shrewdly after him, and then said slowly: "In answer to your question, I shouldn't imagine they get on all that well. They never did when Maggie and I knew them." Perry could well believe that; neither of them was exactly an easy character to get on with. He said as much. Colonel Charles continued: "It's deeper than that, I'm afraid. Since it looks as though the PVB is going to be saddled with that damned woman, I might as well tell you, so you know what to expect. After all, you could say I'm responsible for her being here in the first place."

With no concessions to modern nomenclature, he explained that Yugoslavia had always been an ethnic and cultural nightmare. There had been a lot of old scores to settle, particularly with those who had worked for the government or who had not fitted in in some way. Franjo had become involved in all this, and had been well and truly beaten up. As a result of this, he had come to the attention of the Red Cross, for whom the colonel's wife, Maggie, was then working. Franjo had been brought to England for medical treatment and, in due course, his staunchly English mother and sister had followed as refugees. "Both Maggie and I had known her family for years, so when she needed to come back, I pulled a few strings for them, to help things along. After they settled down in Kent, we kept in touch for a while."

Perry considered these revelations in silence for a few minutes. They explained a lot, but not everything. He asked: "Why don't they get on? After all, they are brother and sister, and they must have been through a lot together."

"I don't know, but I think it stems from something that happened back home. He told me as much once, years ago when he was at home for a spell, and we visited the family. Even then he was bitter about her. Mind you, I always got on with him, but Joan was a different kettle of fish. She was like her mother. She died last year, Joan must miss her."

The afternoon became less sunny and it looked as though they might be in for a storm. The clouds were rolling in from the west, and several of the local organizers declared their intentions of getting away before the storm broke, among them Colonel Charles. Perry and Eric Palmer stood chatting to the stragglers in the lengthening shadows. Franjo had long since wheeled himself off to his greenhouses. Mercifully, Joan Mayflower was nowhere to be seen.

CHAPTER ELEVEN

Following their Saturday morning round of golf, Perry and Jack were sipping their pints in the club house when Jack asked: "How did the meeting with the local fund-raisers go?"

"Not too bad, not too bad at all. They were relieved we'd decided to promote Joan sideways."

"With any luck, we'll be rid of her altogether in a few months."

Perry, grateful for the opening, asked his question. "Several of them wondered how on earth we could have employed someone like that in the first place. She's so unsympathetic towards disabled people. I know you weren't in favour of her, but it's hard to think who would be."

Jack took the bait: "Palmer, the chairman, mostly. He said she'd had such a hard time of it, being a refugee and all, and then losing her job as a teacher. It can't have been easy to start all over again in middle age."

Perry considered for a minute or two. "I didn't realize she'd lost her job as a teacher. I thought she'd simply got fed up and resigned. A lot of them do. I can't say it's a job I'd like, not these days." He paused. "Why did she lose her job, do you know?"

"Oh, it was nothing to her detriment. She'd been at the same school for years; she went there just after she qualified. It was a girls' grammar school then. After the re-organization, when the schools here finally went comprehensive, it was really surplus to requirements. The town already had two large sec-mods, one for girls and one for boys. They'd traditionally had much wider catchment areas than the grammar and, after a while, the grammar school closed. She was made redundant."

"And they couldn't get her a post in one of the other schools?"

"Apparently not. I remember at the time quite a few of the teachers lost their jobs, including the headmistress, Miss Robertson. She gave Miss Mayflower a good reference when she applied to us. I suppose the other schools already had full complements of staff. Perhaps she couldn't fancy starting off again in a new school somewhere else and thought she'd have a complete change, so she went to the Martin Luther Missions."

"More's the pity for us. Can I get you a refill, Jack?"

"Thanks." Perry couldn't put his finger on the reason, but he felt Jack was being evasive. Unlike Perry, Jack was a local man and could probably have told him a great deal about Joan if he'd had a mind to. After all, Perry seemed to remember him saying his step-daughter had gone to school locally. She'd grown up now, of course. But for some reason Jack hadn't been very forthcoming. Perry wondered if he knew Franjo was Joan's brother. He decided not to mention it.

Despite himself, Perry found he was developing an interest in his soon to be ex-fund-raiser. There had definitely been something less than frank about the way Jack had described her teaching history. As he drove into work on Monday morning, he spotted her car in the small car park. Sonya was just arriving ahead of him. He thought she must have been at school around the relevant time, and decided to ask her about the demise of the old grammar school and the fate of its German teacher. All in all, Perry was quite looking forward to the next week. The threat of Joan taking his job was gone, and Barry and his antics were a thing of the past. The last week had been difficult, but he felt proud of the way he'd coped. The board had obviously been pleased with him. He'd felt his confidence surging as, one by one, he'd waded through the morass of problems. It had been like the old days, the good old days, when business had been booming and life had been an endless stream of achievements, with no clouds on the horizon. Seen in this new light, even Sonya looked good. Perry had noticed that over the past few weeks she too had gained in confidence and had smartened herself up.

One of Perry's first duties was to check the work on the new block, which he did every week, while on his morning constitutional. Knowing builders as he did, he thought it best to let them know he was keeping an eye on them. It never did to let them think they could get away with anything. On his rounds he bumped into Franjo. "How did you enjoy your little talk with the good colonel?" he asked slyly.

"Colonel Charles has taken over as the local fund-raiser for Mid-Kent," replied Perry non-committally.

Franjo's upturned face scrutinised him. "Oh yes, he is a great organizer, that one. You can rely on him to do his duties to our PVB."

"I hope so." The two men remained in awkward proximity, neither of them speaking, until Perry continued. "Miss Mayflower will be resigning her post as fund-raiser at the end of this month and she will then become our new education officer."

Franjo snorted. "This I know, but how long will it last, my friend? How long before you get rid of her altogether?" Perry couldn't answer that one. "Well, let me tell you, you may think you know. You may think you know all. You do not. You never can get rid of her. She is here for ever, you will see."

"We can none of us see into the future, Franjo; it is quite possible that Joan herself may find that in a few months' time she would like to take on fresh challenges. I wouldn't be at all surprised." Perry wondered where this conversation was leading him.

Franjo laughed a little. "Oh no. She has it too good here. She will never leave. You be careful."

"I will," promised Perry. Throughout their conversation, neither had mentioned that Joan was Franjo's sister. Perry noticed that Franjo had a miniature rose in a pot on his lap. "I didn't know you were doing those now."

"Yes, we have only a few, to see how they go with the shops. If they sell well, we could get more."

"If you have any spare in that sort of pink-red, I'd like to buy one for Pam, she's very keen on that sort of thing right now."

"I put one away for you," offered Franjo. "When you come tomorrow, you can have it. When you tell me how Mrs Jackson goes." With that cryptic remark, he wheeled himself away.

Perry understood that he was supposed to go and see Wendy Jackson. He couldn't think why, but he went just the same. The leather-craft workshop was a hive of happy industry, with Classic Radio accompanying the chattering of the workers. Some of them were singing along. As usual, Wendy was keeping a conscientious eye on them and helping some of the most disabled ones with their more difficult tasks. It was a far cry from the scene after Barry had threatened her. "Good morning, Wendy; good morning all," Perry called out as he entered.

They all chorused "Good morning," in reply.

"How are you getting on, then?"

"Freddie's starting on the new range of handbags for the Christmas market," replied Wendy.

Freddie moved over so that Perry could draw up alongside him and watch him assemble a small, dark brown leather handbag with a long shoulder strap. It was a relatively simple job and the result was remarkably handsome. "Isn't that shoulder strap a bit long?" asked Perry. "There's no buckle or anything, no way of shortening it."

"They wear it across the body, like this," said Freddie, holding up one of the finished bags to demonstrate. "It's safer that way. They can't get it pulled off their shoulder, like they could if they didn't wear it over the body."

"It's all the fashion now," remarked Cedric, who was polishing the finished articles and checking them before they were packed into large boxes.

"I must look at what Pam does with hers next time we go out," said Perry.

61

"Besides, have you seen the young girls these days?" asked Wendy. "They're six feet tall and broad with it. Not like us delicate flowers." They all laughed.

"So everything's settled down again?" asked Perry.

"Yes, we're all back to normal now."

"Well, let's hope it stays that way. With a bit of luck, we've heard the last of Barry. If he continues to plead guilty, we won't have any more trouble." Perry noticed that at the mention of Barry, Wendy had begun to look evasive. He wondered what was going on and drew her to one side, out of earshot of the workers. "What's the matter, Wendy? You don't look too happy."

"It's just that when I thought about it, I feel a bit of a creep, having a bloke in a wheelchair prosecuted. I've half a mind to go to the police and ask them to drop the complaint. After all, he's being done on the arson charge and he won't ever come back here." She looked hopefully at Perry.

"Wendy, you know as well as I do, that if he gets away with it this time, he'll just go and do the same thing to some other poor patient or therapist or doctor. Besides, he's the sort that would promise to plead guilty to the arson and then turn up in court with some sob story saying you'd upset him, driven him to it, and if you withdraw your complaint on the assault charge, he might well be believed. You'd probably end up being made the villain of the piece."

Wendy muttered something Perry couldn't quite catch. He asked: "You don't want that to happen, do you?" She shook her head. "So tell me what's going on."

"Sit down," she invited reluctantly. They cleared spaces in the corner of the workshop by the kettle and tea-making paraphernalia. Wendy didn't say anything for a few minutes. She was obviously finding this difficult. Perry allowed her to take her time. Finally, she began: "She's doing it to me again, just like she did before." Perry had no need to ask who "she" was. "When I was at school, I was bullied something rotten. I was different, you see; I had a foreign name and I was a Catholic. We didn't go into assembly or anything; we used to have separate religious instruction from the local priest, who came in twice a week for the half dozen of us who were Catholics. And I was different in other ways too: I was quite clever and a bit of a swot; on top of that, my parents were better off than most. We owned our own home and ran a small car."

She paused to see if Perry was taking in what she was saying.

"So there was quite a lot of jealousy," he said, encouragingly.

"Yes, I suppose that was at the bottom of it," she replied. "At the time, I used to think it was me, that there was something wrong with me. I had absolutely no self-confidence. The worst of it was that I had to travel about ten miles by train to school. A whole load of the pupils came from Cansterville, and we all had to travel on the same train to and from school. Those ten miles were a nightmare every day. In the mornings they used to rip up my homework and in the afternoons they used to thump me on the way home. There was no way out, the trains were so few and far between that I couldn't just take another, and there were never any witnesses. And it wasn't only that; I can't remember the number of times I had pens and money stolen; the entire PE kit I kept at school was filched a couple of times, and they weren't cheap. Then my train season ticket, provided by the local authority, was stolen at the beginning of one term, so my parents had to pay the fares all that term."

Perry interrupted: "But couldn't you do anything, even if your teacher wasn't sympathetic? That sort of thing simply shouldn't be permitted by a school."

"Of course it shouldn't. But things were a lot more rough and ready then. You were expected to be able to look after yourself and it was your own fault if you didn't."

"That's rubbish," protested Perry. "One person can't stand up to physical violence and theft organized by a gang like that. No one expects an adult to do it. That's why we have a police force."

Wendy shrugged. "Of course, we did complain. First of all, I complained directly, and then my parents went to the school to see Miss Mayflower, who was my form teacher then, and the headmistress. Miss Mayflower simply told my parents and the headmistress I was making it all up. According to her, I'd never been beaten up, and I'd carelessly lost my PE equipment and my season ticket myself. That was despite the fact that the PE equipment had once gone missing when I was away from school with flu."

"I'll never know why, but Miss Mayflower hated me. I'd never done anything to her, but after that she made my life a misery. She was always pulling me up in class, making derogatory comments about me in front of the other girls and giving me all the rotten jobs to do. It just wore me down, I was like a shadow. In the end my parents took me away and sent me to the local Convent School. Fortunately, they could afford to; God knows what would have happened to me if I'd stayed in that place. You see, I had absolutely no protection. Not only were the other girls still bullying me, but now they knew they had a free hand. Their form teacher was joining in the sport."

Perry shook his head in disbelief. "I can't understand how someone who was as bad a teacher as that was allowed to continue in her job. She allowed the situation to develop and then made it worse by deliberately encouraging the bullies. What was the headmistress thinking of? Surely she must have seen there was something wrong? Why didn't she do something?"

"I don't really know the answer to that. Maybe she really didn't believe me, maybe she did believe Miss Mayflower, maybe she didn't care any more. She wasn't a well woman. She'd been in a serious car crash some years before and she was always having months away ill. She probably just couldn't cope. Looking back on it all, I think Miss Mayflower was more to blame than anyone, including the girls. She knew better, and she was in a position to stop it and she didn't. Instead, she went round behind my back, running me down and making me look guilty, when I was the victim. It wasn't very pleasant, I can tell you."

"And now you think she's doing the same kind of thing all over again with this business with Barry?" asked Perry cautiously.

Wendy nodded. "Last thing on Friday, Mr Manning, our administrator up at St. Luke's, called me into his office and asked for details of my complaint against Barry." Perry was surprised and he showed it. "I asked him why he wanted to know. It's not really anything to do with St. Luke's, even though Barry was briefly a patient there after the fire."

"I should think not," retorted Perry. "And what did you tell Mr Manning?"

"What I've said to you: that it wasn't really any of his business. It was then that he started on about knowing that I'd had an 'unfortunate history', as he put it, how, perhaps, I tended to see things as more serious than they really were, and how he wouldn't like to see a member of the staff of St. Luke's put in an embarrassing light, if it ever came to court. He asked me whether or not the matter had really been all that serious, and whether I wasn't in some measure to blame, provoking Barry and all that. I was so upset, I was nearly in tears when I bumped into Freddie. He was up there for his weekly physio. and offered to buy me a cup of tea. Wasn't that sweet of him?"

"That Manning's got a damned cheek," fumed Perry. "It's got absolutely nothing to do with St. Luke's, and if I didn't think you were an entirely reliable person, incidentally supported by witnesses, I wouldn't have pressed you to put the matter in the hands of the police. And don't forget, as far as we know, Barry himself is willing to plead guilty. In the circumstances, he could hardly do otherwise."

Wendy looked relieved and a lot happier. "I understand, Perry, I do, but the thought of going through all that unpleasantness again is putting me off."

Perry was puzzled: "Why do you think Miss Mayflower has been at Manning? Couldn't he have got his information from somewhere else?"

"She lives next door to him," replied Wendy shortly.

Perry nodded. "Well, Wendy, the thing to remember is this time you're not alone: you've got witnesses and me to support you. With your permission, I'm going to put a stop to this once and for all. I'm going to phone your Mr Manning and advise him to stick to administering St. Luke's hospital and to leave administration of the PVB to me. I'll also give him a friendly lesson on the perils of listening to unsubstantiated gossip." Perry was feeling really angry, but, strangely enough, his heart wasn't playing him up at all. He even thought he could feel the blood coursing healthily along his arteries. Wendy gave him Mr Manning's work number. Before they parted, he instructed her: "If you get any more trouble from the same source, come to me straight away, and I'll back you all the way; don't try to fight it alone, you don't have to." She looked grateful and smiled.

As Perry was about to return to his office, he paused for one last question: "Do you know Franjo, by the way?"

"The gardener in the wheelchair? I've seen him around, but he's never been in craft therapy, at least not during my time. Why do you ask?"

"He comes from the former Yugoslavia, you know, like Joan and your parents and I think he keeps his eyes open for you."

"That's kind of him, but why?"

Perry smiled. "I've an idea he knows our friend of old, but anyway, don't you worry, I'm off to talk to your Mr Manning now." As he ambled back to his office Perry thought that Wendy clearly didn't know Franjo was Joan Mayflower's brother.

It transpired that Mr Manning was in a meeting when Perry called, but about an hour later Sonya managed to get him. "Mr Manning, Perry Barrett here from the Princess Victoria's Bounty."

"Oh good morning, Mr Barrett, what can I do for you?"

"I understand you've been making enquiries about our recent spot of bother." Mr Manning didn't reply; there was a silence. "Mr Manning, are you still there?"

"Yes, I'm here, Mr Barrett, and yes, I did just mention it to Mrs Jackson when I happened to bump into her on Friday, just as a matter of general interest, you know. After all, it's been in the papers." Mr Manning was clearly not very verbally skilled.

Perry paused, and then said: "Yes, I am aware that the newspapers reported both the facts that the young man threatened a member of staff with a knife in front of several witnesses and that he later set fire to his own room here. Perhaps they failed to make it clear that the PVB regards both incidents as very serious and is very anxious for the police to prosecute on both charges, most particularly since there may be an unsavoury drug connection to both incidents, as I am sure you are well aware."

"Yes, the boy, after all, did come to St. Luke's, so I do know about that," agreed Mr Manning.

He'd fallen into the trap. "Presumably whoever was providing him with his drugs or the money to buy them would be very keen on not having him prosecuted in case he decides to spill the beans as a means of getting a lighter sentence."

"Sorry, you've lost me, Mr Barrett."

"I was just pointing out, Mr Manning, that the police would undoubtedly be very interested in hearing about anyone attempting to bring pressure to bear on any of the witnesses."

"Oh, I say, Mr Barrett, that's a bit strong. I mean it was just that I'd heard Mrs Jackson was sometimes a bit inclined to over-dramatize. I didn't want her to get into difficulties, that's all."

Perry was rapidly concluding that Mr Manning was an idiot. "We think very highly of Mrs Jackson here, Mr Manning, and, in future, may I suggest that you restrict your activities to the administration of St. Luke's and leave me to administer here? As I am sure you would agree, unsupported and unsubstantiated gossip is an evil and pernicious thing."

"Oh quite, Mr Barrett, quite. It was just that one of your own people asked if I couldn't help out, in view of the facts, that's all."

He sounded plaintive, but had obviously chosen to ignore Perry's remarks about gossip. "What facts would those be, Mr Manning?" Perry enquired coldly.

"Well, perhaps someone just got hold of the wrong end of the stick; I don't know anything about Mrs Jackson personally. I was just going by what I was told."

"By whom, Mr Manning?"

"Well… er… I don't know if I should disclose that. Best just to let it drop, eh? Now that we've cleared the air a bit." He sounded quite hopeful.

Perry thought he would press a little harder. "I'm afraid it's not that simple, Mr Manning; if someone purporting to speak on behalf of the PVB has been inviting you to put pressure on Mrs Jackson to withdraw her complaint, then I think I should be informed."

"Well, it was just a friendly conversation, really. I don't think there was any ill intent, nothing like that." Mr Manning was clearly not relishing the prospect of having Joan Mayflower as a neighbour if she ever found out he'd shopped her.

"Yes, Mr Manning?" There was a pause. "Look, if you don't want to tell me, I'm afraid I shall just have to inform the police, and let them deal with it."

Mr Manning caved in. "It was my next door neighbour, Miss Mayflower, your fund-raising officer."

"And did Miss Mayflower happen to disclose her interest in that young man?" Perry tried to sound as menacing as possible.

"No, not at all," replied Mr Manning quickly. "It was just that I think she was concerned for Mrs Jackson."

"I think in future, Mr Manning, it would be safer to assume Mrs Jackson can look after her own interests, and that I speak for the PVB in this matter, not Miss Mayflower."

"Yes, yes, I understand, Mr Barrett. I was only trying to help," agreed Mr Manning.

"As long as that is clear, Mr Manning, I'm prepared to leave the matter there, but I must warn you that any further attempt to influence this matter by yourself or anyone else will be reported directly to the police. Goodbye." Perry dropped the receiver before Mr Manning had a chance to reply. He thought Manning was a spineless little twerp, the type who would cheerfully go round causing misery by repeating gossip, and then claim he was "only trying to help", when he got caught out. He was just the sort of person Joan Mayflower would pick to do her dirty work. Really, that woman was getting worse.

CHAPTER TWELVE

Perry called Eric Palmer and laid the latest discoveries before him. He thought that with Mr Manning's admission of the involvement of Joan Mayflower in attempts to prevent the successful prosecution of Barry there was good cause to have her dismissed. The chairman's response was disappointing. He hemmed and hawed and pointed out that Perry only had Mr Manning's verbal admission. "But he did talk to Mrs Jackson, and he had gossip that he could not reasonably have got from any other source. I've got him good and scared; I'm sure he'd repeat his story for the board's benefit, if we act quickly. We could get rid of her in a manner which would make it impossible for her to go to the press over that business with Paul Russell. Take it from me, Eric, she's poison. She's creating havoc here and she'll go on doing it as long as she continues to work for us."

The chairman sighed. "Look, Perry, is there anywhere we could meet for lunch?"

"What about the Thai down by the floral clock in town?"

"Yes, I know it. I'll see you there about one and we'll talk this over then. OK?"

"Fine." Perry was mystified. No doubt all would be revealed over lunch. Not for the first time, he found himself wondering why the chairman was being so benevolent to Joan.

The Thai restaurant was practically empty, even at the peak of the lunch hour. It was a good restaurant, but Perry thought it suffered from the fact that most people couldn't tell the difference between Thai cuisine and Chinese, and there were any number of cheaper Chinese restaurants around. However, since the chairman had once expressed an admiration for Thai food, Perry thought it a good choice to put him at his ease. Much to his surprise, Eric was waiting for him when he arrived at five past one. They ordered a satay *hors d'oeuvre* and a Thai curry apiece. Eric ordered a bottle of Muscadet. Perry thought the food was very good; maybe he'd bring Pam there on their anniversary.

The chairman opened the batting. "What you were saying earlier, about getting our good lady dismissed, I don't have to tell you I'm not a great fan of hers myself, that's obvious."

"I did wonder," replied Perry evenly.

The chairman plunged on: "But, well, I'm telling you in the strictest confidence, just so that you don't overplay your hand with her, that I couldn't support you in any attempt to get rid of her." Perry didn't reply, he wondered how someone as successful as Eric Palmer could be so naïve. He thought it was one of his chairman's more endearing traits. "After all, I was the one in favour of giving her the job in the first place."

"But look," argued Perry, "that's no reason to support her if it doesn't work out. We all make mistakes. Maybe she was the best candidate at the time, I don't know. But she isn't the best choice now. It was a mistake. We all make 'em," he said sympathetically. God knows, he thought, I've made enough in my time.

The chairman dipped his meat in his peanut sauce. He looked older and sadder, as if all the energy had drained out of him. "Yes, we all make mistakes, and I've been paying for mine ever since. Me and Helen."

Perry knew that the chairman's wife had arthritis and that she'd been in and out of various hospitals for years. That was how Eric had become interested in the work of the PVB in the first place. It had all been before Perry's time, but Jack had told him. For one absurd moment, he pictured Eric having a bit on the side with Joan Mayflower. The vision was soon dispelled.

"It all started before we were married, when she was the headmistress of the local girls' grammar here." Perry had an unpleasant idea that he was being taken down a familiar road. Eric was still speaking: "Her maiden name was Robertson. She had it all: a good career, friends, a nice cottage on top of Love In Vain Hill, you know the place?"

71

"Yes, it's that steep incline on the old coast road, isn't it?"

"That's the place. Neither of us had married before; she was married to her career, and I was working twenty-five hours a day on the business. You know how it is. It was through the business that I met her: she wanted some landscaping at the back of the cottage. We liked each other, and eventually, we decided to get married. We were both in our middle thirties then." Perry mentally adjusted that to late thirties. He said nothing.

"The summer before we married, she'd been to an evening parent-teachers' meeting, and had just driven home. It had been a long day and she was dog tired. She parked the car at the top of the hill outside the cottage; there wasn't a garage. As she was getting out, the car started to slip forward down the hill. She struggled to get back in and behind the wheel to stop it. She didn't make it; all she succeeded in doing was getting herself dragged along the ground, trapped by the car door."

He paused as the curries appeared; he clearly didn't want the waiter to overhear. Perry poured them both some more Muscadet. Eric continued: "She spent months in hospital and had to have a minor operation on her brain. She even had to wear a wig for a while." Perry showed his sympathy rather than speaking it. "Anyway, she appeared to make a complete recovery and went back to work. In due course, we got married, much to the delectation of the kids." Eric smiled in remembrance, but appeared unable to continue.

They ate in silence for about ten minutes and then he tried again. "Of course, we didn't understand at the time, but she was ill, mentally ill. The smash must have affected her more than we realized. On the surface, everything was all right. She had to return to the hospital occasionally for minor bits of cosmetic work, but she seemed quite OK. Then the problems started. She couldn't cope with her job any more. It was too much for her, but she wouldn't give it up. It was her life."

Eric seemed to be choking on his own words. "She was really fond of the girls, I don't care what anyone says, she really was, but one or two of them just rubbed her up the wrong way. She developed an irrational dislike of them; she couldn't help it. I can see it now, I couldn't then." Perry wondered if this was leading in the direction of Wendy Lalovic, but he was to be surprised. "There was one girl, Anne Baker; her parents were members of the Plymouth Brethren. She was a very clever girl and she should have tried for a scholarship to Oxford or Cambridge, but her parents wanted her to go to London University, so she could live at home. In the lower sixth, as it was then, they all had an interview with Helen to sort out their career options. She was very conscientious like that." Eric made another choking sound, but managed to continue: "This Anne explained to Helen that she didn't want to live away from home. Helen lost her temper and said she was being childish. One thing led to another and she struck the girl."

Perry couldn't help himself: "Oh no. How awful." He regretted the words the moment they were uttered.

Eric understood his repugnance, but worse was to come. "Unfortunately, she didn't stop there. She laid into her quite a bit." Perry couldn't believe his ears. Eric was sounding bitter now. "Miss Mayflower was coming back from hockey practice and she had to pass the window of Helen's office to get back to the staff room. She saw what was happening and rushed in to put a stop to it. Fortunately, the girls' changing rooms were in the opposite direction and she was the only one who saw anything. Thank God, Anne was only bruised. There was no serious damage, but it was enough. If it had come out, Helen would have lost her job, maybe even been prosecuted."

Perry interrupted: "Surely not, it must have been obvious she was ill, that the crash had damaged her brain. Wouldn't she just have been pensioned off, due to ill health?"

The chairman looked thoroughly miserable. "Looking back on it now, it's easy to say that. I suppose we should have seen it at the time. But we couldn't. At the time, the most important thing was to protect Helen. At least, that's what I thought. Joan Mayflower phoned me from Helen's office and I came over at once. I took Helen home and Joan said she would take Anne home and explain everything to her parents."

Perry said: "She would." He was beginning to smell a rat. Although he was far from agreeing with Eric in his obsessive need to protect his wife at the expense of her pupils, he could sympathize with him.

"Yes, I can see you understand," he said wearily. "After that Helen was completely in her power, and me too; I'd compounded the felony, so to speak. She's had us just where she wants us ever since."

Perry asked the obvious question: "What about this Anne Baker and her parents, did they never complain to the authorities? Or did Joan have some way of fixing them too?"

"There was no chance that she could have had anything on them. They were real Christians; they forgave Helen, both Anne and her parents. They were genuinely decent people. They even phoned me up at home to ask how Helen was getting on. They made it quite clear they wouldn't 'add to my burden,' as they put it."

"It's not often you find really charitable Christian people like that these days," remarked Perry. "I know it's none of my business, but what happened to Anne? Did she go to university in the end?"

Eric's face showed that the question was not a welcome one. "No, that was the awful part about it. Within nine months she was dead. She'd had TB as a youngster and had been cured. But it came back and she died; they couldn't save her. I don't know the ins and outs of it, but her death really did for Helen. She felt responsible, as if hitting Anne had brought the illness on again."

"Surely not, that couldn't happen."

"No, I don't think it could, but you see, by then she wasn't rational. To make matters worse, she confided her fears to Joan; she thought she was her friend."

"She couldn't have picked a worse one."

"We know that now. She's never let us forget it. First of all, it was a cracking good reference when the school closed down, then when she couldn't get another teaching post, it was the same again when she applied to the Martin Luther Missions, and again when she came to the PVB. So, you see, she's got me. She's got me because she's got Helen."

"But not after all these years; all this is old history. Joan could never prove any of it. No one would be remotely interested, especially now that Helen is no longer working and, sadly, Anne Baker is dead. No one could hold Helen responsible for that."

"She holds herself responsible, Perry, and that's enough. She's got arthritis now, as a result of the crash. Otherwise, her doctors say she's coping very well, but she couldn't stand to have it all raked up again. I can't let anyone…" He didn't finish his sentence. "Joan need only put a few words of gossip round; that would be enough."

They ordered Thai custards for dessert, which proved to be very similar to English custards, and Perry sat silently, absorbing everything he'd been told. He could understand that Eric was only trying to protect his wife, but he also had a duty to protect the staff of the PVB from the predations of Miss Mayflower. Most immediately, there was a duty to protect Wendy Jackson. Trying to put as much compassion into his voice as possible, Perry said: "I understand what you're trying to do, but it's not that simple. For some reason, Joan Mayflower wants Barry to get off as lightly as possible." He carefully avoided elaborating on what that reason might be; he didn't want to lay a trail that would lead Eric to Barry's activities on the switchboard. They were best forgotten. Instead, he said: "No doubt she has her own peculiar reasons, that we won't ever know about, but to achieve her ends, she's applying the most unethical pressure on Mrs Jackson to get her to withdraw the assault charge. First of all, she tried a direct confrontation and, when Wendy courageously stood up to that, she started a gossip campaign, just like the one you're afraid of. As far as I can see, she's using the same method that she's always used. Blackmail." The chairman winced. "Eric, there's no good trying to cover it up. That's what she is, a common blackmailer. She doesn't blackmail for hard cash, at least not as far as I know, but she does it to get what she wants in life, and the more people give in to her, the more she preys on them. Surely you can see that?" he asked gently.

"I do. I know you're right, but I just can't put Helen through that, not again."

Perry thought this was getting to be very hard going, but he had to try. "Look, you've said that Helen feels guilty about what happened to Anne Baker; there's nothing you or I or anyone can do about that now. But what about Wendy? Surely if Helen could help her now, by standing up to Joan, with you to help her, that would at least make her feel better about what happened to Wendy."

Eric looked puzzled. "I don't think I'm following you."

"Sorry, perhaps I didn't put that very clearly. If Helen could help Wendy now and, incidentally, help the rest of us, by letting you move against Joan, surely it would help to make up for that time when Wendy was being bullied at school, and Joan encouraged it, while Helen did nothing."

Eric looked to be thinking. "Wendy. Wendy Jackson. Wendy. That Yugoslavian girl. Yes, I remember. But surely… I'd no idea that Wendy Jackson was the Wendy from Helen's school. I've never thought of her as anything but English."

"She is," said Perry shortly. "It was only her parents who came from abroad."

"I do remember the case," continued Eric slowly. "It was towards the end of Helen's time at the school, but I never thought there was much in it. Just one of those things that happen at a school. It was all sorted out anyway. I seem to remember she left and went to a private school. But I'd no idea it was our Wendy."

Perry was getting towards the end of his sympathy with Eric's absorption in his none too lovable wife. "Bullying is a rotten thing, and in this case it was made far worse by a form teacher who encouraged it and a headmistress who wouldn't stop it because the form teacher told her not to."

"Oh no, surely not. I can't believe Helen would ever allow anything like that to go unpunished. I just think there was never any proof. Despite her own problems she really cared about the girls, that was what made it all so sad."

Perry was rapidly coming to the conclusion that the only person Helen Robertson had cared about in that school had been herself. He pressed his point home. "Wendy tells me she was beaten up repeatedly and her personal property stolen on several occasions. Her parents went to the school, but Helen wouldn't do anything, so they simply took her away. That's what Joan did to Helen, what she made her into. It's what she's still doing now. She's just gone through life leaving a trail of victims in her wake because no one has ever stood up to her."

The chairman looked thoroughly crushed. "I know what you're saying must be true; I can't imagine Wendy Jackson making a thing like that up, least of all now. She's got no reason to. Poor Helen. What do you suggest we do?"

Perry was relieved to have won the chairman round and he explained his idea slowly. "The important thing, from the point of view of the PVB, is to get rid of her in such a way that she can't go telling tales to the press. She's completely out of sympathy with the aims of the charity and she's created a lot of ill will in the short time she's been with us. She just cannot do the job. That in itself is ample grounds for dismissal, but on top of that, she has behaved in a professionally irresponsible way towards one of our employees, and has misrepresented the PVB's position to outside parties, i.e. Manning. If necessary, I'm sure we could get evidence to that effect from both him and Wendy."

"I think we should go for dismissal on the grounds of unprofessional conduct with, in the background, the implication that she couldn't do the fund-raising job properly, and was only given the education officer post out of kindness. That should stop her running to the press, and I don't think we should even give her a reference; that would just be passing the problem on to some other poor suckers. What we've got to do, you and me together, is put it to the board that this latest outrage is one too many. I'm sure the majority of them would be only too glad to see the back of her. You've got to stand up to her, you and Helen together, otherwise, you'll never be free of her."

"But Helen—"

Perry interrupted: "I'm sorry for Helen; I'm even more sorry for you, but can't you see how much damage she's doing to the PVB?" He tried to stiffen the chairman's resolve: "We've got to stop it. You and I. And it won't only be the PVB which benefits; it will help Helen too. By letting you go ahead, she'll be doing something to help someone she should have helped all those years ago. She can make something decent, something positive, out of all that sad mess." Perry was beginning to feel like an evangelical preacher.

At last, the chairman nodded. "I'll talk to Helen, get her to see it my way, and then you and I can talk to the board. You've convinced me; it's only what I've always really known anyway. I've just shut my eyes to it, but I won't any more." He paused, and then, in a more business-like tone, added: "I'll get back to you before we hold the board meeting."

When Perry returned to his office in the middle of the afternoon he had a whole day's paperwork to catch up on, and Sonya was being even more inefficient than usual. She'd done something strange to her computer again, and was waiting for Mr Barber, the engineer. Since she couldn't send out any letters until it was mended, Perry decided that, after his huge lunch, he wasn't feeling able to concentrate anyway. Convincing Eric Palmer of the necessity of getting rid of Joan Mayflower constituted a good day's work in itself, and he decided to go home early. He told Sonya to go as soon as Mr Barber had finished. They could catch up tomorrow.

The next week was due to be Miss Mayflower's last as fund-raiser, and Perry was hoping against hope that the board would get rid of her before she got her feet under the table as the education officer. He was beginning to doubt that he really had won the chairman over, when he received a phone call from Helen, whom he'd never actually met. She sounded like a charming middle-aged lady, someone whom it would be hard to imagine ever losing her temper, let alone hitting a schoolgirl. Her diction was excellent and she was succinct: "Mr Barrett?"

"Yes, Perry Barrett speaking."

"It's Helen Robertson-Palmer here; I was just calling to let you know my husband and I have discussed your proposal concerning future developments at the PVB." Perry thought she sounded like a lady planning officer considering the suitability of a new out of town shopping complex. He wondered if she thought she was being overheard. "I wanted to inform you that I am fully in agreement with your suggestion and will support you in its execution. This unfortunate matter has really dragged on long enough." Before Perry could reply, she rang off.

About ten minutes later the chairman himself called and said that the board meeting which would end Joan Mayflower's employment with the PVB would take place on Thursday at the usual time. He would be grateful if Perry could attend. He'd already spoken to enough of the board members to ensure an overwhelming vote for dismissal, and it would not be necessary to involve either Wendy or Mr Manning directly. Perry expressed his heartfelt thanks. The businessman in the chairman then took over, and pointed out that it was fortunate that the necessary forms and job description for the post of education officer had not been produced by admin., so there was nothing legally binding for the new post. There was no need for a period of notice: Joan could leave immediately. Perry had to smile: saving a buck all round. Still, money saved from Miss Mayflower's salary could be better spent on the patients.

On the afternoon of the board meeting Sonya excelled herself. She remembered to put out all the blotters and agendas and she even had the coffee on the boil before they all settled down and went in. Perry thought they were like a bunch of schoolboys plotting to escape from the dorm. and hoping the house master wouldn't find out. They had arranged to run a brief normal meeting in the presence of Miss Mayflower and then, at the end, under "Any Other Business", to raise a motion for dismissal. That way she was not forewarned by the circulated agenda. Perry wasn't looking forward to the meeting and, judging by the looks on their faces, neither were the other board members. By contrast, Sonya was cheerfully adjusting the chairs at the boardroom table and was lightly singing to herself. She didn't know what was going to happen. Perry thought it was going to be very unpleasant.

In the end it was far briefer and far more unpleasant than he had thought possible. Councillor Fairbrother had drawn the short straw: he proposed the motion to dismiss Miss Joan Mayflower from the service of the Princess Victoria's Bounty on the grounds that she had not conducted herself professionally in a way compatible with the aims and organization of the charity, and that she had, moreover, failed to carry out adequately those duties entrusted to her. Jack quickly seconded the motion and, before she could start a row, the chairman asked for a show of hands. It was unanimous.

Miss Mayflower realized she had been set up and that the contract for the new post hadn't been completed. She didn't argue or shout. She merely sat back in her chair and looked at each of the board members in turn, as if making sure she would remember their faces. She spoke only once: "I see. You'll regret this, all of you." She then stood up and, leaving her papers behind her, walked from the room.

Perry shivered. He suddenly felt cold. He thought the others did too.

Sonya was still writing. "How many s's in dismissed?" she asked quietly.

CHAPTER THIRTEEN

At about five o'clock that afternoon Perry was alone in the office with Sonya. She was tidying her desk for the day and Perry was standing looking out of her window at the main road. "Quite an afternoon, eh?" he asked.

"Oh yes, quite an afternoon."

"Still, at least we're rid of her once and for all now."

"I hope so," she replied, a little uncertainly.

For the first time, the euphoria drained away from Perry, and he asked quickly: "What do you mean? She's gone now; there's nothing more she can do to us."

Sonya sighed. "I didn't like her, I can't pretend I did, but I wish I'd known what you were planning to do this afternoon."

"Why, what difference would it have made?"

She shrugged. She was in one of her self-effacing, never mind me, moods, which Perry always found difficult to cope with. It was this aspect of her character which tended to make people view her as a little maid, old before her time.

"Sonya, you didn't want her here any more than the rest of us. You can't have forgotten how she's treated you."

"I haven't. Oh no, I haven't; you can be sure of that."

Perry was disconcerted by her words and the tone in which she spoke them. "Then what is it?" he asked.

"Miss Mayflower is bad enough to work with, I grant you. But Miss Mayflower when she no longer has a use for you is pure poison."

"I don't follow," said Perry, beginning to think that he might.

"Now that you've got her dismissed, she's going to find it very difficult to get another job after this."

"Yes, but that's not our problem."

"Oh yes it is," replied Sonya. "She'll make it your problem. After all, she's got a mortgage to keep up, like the rest of us, and if she can't get the money one way, she'll get it another."

"You mean by trying to blackmail someone into giving her a good reference?"

Sonya shot Perry a shrewd glance. "Something like that," she said. "And then, when she's got no further use for you, she'll spill the beans and blacken your names from here to Timbuktu."

"You sound as though you're speaking from experience," he ventured.

She smiled, her old self again. "Oh no, well anyway, not mine. It wasn't until Mrs Robertson-Palmer phoned you the other day, that I was reminded of the connection between her and Miss Mayflower."

The light was beginning to dawn on Perry, although he couldn't be quite sure what Sonya was getting at or how much she knew. "You've no need to worry on that score, Sonya. I had a little talk with the chairman before we decided to hold the board meeting, and I convinced him that, despite the fact that Helen had given Miss Mayflower a good reference, and he himself had been in favour of appointing her, it was a mistake and she wasn't a suitable person for the PVB." He hoped this carefully edited version of the truth would put Sonya at her ease and still preserve Helen Robertson-Palmer's secret.

Sonya looked thoughtfully at him for a few minutes, and then carefully asked: "Did you know Miss Robertson and Miss Mayflower didn't get jobs when the grammar school closed down?"

"I heard they were both surplus to requirements, that the other, larger school already had all the staff it needed."

Sonya shook her head. "The headmistress of Westfield was due to retire, and they hadn't got a German teacher at all. They had to advertise for one. Most of the other teachers got jobs in either Westfield or Eastfield; some of the older ones retired early, but most just transferred to the new schools." Perry's interest was beginning to quicken. "Miss Mayflower didn't get a job because of that business with Wendy. Her parents were disgusted by the way she'd been treated, and wrote to the Local Education Authority. They were reluctant to intervene in the school, which appeared to be otherwise well run and, as Wendy had already left by then, that was the end of it. But when it came to appointing teachers for the new schools, they gave Miss Mayflower a miss."

Perry couldn't help laughing. "So in the end, Wendy got her revenge, although she didn't set out to do it. I'm glad. I wonder if she knows."

"Who? Wendy? I doubt it. There's no reason why she should. I only know because my Auntie Bernie was on the Local Education Authority at the time."

Perry was feeling cheerfully malicious. "I don't suppose after all these years it would do any harm to inform her, do you think?"

"No, it might even cheer her up a little, make her realize that not everyone was against her, even then," replied Sonya brightly.

She continued tidying her desk while Perry continued to think things over and pack his briefcase. Then something dawned on him. "What about Helen Robertson, then? Why didn't she get the job of the headmistress who was due to retire? Was it due to her ill health?"

Sonya smiled a worldly smile. "I wondered if you would get on to that. She didn't get the job because someone wrote and told the LEA that she'd attacked a girl called Anne Baker, one of her own pupils."

"Ah. And did they have any idea who this someone was?"

"I don't really think so," replied Sonya slowly. "It could have been anyone: Anne's parents, another girl, a teacher. The letter was anonymous, but the point is, that as soon as Miss Mayflower realized she wasn't going to get anything in the new school, someone informed the Local Education Authority about Anne Baker. An interesting coincidence, wouldn't you say?"

Perry didn't reply immediately, then he enquired, without hope. "I suppose it's possible Anne Baker's parents wrote that letter, thinking perhaps that Helen Robertson shouldn't be given the new job, with even greater responsibilities than she had at the grammar."

"It is possible, but my Auntie Bernie always said she didn't think it was them. The LEA contacted them when they received the letter. They said that Anne was dead and that they had forgiven Helen Robertson. They were not interested in stirring up unhappy memories again. Auntie Bernie thought they were telling the truth. Officially, no one has ever discovered who sent that letter."

"In any case, Sonya, what you're saying is that I should be careful for a while, just in case Joan tries her tricks on me?"

"Yes, you and the others, Mr Barrett. It's a good thing that you all acted together like that, so she can't go running behind anyone's back, but don't forget that when it comes to spilling the beans, you may have stopped her for now, but there may well be other cans in the future."

"Thanks for the tip, Sonya. I'll be on my guard." Perry was beginning to think Sonya was a very shrewd young lady and Joan Mayflower wasn't just a louse, she was evil. Evil in a way he hadn't encountered before. Thank God he had Sonya and Jack.

CHAPTER FOURTEEN

The next two weeks passed relatively quietly. Perry made his daily rounds of the complex, chatted with the patients and staff, and noted that the atmosphere seemed lighter and people were more relaxed. The whole place was happier. Even Franjo was positively light-hearted, when Perry finally called to collect the miniature rose he had forgotten. "I keep him for you. Beautiful little plant, your wife will like him, I am sure."

"I am sure she will, Franjo, thank you very much." Perry dropped his payment into the box placed on the greenhouse work bench for the benefit of those who wished to purchase house plants.

"It is a beautiful summer, is it not?" remarked Franjo.

"It certainly is; I think we could be in for a thoroughly pleasant year."

The gardener asked suddenly: "Tell me my friend, how did you do it? How did you get rid of her?"

Perry was only surprised he hadn't asked sooner. "I discussed the problem with the chairman and he contacted the other board members. We all acted together and sprang a little surprise on her."

"Good. Good. I am glad, so glad." With a quick smile in Perry's direction, Franjo wheeled himself away. Perry thought he was almost as much of a curiosity as his sister. Even now, he still didn't admit to the relationship.

When he returned to his office, Dilys Owen, the new fund-raising officer was waiting for him. She was a slightly overweight, middle-aged spinster, who wore gold-rimmed spectacles and had her hair drawn back into an old-fashioned bun. Despite having lived most of her life in the south of England, she still retained more than a trace of her sing-song Welsh accent. She was chatting amiably to Sonya as he came in, and Sonya offered to make coffee for them all. Dilys explained that she'd just dropped by to see about some publicity photographs of the patients for the new brochure. "The old ones are looking a bit dated now, you see. You can tell how old they are by the clothes and people's hairstyles. I thought, being as they are for the anniversary brochure, it would be best to be really up to date."

"Good idea," agreed Perry.

"Well the problem is, you see, I don't really know the residents that well, being new here, and I wondered if you might be able to guide me in the right direction. I just need about five or six of them, photogenic types, who won't mind being used in publicity material. Not everyone would want to."

"I'll see if I can round up a bunch for you. When is the photographer coming?"

"Wednesday next. I thought I'd better get it done while the grounds look so nice; he's going to do some outside shots as well." She accepted her coffee from Sonya and the three of them sipped in companionable silence. Perry thought how nice it was to have this thoughtful-natured soul as a fund-raiser and colleague instead of the evil Joan Mayflower. He was sure she was going to be a great success and she looked so wholesome, just right for the PVB. How fortunate it was that Give Kids a Hand had decided she was simply too old for their public.

The phone rang and Sonya entered into an earnest conversation, punctuated by sidelong glances at Perry, as though she were deciding whether or not to trouble him with the call. Perry thought it was another of life's current joys that the switchboard was now run with military precision by Brenda. Ever tactful, Dilys said: "Look, I've loads to do this morning, so I'd better be doing it. I'll see you both later. Thanks for the coffee." As she closed the door behind her, Sonya handed the receiver to Perry.

It was a call from the special hospital which had taken Barry. A Mrs Morris reported that they were very pleased with his progress. He'd made great headway with his battle against his addiction and would be fit to attend trial in a few weeks.

Perry voiced the obligatory congratulations and only hoped this wasn't a prelude to asking him to take Barry back to the PVB or to say nice things about him at his trial. The tactful young woman at the other end of the line made her request: "I'm sure Barry has given you enough trouble already, Mr Barrett, but he did request me to ask you if you could call by and see him here before the trial. He says he's got something he wants to tell you."

Perry sighed: "Really, Mrs Morris, I think it would be better if I didn't. Not with the police involvement; we are, after all, on opposing sides, so to speak. I might find that I'd have to pass on what he told me, and I wouldn't like to be in a false position. I think it would be much better if he were to confide in your people or in his solicitor."

"Naturally, Mr Barrett, I understand your reluctance to get involved. I'd feel the same myself. He's not your responsibility any more. He's ours. And that's why I'm calling you now. You see, I think whatever is troubling him may be holding up his progress. He's done very well so far, but it's Doctor Vine's opinion, and mine too, that if he could get this off his chest, the road ahead would be much easier for him. And I don't think you need worry about being in a false position. Barry assures us it has nothing to do with either the attempted assault or the fire, but he won't talk to us about it. He says he only wants to talk to you, that it's something you should know about, and that he always found you very sympathetic."

Perry was surprised and said so. He'd never felt that he'd got on particularly well with Barry, but faced with a genuine humanitarian request, he couldn't refuse. It looked as though Friday afternoon was going to be slack and he agreed to drive up and see Barry at four o'clock. Mrs Morris thanked him profusely and gave him directions for finding the hospital from the main road, once he'd got to Middlehampton.

By the time Friday afternoon came, Perry was almost certain Barry was going to treat him to some revelation about Joan. It was just the sort of spiteful thing he would do. He'd already shopped his old friends who had supplied him with drugs while he'd been at the PVB; now he was presumably going to shop the woman who'd provided him with the money to buy them. It was likely Barry didn't know she'd already been dismissed and was willing to try and bring about that happy event by his own efforts. Perry was quite looking forward to having something to hold over the head of the arch-blackmailer. It would be an insurance policy.

The mid-afternoon was hot and airless in a way that only London during a heatwave can be. It seemed to Perry that the whole city and its outskirts were quietly boiling away, evaporating into the cloudless blue sky. Since it was the end of the week, Perry asked Sonya along for the drive. At least that part of it before they hit the suburbs would be pleasant enough, and Perry didn't like driving alone.

They speculated cosily on what it was Barry might have to confide. Assuming the whole thing wasn't a wind-up, Sonya had reached much the same conclusion as Perry. Driving along the motorway, with the sun roof open and the green embankments flying past them, it was a joy to be out and away from the office. The spring of joy dried up very quickly as they neared the M25. Perry hadn't driven this route for a long time and he simply hadn't counted on the volume of traffic that a Friday afternoon in the summer could generate. They were not held up by road works or an accident, but they moved with frustrating slowness.

"I suppose it's due to people getting off work early for the weekend and using the motorway to get to Heathrow for their holiday flights." Sonya fanned herself with an old PVB brochure.

Perry looked at his watch. "We're going to be late; we'll never make it by four now."

"I don't suppose it matters too much. He won't be going anywhere and they'll probably realize we've got stuck in traffic."

When they finally left the M25, the traffic began to flow more easily, particularly as much of the rush hour flow now appeared to be heading in the direction opposite to Perry and

Sonya. "I only hope that lot's cleared by the time we have to drive back," remarked Perry.

Sonya looked none too hopeful. She was keeping her eyes peeled, but it was Perry who spotted the road leading to Virginia Wood Hospital. Mrs Morris' instructions had been remarkably accurate. It was just a quarter to five when they drove slowly into the hospital car park. The hospital itself looked like a large converted private house. A discreet blue and white sign announced its name, but not its function, to the world.

"I'll stay in the car," said Sonya.

"Are you sure? I expect they'd get you a cup of tea or something."

"I'm fine as I am, thanks."

Perry put on the jacket of his suit and made for what was obviously the main entrance. To his surprise, a small, thin woman with straw-coloured hair came out to meet him. "Mr Barrett?" she enquired.

Perry thought she looked very upset. "Yes, I'm Perry Barrett; you must be Mrs Morris. I'm pleased to meet you." It was then that he caught sight of two uniformed police officers standing in the cool of the vestibule.

Mrs Morris shook his extended hand and said: "I'm so sorry, Mr Barrett. Something quite awful has happened. I'm so sorry." She abandoned Perry to a plain clothes police officer, who had been hidden from view by his two colleagues.

"Mr Barrett, from the Princess Victoria Hospital? I'm Inspector Henderson."

"What can I do for you, Inspector? What's happened?"

"This young man, Barry Kemp, was he a friend of yours, sir?"

Perry thought he was hardly a friend. He said: "He lived for a while at the Princess Victoria's Bounty. I'm the administrator there. Why? Is he in any trouble?"

"I'm sorry to say, sir, the young man is dead. At first sight it looks as though he killed himself."

"Good God." The Inspector's words had taken Perry completely by surprise. "Do you know why? Did he leave a note? I understood from Mrs Morris here that he was well on the way to making a recovery." Mrs Morris nodded in agreement.

"We were wondering if perhaps you could throw some light on that, sir. There was no note. Do you know why he wanted to see you, sir?"

"I've no idea, Inspector, I only know what Mrs Morris told me on the phone last Wednesday."

Mrs Morris said: "I've explained his history to Inspector Henderson already, in as far as it is known to me."

"He seems to have been a most unhappy and unlucky young man," remarked the Inspector dryly. "I suppose it's possible he didn't think he had a future, stuck in a wheelchair for the rest of his life, in trouble with the law, and no drugs to soften the blow, but the real puzzle is what he wanted to tell you so urgently and why."

"There, I can't help you, I'm afraid." Perry was full of questions. "How did he die? How did he manage to kill himself in a hospital?"

Mrs Morris thought the hospital was being criticized and leapt in. "It was awful. Quite terrible. He had a room on the third floor. That is the most secure floor we have."

"Especially for someone in a wheelchair," chipped in the Inspector unkindly. Perry had the impression Inspector Henderson didn't regard the demise of Barry as much of a loss to the human race.

Mrs Morris hastened to explain: "As you can see for yourself, this place isn't really suitable for wheelchair bound and severely disabled patients. We've been trying to get a ground floor suite for years, but there's never enough money. You know how it is." Perry nodded sympathetically. The Inspector looked carefully at the facade of the building, in an abstracted way, as if to imply that any amount of money spent on the hospital was doomed to be wasted. Mrs Morris continued: "As you can see, if you look round the corner, we have the old-fashioned wrought iron fire escapes, with platforms on every floor. Barry simply wheeled himself on to the platform on his floor, and kept going. There was a chance he might not have died from a fall from that height, but he was unlucky; for one thing, half of him was dead weight, so to speak, and he couldn't even attempt to save himself on landing, and then he must have caught his back on the iron work as he fell. His wheelchair fell on top of him and he sustained severe head injuries."

"What a horrible way to go!" exclaimed Perry.

The Inspector looked at him shrewdly. "Yes, we rather thought that, sir; even in his present circumstances, there must have been easier ways available. That is why we're so interested in what he might have had to tell you, Mr Barrett. You see, sir, he landed quite a way from the bottom of the fire escape, so he must have gone over the edge of that platform at a good speed. A good shove would have done it."

"Oh surely, Inspector, you're not suggesting anyone would want to kill Barry," expostulated Mrs Morris. She was rapidly coming to the conclusion that this situation was running away from her control.

"I'm keeping a very open mind at this stage," replied Inspector Henderson evenly. "In my experience, normal middle of the road, honest citizens don't usually get themselves killed. On the other hand, drug users and pushers often do."

"But Barry was round off all that."

"Are you sure, Mrs Morris?"

"He certainly had no chance of getting hold of anything in here," she replied firmly. "We're very strict about that, bearing in mind the kind of patients we have here. Visitors are by prior arrangement only and recorded in the book."

Inspector Henderson turned his attention once more to Perry. "I understand he was able to get hold of drugs while living at the Princess Victoria's?"

Perry thought it was his turn to be firm. "The PVB provides housing and employment opportunities, as well as medical care, for disabled people. It is neither a prison nor a drug rehabilitation centre. We encourage our clients to have as much contact with the wider community as possible. Inevitably, some of them will abuse this policy."

"Quite so, sir." It was impossible to tell whether or not the Inspector agreed with the PVB's policy towards its clients. He changed tack. "You say you weren't particularly close to this young man while he was resident with you, sir?"

"I wasn't, Inspector, and I've no idea why he wanted to see me." Perry was not going to be drawn into speculation about Joan and her involvement with Barry.

Inspector Henderson thought for a few minutes and then asked: "Who else knew about your proposed visit this afternoon, Mr Barrett?"

"As far as I know, only Sonya, my secretary. She came with me for the drive," explained Perry, indicating the lone figure sitting in his car. "She would have put it in the diary, so I suppose anyone at the PVB who came into her office might have seen it, but I can't think of anyone who remarked on the fact."

Sonya must have noticed the Inspector staring at her, and she left the car and walked over to the little group. "What's up?" she asked.

Perry got in first. "Barry's dead. He fell off the fire escape from the third floor. Inspector Henderson here seems to think someone may have assisted him."

"Oh no!" she gasped, putting her hand over her mouth.

The Inspector calmly turned his attentions to the newcomer. "I understand you are Mr Barrett's secretary at the PVB, Miss…?"

"Bishop, Sonya Bishop. Yes, I am."

"And you made the arrangements for this afternoon's visit to Barry?"

"Of course. I took the phone call from Mrs Morris."

"How do you do?" offered that lady inconsequentially.

"And you presumably knew the lad when he was living at the PVB?"

"I knew him, but not very well. I work mainly in the admin. block with Mr Barrett. I don't often come into direct contact with the patients."

The Inspector appeared to consider this information. "And have you any idea why Barry asked to see Mr Barrett this afternoon?"

"None at all, I'm afraid."

Perry had wanted to shield Sonya from Inspector Henderson; he hadn't thought she would be able to cope very well with his strong personality. But here again, he reflected, he had underestimated her. She was making a very good job of coping with the Inspector. It was Sonya who asked the pertinent question: "When did Barry fall, Inspector, do you know?"

The Inspector consulted his notes. "About ten past four, according to Mrs Morris. He'd had a cup of tea served to him by the new volunteer assistant at a couple of minutes before four. She told him she'd bring some more when his guest arrived and he even managed to thank her. That was the last time anyone saw him alive. Why do you ask, Miss Bishop?"

"He died about the time when Mr Barrett should have been with him but, in fact, we were stuck on the M25, worrying about being late for the appointment here. It looks as though we were fortunate in being late, and Mr Barrett is also lucky I came with him, so he has a witness to his whereabouts at the relevant time."

While admitting the truth of this statement, the Inspector was clearly not going to be bested by a secretary. "And so do you, Miss Bishop; I congratulate you both."

After leaving their names and addresses with the Inspector and bidding farewell to Mrs Morris, Perry and Sonya climbed back into their sweltering car and set out on the long journey home. This time they were fortunate in that the traffic had subsided, and they had a relatively clear run. The heat of the day had built up on the outskirts of London, and lay heavily on them. It wasn't until they were well clear of the southern suburbs that Perry brought up the subject of Barry. "What a rum do. That Inspector obviously didn't think he'd managed to kill himself. The question is, if he didn't do it himself, who did?"

Sonya said thoughtfully: "I can't see anyone trying to kill themselves in that particular way. I would have thought there was more of a chance they'd seriously injure themselves than that they'd actually die."

Perry didn't reply. He was thinking of Per. What had he been thinking about as he calmly got into his car for that last time, knowing what he was going to do? Per must have been thinking about suicide for some time: he'd left his affairs in order, or at least as good order as he could in the circumstances, but in that final moment, when he had steeled himself to do it, all that was needed was one momentary press on the accelerator when he was facing the wall. That was a completely different thing to having to wheel yourself off the top of a fire escape, when the chances were you'd be stopped in your fall long before you reached the ground. Perry agreed with Sonya and the Inspector: at the least, Barry had been helped on his way; at the worst, he'd been murdered.

"Well, if he was killed, or assisted on his way, you and I are in the clear," he said. "It was a good job you came along this afternoon."

Sonya looked sideways at Perry. "Yes, it was, and rather unexpected. I don't suppose she counted on that."

Perry tried to sort out his thoughts. "By 'she', I take it you mean Joan?" he asked.

"You don't think it's a possibility then?"

"I don't see how it can be. I do think it very likely he wanted to tell me something to her detriment, but I don't see how she could have found out. Furthermore, she couldn't have done it herself, all visitors are searched and recorded in the visitors book. There's no chance she could have gone and chatted him up for a few minutes and then shoved him down those steps. For one thing, he would have been suspicious of her turning up out of the blue, when he'd asked to see me, and for another, Mrs Morris didn't say he'd had any visitors this afternoon."

"I agree she couldn't have done it herself, but I bet she's at the bottom of it, and she's very good at getting other folk to do her dirty work for her, remember. I think it's significant he died at about the time you should have been with him. It would have suited her very well to have you suspected of the crime."

"Oh no, I can't believe that, not even of Joan."

"Believe it, Mr Barrett. On that last day, she promised you all you'd regret dismissing her. I think this was one step in her revenge."

"And I think, Sonya, you are getting as paranoid about that woman as I am."

CHAPTER FIFTEEN

It wasn't until Tuesday of the following week that Perry and Sonya received a visit from Inspector Henderson at the PVB offices. Sonya prepared coffee in the new "Saints" series mugs. If the Inspector admired Ben's artwork, he didn't show it. When the three of them were ensconced, with the Inspector's silent sergeant taking notes, he unburdened himself. "There are just a few loose ends to tie up, but I thought you should know how far we've got, and then you might be able to fill in a few details for us." He coughed quietly and referred to his notebook. "We did a little checking with the local police about the lad's background, and we discovered that the parents of the young girl he'd killed with his bus were called Peters. Mr Peters threatened him after he was caught and there was some nastiness at his parents' home. Bearing in mind that visitors are well recorded at the hospital, if he was helped out of this world, logically, it had to be by one of the staff. We found her without too much difficulty. She was working there under her maiden name, in a rented flat."

"Who?" asked Perry.

"Mrs Peters. She was the volunteer who brought him his last cup of tea, laced with the tranquillizers she's been taking since her daughter's death. Together with the medication the hospital had been giving him they put him out in no time. Mrs Peters admits openly to having wheeled him out on to the fire escape and to giving him a good push to send him on his way. That statement fits in with the forensic evidence; and he couldn't have done the deed simply by wheeling himself off that platform, a good push was necessary."

Perry was shocked. "How awful, Inspector, how absolutely tragic. To lose her daughter and then to go and do a thing like that. The poor woman; she must have been driven to despair."

"Hm," said the Inspector non-committally.

"Barry didn't come from Middlehampton, did he?" asked Sonya. "What I mean is, if Mrs Peters was living near to Barry when he had his accident, what was she doing working up in Middlehampton?"

Inspector Henderson was warming to her. "My question exactly, Miss Bishop. My question exactly." Perry looked at him cautiously; he had a nasty idea he knew what was coming. The Inspector continued: "Unfortunately, Mrs Peters was less than forthcoming on that point, but she did go so far as to tell us that someone phoned and told her when and where he'd been transferred after he'd left hospital."

"Did she say who?" enquired Perry.

The Inspector didn't reply at once, instead he let his gaze wander over Perry and Sonya. Then he said: "She says she doesn't know, the call was anonymous, but she did let slip that it was a woman." Neither Perry nor Sonya could stop themselves; they both let out a sharp breath, and looked at one another. Inspector Henderson waited politely for the explanation.

Perry felt obliged to provide him with an edited and abbreviated version of Joan Mayflower's history with the PVB. He explained that she had been engaged as the chief fund-raiser, but had proved totally unsuitable, being unable to get along with either the other paid officers or the clients. He related that she had taken her dismissal very badly. This explanation clearly begged more questions in the Inspector's mind than it answered. His sergeant looked up from his notebook, as if waiting for the second instalment. It didn't come.

"I'm sorry, sir, but I don't see the connection between this woman and Barry, other than the fact that he lived here for a time."

"Strictly speaking, Inspector, we never found one, but she did seem to have taken him under her wing. For example, she tried to put pressure on Mrs Jackson to withdraw the assault complaint against him. We never found out why, but it was that which precipitated the move to dismiss her."

"Ah yes, Mrs Jackson, the therapist he threatened. I remember the case from the file." Inspector Henderson paused again, but this time the tactic was unsuccessful. Perry had said as much as he thought wise. He didn't want to drag Wendy's and Helen's pasts into the daylight for another airing and, most importantly from his own point of view, he didn't want Barry's delinquencies on the exchange and Paul Russell's shabby story brought out for inspection.

The silence lengthened. Finally, the Inspector conceded defeat. "So what it amounts to, sir, is that you had this fund-raiser who was unsatisfactory, and you suspected some connection with the young man, but you never found out what. That about sums it up, sir?"

"Pretty much, Inspector. I'm sorry I can't be more helpful." He thought his last remark sounded grossly insincere; Inspector Henderson was bound to notice it.

He affected not to. "So you think it possible this Miss Mayflower turned on her former friend for some reason and told Mrs Peters of his whereabouts, knowing full well that she might well like to do him an injury?" Perry didn't reply. The Inspector was insistent: "That is what you're saying, isn't it, sir?"

"It was just a thought, Inspector. She was a most unpleasant woman."

The Inspector turned to Sonya. "And you would agree with that, Miss Bishop?"

"Oh yes," she relied quietly.

"You see, if what you are saying is correct, Mr Barrett, I'm beginning to wonder how unpleasant. Do you think there is a possibility that she did not only turn on the young man but, upset by her dismissal, she wanted to get you stuck with the crime. That's not a very nice thought to take home with you, sir, not very nice at all."

Perry felt very miserable. Were they never to be rid of the woman? "At least that didn't work out, Inspector. Thank God,

I had Sonya with me and that we were held up. If we'd been on time, I wonder what would have happened?"

The Inspector consulted his notebook again. "According to Mrs Morris, you'd simply have walked into an empty room. They book visitors in at the main reception desk on the ground floor. They don't escort them to individual rooms. They haven't got the staff. The main desk also deals with the telephone and they can't spare the personnel to go wandering around the building. They just direct visitors to the correct room and give them instructions for when they get out of the lift. The rooms are all numbered and there are no locks on any of the patients' doors. You would have been hard put to to prove you hadn't pushed him down that fire escape. She should have watched you arrive, wheeled him to the exit, waited until she heard the lift and then pushed him out. She could then have ducked into a storeroom until you went to raise the alarm, but her nerves got the better of her."

Sonya once again asked a good question. "Inspector, did Mrs Peters actually say why she chose that time to kill Barry? I mean," she added, blushing, "can you tell us?"

Affected by this becoming display of modesty and shyness, Inspector Henderson managed a watery smile. "No, she didn't. We did ask her, because, in the normal way of things, it should have been the last time she'd have chosen, when she knew he was expecting a visitor who might arrive at any time. She just said one time was as good as any other. We shall ask her again, in the light of the information you've both just given us, but I doubt she'll go any further than she has already. You see, she regards her mystery informant as a friend, someone who gave her a chance to see justice done. She won't want to get her into trouble."

"At the risk of getting me, a perfectly innocent bystander, into very considerable trouble," concluded Perry wryly.

"Quite so, sir. Quite so." The Inspector consulted his notebook again. "You've told us that you yourself weren't particularly friendly with Barry when he was here?"

"Correct."

"So there was no chance of you turning up at the trial to speak on his behalf?"

"Absolutely none. One way and another that young man caused us a great deal of trouble. I'm sorry he's dead, but I'm by no means sorry he's out of our hair. Why do you ask?"

"It was just something Mrs Peters said when we asked her why she'd acted now, rather than before, when she knew he was living here. She said: "Types like that get all the help, Social Services, counselling, everything. What did we get? Sod all. Nothing. It was our daughter he killed, and he gets all the help and all the sympathy. Even now. He sets fire to the place, and they're trying to keep him out of jail. It's not right to let him go on getting away with everything." So it looks, Mr Barrett, as though the idea was put into her head by the revelation that Barry was still causing havoc and being allowed to get away with it."

"That's grotesque, Inspector; neither myself nor any responsible person connected with the PVB would have lifted a finger to help him in that way. I suppose Mrs Peters didn't specify who 'they' were?"

The Inspector shook his head: "No, sir. But if you're right, we have a good idea who put the thought into Mrs Peters' head."

Perry's reassurance on that point brought the interview to a close, and the Inspector and his sergeant retired to interview Mrs Peters again.

CHAPTER SIXTEEN

The following day the photographer came and took the publicity shots of some of the patients and staff. Fortunately the sun was shining and the day was warm. It made everything run so much more smoothly, as Dilys remarked to Perry, as they watched the young man at work in the hard light of the morning. "What about including you two in one of the pictures?" he suggested. They both demurred.

Ben said: "People want to see the types who run these places and spend all their donations. And you two both look so incredibly wholesome." He laughed.

Perry was glad to hear him laugh. What a difference getting rid of Joan Mayflower had made. Dilys was a much better bet, hard-working, kind and popular. And, apparently, very modest. She absolutely refused to be photographed. "You don't want an old spinster like me cluttering up your pictures." She smiled. Perry thought she would have been very attractive if it were not for those spectacles and that bun.

The afternoon was much less pleasant. Perry had no sooner returned from the self-service cafeteria than he was confronted by an irate middle-aged man, who barged into the office, despite Sonya's valiant efforts to prevent him. She stared into the room after him. "I'm sorry, Mr Barrett, I couldn't stop him." She was waving her arms about and looking very distressed.

"It's all right, Sonya," replied Perry, trying to sound calm. "I'm sure I can deal with this."

"Oh yes, you can deal with 'this' as you put it. 'This' happens to be a person. But your sort forget that. Everyone's just an item to you. To be dealt with."

Sonya was hovering nervously in the open doorway. "I'm sorry, you have the better of me," remarked Perry, in what he hoped was a soothing voice. "I don't even know your name."

"Peters, Joseph Peters." He spat the name out, as if merely uttering it should send Perry into a state of terror.

It didn't. Perry was a good eight inches taller than Mr Peters and, for all his heart trouble, he looked a great deal healthier. It was hard to judge Mr Peter's exact age, but he gave the impression of being prematurely aged, in his old-man's worn tweed jacket and pullover.

"Why don't you sit down, Mr Peters, and tell me what this is all about?" Perry waved him to a seat, and nodded to Sonya, to indicate she could go. She shot him a worried look, and retreated.

"What's it all about?" yelled Mr Peters. "I'll tell you what it's all about, Mr Do-gooder. It's about you trying to get that shit off when he comes up for trial, that's what it's about."

"Mr Peters, I can assure you—"

Joseph Peters interrupted him. "Oh yes, you can assure me. That's what they said when that bastard killed June." He took on an imitation upper class drawl. "We can assure you, Mr Peters, that young man will be prosecuted with the full vigour of the law." And what happened? He landed up here, living in the lap of luxury and paid for by the taxpayer. By me and Ruth. That's what happened. And was he grateful? Was he hell as like. He threatens people, and then sets fire to the bloody place. And what do you do about it?" Before Perry could reply, he continued: "You say you're going to stand up and come the sob story for him. Get him put into another luxury hotel. My daughter is dead. Dead. Dead. And you go around molly-coddling his killer."

Perry had let Mr Peters run on until he ran out of steam. It was the only way he knew of dealing with intense anger in others. Now he spoke, before Mr Peters could get his second wind. "Mr Peters, I'm very sorry about what happened to your daughter. I had nothing to do with Barry at that time—"

"Barry," spat Joseph Peters. "It's Barry, is it?"

Perry continued in his most soothing voice. "Yes, it was Barry. We're all on first names here." Before Mr Peters could interrupt again, Perry raised his hand to indicate silence. "Now, that young man caused a lot of trouble here, one way and another, but he's dead now. I don't approve of what your wife has done. I don't approve of private revenge, however badly you feel treated by the system, however you feel about Barry. One thing I can tell you, though: neither I, nor any responsible member of my staff, nor anyone else here at the PVB would have done anything to help Barry out of that mess."

Mr Peters' anger had subsided somewhat and, although it was difficult for Perry to gauge how much of his speech had gone in, he was sure the last sentence had struck home. "That's not what we heard. We were told you were going to go to court and put in a good word for him; that you were going to say that therapist had wound him up and that the fire could even have been the result of an accident while he was upset."

"Who told you that, Mr Peters?" asked Perry gently.

"The woman who called Ruth. She told us where he'd gone and that he was going to get away with it again, just because he was disabled. She told us you'd tried to persuade that woman to withdraw the charge."

"Mr Peters, I can honestly tell you I did nothing of the kind. In fact, I persuaded her to go ahead with it. You can ask her if you like. I had absolutely no reason to plead for clemency for Barry. Why should I?"

Mr Peters seemed disconcerted by this. In his turn, he asked: "Why should she lie to us?"

"Maybe she has her own reasons, Mr Peters. Do you have any idea who it was that called you?"

Joseph Peters shook his head. "She never gave her name."

"Did she happen to tell you how she got her information concerning Barry's whereabouts? I imagine that information was known to only a limited number of people."

He shook his head again. It was difficult for Perry to decide if he was being truthful with him. Mr Peters tried again: "And you say you weren't going to try and get him off?"

103

"Absolutely not, Mr Peters."

"If that's what you say, I suppose I've got to believe you." Mr Peters sounded very bitter and far from convinced.

Perry was uncertain as to whether anything could be gained by prolonging the interview, but as he and Mr Peters were unlikely ever to meet again, he thought the chance of some extra information would be lost if he didn't ask now. "Mr Peters, did you know what your wife was planning when she volunteered at Virginia Wood?" The question was a mistake.

Joseph Peters became wary. He was obviously not going to admit to anything which would incriminate him. Perry thought it likely that he and his wife had arranged to keep him out of it. For some reason she had elected to do the deed and take the consequences alone. Abruptly, he replied: "No."

Perry toyed with the empty coffee mug on the table between them. "You see, unfortunately for me, your wife took her revenge on Barry at a time when I should have been visiting him. If I had not been late for that interview, the consequences for me could have been very serious. I was just wondering whether the time as well as the place was suggested to your wife by your anonymous friend." Mr Peters did not appreciate the delicate way in which Perry had phrased his question. He looked blank by way of reply. Perry continued. "You see, it may be that the same person who misled you about my involvement with Barry was trying to implicate me in his death."

Mr Peters looked as though he would have been glad to see Perry implicated, if it meant that his wife went free. "Implicate you?" he asked. "And you an innocent bystander?"

"Well, yes." Perry didn't really follow Joseph Peters' line of thought.

He said, with considerable satisfaction: "Well now you know how it feels." Before he could say more, there was a knock on the door.

Perry shouted: "Come in." Mr Peters, his harangue interrupted, drew a deep breath, as if winding himself up for the next blast. Looking over the top of Mr Peters' head, Perry could see Sonya in the doorway. Behind her she appeared to have an office full of burly middle-aged men in blue uniforms. He almost burst out laughing. Sonya had called Nite-Safe and the security men had turned out in force. Perry acknowledged them and said: "Thank you, Sonya. I think Mr Peters and I have just about finished our discussion."

Mr Peters obviously didn't agree. He'd worked himself up to vent his spleen on someone and he wasn't going to be done out of his chance. He turned round, and looked at Sonya and saw the security men. "Oh yes, that's right, call the heavies when someone tries to stick up for their rights. That's you lot all over."

Perry had had enough. He felt sorry for the Peters, but there was nothing he could do to help them. He stood up, to indicate the interview was at an end. Bearing in mind the contents of Sonya's room, Mr Peters felt it prudent to do likewise. He did not accept Perry's proffered hand and, muttering "silly little bitch", practically ran out of the offices.

"I hope I did the right thing, Mr Barrett?" asked Sonya, when he'd gone.

"Oh yes, quite right, Sonya. Thank you."

Mr Cielo, the proprietor of Nite-Safe, put in: "You never know how people like that will turn. Nice as pie one minute, and the next…" He shrugged his broad shoulders.

"I agree," said Perry, "Except that Mr Peters was never nice as pie. I suppose we must be tolerant; he and his wife have been through quite a lot, one way and another. But thank you for coming. It's reassuring to know you take such good care of us."

They all laughed and Sonya offered coffee. Mr Cielo generously admired the design of the mugs. It seemed that drinking coffee or, as Mr Cielo out it, "getting to know our clients", was an important part of Nite-Safe's services. Dilys Own stuck her head round the door. She had copies of a newspaper advertisement from the local paper but, when she saw the assembled uniforms, modestly withdrew without even taking coffee. Perry felt that some explanation of Mr Peters' visit was necessary, and he briefly explained that Barry had been responsible for the death of Peters' daughter and that Mrs Peters had, in turn, been responsible for Barry's demise.

"Trouble all round, that lad. Nothing but trouble. No good to himself or anyone else," volunteered the youngest security guard.

Mr Cielo seemed distracted, but agreed: "Look at the problems he's caused you."

"Well, hopefully, it's all over now," replied Perry.

CHAPTER SEVENTEEN

The following day, on his rounds, Perry bumped into Wendy as she was helping Freddie load boxes of handbags into a Bedford van. "That's the first lot out for trial in the St. George's Stores, just to see how they go down," she remarked cheerfully.

Freddie looked pleased with himself. "That's a good job jobbed."

"I'm sure they'll do very well," said Perry. "Do you know, when I checked with Pam last weekend, she assured me you were right about the straps being long enough to go across the body. She showed me her shoulder bag. I don't know how many times I've seen her wearing it, and I'd never noticed."

"Typical male."

"By the way," said Perry, on a more serious note, I suppose you know young Barry's dead?"

"We heard," replied Freddie. "It was on breakfast news."

"I had the police round at the hospital," said Wendy. "They told me what had happened. They said it was the mother of that girl he killed. Is that true?"

"Yes, I'm afraid so."

"I don't understand it," she continued. "That won't bring her back, and now they've gone and lost whatever bit of happiness they could have built up again together. I suppose she'll go to prison?"

"I would assume so," replied Perry. Out of the corner of his eye he spotted Franjo none too subtly hoeing the grounds.

With a brief: "Excuse me." Freddie wheeled himself in Franjo's direction.

Wendy looked after him indulgently as he made his ungainly way, jerking his wheelchair in Franjo's direction.

"Freddie's really sweet when you get to know him. He sort of keeps an eye out for me now."

"Well, let's hope you won't be needing too much of that in the future." Seizing the opportunity, now that they were alone, Perry told Wendy about the effects of her school days' traumas on Joan Mayflower's career.

"You know, I'd no idea about that; having left before the school closed down, I missed all that gossip."

"I don't think it was general gossip. Sonya only knew about it through her aunt, who was on the Local Education Authority at the time. But it at least accounts for the way she still seemed to have a down on you. Without trying to bring it about, or even knowing it, you'd managed to lose her her job. And quite justifiably so, but she wouldn't see it like that. She could only think of taking her revenge on you when the chance arose."

"Ah, the revenge," she said slowly, giving Perry a sideways glance.

"Eh?"

"Just something Franjo said to me one day. Freddie must have told him about that time she came round rowing me and the time he saw me after the contretemps with Mr Manning. Franjo warned me about her. He said she was one who enjoyed taking her revenge."

Perry smiled. "It certainly seems as though those two are out to look after you." He nodded in the direction of the two wheelchairs.

Freddie was very kind to me that day after I saw Mr Manning. I told you. He was in physio that afternoon, and we had quite a long chat afterwards."

Perry thought: Well that accounts for how Franjo got to hear of the way Joan used Manning. He asked: "Did you get any more trouble from Manning?

"No, I didn't. He avoids me like the plague now. But I don't mind that. He's the sort of person I can well live without. I don't know what you said to him, Perry, but it certainly did the trick. Thanks."

"Only too glad to be of help. In fact, I rather enjoyed myself," he admitted.

"And the sad and sorry thing is that it was all so unnecessary." Wendy shook her head as they parted.

As Perry started to walk back to his office, Franjo called out: "She is all right now, your little flower?"

Misunderstanding the question, Perry replied: "Fine thanks. I told Pam to be careful not to over-water it, like it says on the instructions. It's blooming away in the front bay window. It looks just fine."

Freddie laughed, and Franjo said quietly: "Not him. I know he is fine. I grow him. I mean the little Wendy flower."

Perry nodded and said, laughing: "Yes, thank you, that little flower is also blooming."

Back in the office there was deathly silence. Sonya had broken her printer. "I just don't know what I did, Mr Barrett, I don't understand it. It just underlines everything. I can't stop it." Perry deftly pressed a few keys. As the printer then not only underlined everything but also spelt it out in capitals, he deduced it was time to call in the engineers. There was no doubt about it: whatever Sonya's other talents, handling machinery wasn't one of them.

Being unable to send out any correspondence or to concentrate on clearing the final bills for the new wiring from the builders, Perry nosed around his appointments diary. Sonya, meanwhile, was chattering away: "Oh I know, Mr Barber; it was only the other week you came, but I can't do anything with it. It keeps underlining everything and it's making a funny noise. This afternoon? Oh, thanks, thanks a lot." Perry wondered how much the bill from Mr Barber would come to this time. Had they even paid the last one? He couldn't remember. It was then, as he was flicking through the diary, that a question which had been nagging at the back of his mind came to the fore.

"Sonya, can you remember who came into the office last week, before we went to see Barry?"

She looked helplessly at him and replied: "No, I don't think I can."

"It was only a few days ago," he encouraged.

"I know, but people are in and out of here all the time, Mr Barrett. Some days it's just like Piccadilly Circus in here. Anyone could come in. Anyone from here, I mean."

"I know," he sighed. "And they needn't even come in while you or I are here. They could come in when we'd gone to lunch, for example. I just wondered if you'd noticed anyone who doesn't normally visit us?"

"Is it that business with Barry that's still troubling you?"

"Yes. I can't get it out of my mind. If, and I know it's only if, our friend was responsible for winding up Mrs Peters who told her I was going to see Barry?"

"A good question. A very good question. It wasn't me. I can assure you of that."

"Oh, I know that, Sonya. I never dreamt for a minute that it was. But I can't help wondering who it was."

Just then the telephone rang. It was Mr Cielo from Nite-Safe. He wanted to come and see Perry. Urgently. Before lunch if possible. Perry was intrigued and agreed. He'd been impressed by the way Nite-Safe had turned out to protect him at Sonya's request, and Mr Cielo didn't strike him as a man who made mountains out of molehills. All the same, Perry couldn't imagine what he wanted.

Within thirty minutes of his telephone call, Mr Cielo was once more seated in Perry's office, cradling another cup of coffee. "St. Anthony, the first hermit," he remarked, looking at the design on the mug. "You see what comes from being a member of a large Catholic family."

"Oh yes, Spanish, of course, I never thought."

Mr Cielo was obviously trying to soften some blow or other. He replaced the mug carefully on the low table and began: "You know, Mr Barrett, I used to be a police officer, before I got too sick."

"I think I remember you saying so when your company applied for our security contract, yes."

"In that job, you know, you develop a good memory for faces, and yesterday when I was in your office, I thought I saw someone I recognised."

"Sonya?" Perry was surprised.

"No, no. Not that young one. She came in only for one minute; she just put her head round the door and went away again."

Perry couldn't think who it was Mr Cielo had seen. "I don't remember," he said.

"She had her hair done tight behind her head, in a bun."

"Oh, Dilys. Dilys Owen, our new chief fund-raising officer."

Mr Cielo nodded sagely. "She looked different, but I never forget a face, Mr Barrett. She has one of those unforgettable voices too, doesn't she? Beautiful Welsh accent, yes?"

"She does, Mr Cielo, but how do you come to know her?"

Mr Cielo pulled a photocopy of a newspaper cutting from his jacket pocket. The cutting comprised a photograph and two half-columns of print. The photograph was somewhat blurred, and had been taken a few years previously, but the figure in it was clearly recognizable. The text told its own tale: Miss Olwen Davies was today found guilty of stealing £20,000 from the Fighting Hunger Now project and was sentenced to 9 months' imprisonment. Scanning the cutting, Perry could see that the judge had remarked on the particularly despicable nature of the crime and had deemed a prison sentence necessary, despite the fact that the prisoner was truly remorseful and that there were certain mitigating circumstances for this first offence. Just by looking at the photograph, Perry decided that he couldn't really say Olwen Davies a.k.a. Dilys Owen looked particularly remorseful. He thought she just looked rather relieved.

Mr Cielo looked intently at him. "I'm right, aren't I, Mr Barrett? She works here, doesn't she?"

"Oh yes, you're right. Oh God, what a mess." Perry was reaching for his bottle of tablets.

"Certainly it is a mess, Mr Barrett. That is why I came to you privately, so that you could handle it discreetly."

"Thank you, Mr Cielo. I appreciate your thoughtfulness. And you certainly must have a terrific memory."

Mr Cielo accepted the compliment with pleasure. "What will you do, Mr Barrett?"

Perry replied cautiously: "I shall have to consult the board of trustees, of course; hiring and firing is their prerogative not mine, but I can't see her being allowed to continue here. She wouldn't have got the job in the first place if we'd known about this. It's a pity really, because otherwise she seemed ideal."

"That's no doubt what the Fighting Hunger Now project thought," remarked Mr Cielo dryly.

"You know what puzzles me, Mr Cielo? She came to us, as I remember, with excellent references. How did she manage that? She'd been working for Give the Kids a Hand before she came to us. How did she get the job with them? Does she just lie about her background all the time?"

Mr Cielo shook his head sadly, as if depreciating this last example of the dishonesty of man, or, in this case, woman. "Probably. It wouldn't surprise me if she got some shady friend to provide her references. All it takes is a bit of headed notepaper or a mate on the other end of a phone or e-mail. These days a lot of people take references that way. They just use the information provided by the candidate. Nine times out of ten they don't check any further. Who's to say who is on the receiving end of a phone call or e-mail?"

Perry thought for a few minutes. It was somehow impossible to connect the charming Miss Owen with any degree of dishonesty. But, on the other hand, she had been strangely reticent about having her photograph published in the PVB's literature. He asked: "How much do you know about the case, Mr Cielo? Was there any more to it than appeared in the paper? What about these extenuating circumstances?"

112

Mr Cielo smiled broadly. "I thought you would ask about that, Mr Barrett, so I did a little bit of research for you." He consulted a small notebook. "As far as anyone could tell, the mitigating circumstances amounted to no more than the desire to help a friend, a female friend, who was in financial difficulties. I couldn't unearth the name of the friend without arousing suspicion, which I thought it best not to do, but the view of the police was that said friend never did get any of the money. It was just an excuse to make her look good. The friend had conveniently disappeared before the trial and so couldn't vouch for her story."

"She sounds quite devious, Mr Cielo."

"Quite so, Mr Barrett, and very plausible. Very plausible indeed. May I give you some advice?"

"Certainly, please do."

"Without telling her you know, or arousing her suspicions, go through your accounts. Get your local fund-raisers to let you know how much they've handed over to her. Then, if it looks as though anything has gone wrong, you must call the police at once, you must not wait. Not one minute. Do not fire her until you have checked the accounts; if you do, she will simply take any money she has already, and run. If she has stolen anything from you, you would lose all chance of recovering it."

"You know, I'm sure you're right, Mr Cielo, and I will do as you suggest, but it's very hard to think of her stealing from us. Surely she wouldn't be so stupid as to do the same thing again?"

Mr Cielo replied slowly and firmly. "Mr Barrett, it wouldn't be stupid. Not by any means. It's a job to her, like administering is to you. For as long as it lasts, she gets a good salary; when and if she gets caught, she just goes to jail for a short time, if they manage to convict her. Last time, she made an extra £20,000 tax free, for 9 months being kept by the taxpayer, minus time off for being a good girl. It's an industry and a very profitable one. It's not stupid."

Perry's heart was churning over in his chest. He managed to reply: "Yes, I see, Mr Cielo. Looked at from that point of view, it's a very profitable way of working. I'll check with the board, but I've no doubt they'll take your advice."

"Make sure you make it clear to them, Mr Barrett, how unfortunate the consequences could be if she were allowed to get away with stealing from the PVB. You must act quickly and discreetly. If she has not already stolen, quick action will rob her of the chance. If she has, you will stop her stealing even more, and you may stand some chance of recovering some of the money."

"Do you know whether the Fighting Hunger Now project ever got any of their money back?"

"I can tell you that they didn't. In all probability she simply opened a bank account under a false name in a town where she wasn't known and put the money in there to gain interest during her stay in Her Majesty's Hotel. The police investigated her known accounts thoroughly at the time, but they found no trace of the money under her own name or evidence of heavy spending."

Perry wrinkled his nose in disgust. "Which is her own name, Dilys Owen or Olwen Davies? I know it's a long shot, but could she have banked the money under the name of Dilys Owen last time?"

Mr Cielo smiled again. "If she did, you can bet it's not under that name any more, and as to her real name, the one she was born with, it's probably Mary Jones or some such. If I were her, I might bank my ill-gotten gains under that name, but I'd never expose it to the public in any place where I committed a crime."

Perry was very grateful to Mr Cielo for spending so much of his time on the PVB's business and for being so thoughtful in his advice, and he said so. But Mr Cielo hadn't finished his good advice for the day. "You must be very careful, Mr Barrett. If the press get hold of this, it could be very bad for you all here. Very bad indeed, coming on top of the news about that awful youth. It is not that your charity has done anything wrong. Not at all. But it is guilt by association, if you follow me. It is not true for you that any publicity is good publicity. If you can dismiss her before she commits a theft on you, so much the better. There is no crime. There is no interest for the newspapers. It is simply a domestic matter. But…" He paused significantly. "But, if she has stolen from you, you must come clean and go to the police straight away. Minimize the damage that way. The worst your PVB is guilty of is not checking her references properly. It is not a major crime." He smiled. "Do not try to keep it quiet, dismiss her, and let her get away with it. It will only come out in the end, maybe when she gets caught next time. And then you would all be guilty of facilitating a despicable felony. Do you understand me?" he asked earnestly.

"Perfectly," replied Perry. "Would it be indiscreet to ask if the poor devils at Fighting Hunger Now got it right?"

"No, Mr Barrett, they did not and it is now public knowledge. The crime was discovered by their accountants. They had it brought to the attention of the police to protect themselves. The charity was very damaged by it." Perry thanked Mr Cielo again for his time and consideration, and promised to let him know how things developed. Mr Cielo left the copy of the newspaper cutting with him.

When Mr Cielo had gone, Perry sat back and stared at the cutting. It was all so hard to believe. The whole episode had a nightmare quality, as if he were being sucked down a huge drain. There was no doubt that the modern spinster was a creature to be reckoned with. First Joan Mayflower and now Dilys Owen. The phrase "compounding a felony" swam before his eyes. He thought back to poor Paul and his petty thefts. What was the difference between him and Dilys? It was only a question of degree. Degree of desperation and degree of theft. And degree of remorse? He'd compounded Paul's felony. Wasn't that the same thing as compounding the same felony for Dilys? Perry's head began to spin. Eventually he let himself off the hook with the thought that in cases like this, the degree was all important. There was a great deal of difference between a hundred or so stolen in need and later returned and the unrepentant, planned theft of thousands.

After snatching a hasty lunch in the cafeteria, Perry called Eric Palmer and suggested he call round to see him in his own office, away from the PVB. The chairman hesitated; he had a busy afternoon ahead of him, but Perry stood firm. This was one problem he was certainly not going to discuss over the phone, no matter how much he trusted Brenda on the switchboard. Palmer couldn't fit him in until after six o'clock, but Perry assured him this was fine. Privately, he thought it would be better the fewer people who were around when he broke the news.

CHAPTER EIGHTEEN

The afternoon crawled by, alleviated only by the appearance of Mr Barber to repair the printer. He diligently and patiently explained to Sonya where she was going wrong and remarked that, although computer technology was almost fool-proof and very robust, there were certain things even the strongest equipment couldn't withstand. "The funny thing is, Mr Barrett, I don't remember doing anything like that," Sonya protested, after Mr Barber's departure.

"You can't remember everything, Sonya. You probably didn't notice touching the wrong keys accidentally."

"Oh, but I'm most careful, really I am," she persisted, in the face of the facts. "After all, I don't want to have to input all those names again."

"What names?" enquired Perry absently.

"You remember, the mail shot names. The people who've given to us before. We keep all their names on disc and now and then we send them nice letters to ask for more money. Maybe just once or twice a year, whenever the fund-raiser thinks we should. Really, it's nothing to do with your work, as such, but the fund-raiser never has a secretary, so I do it when I've got a bit of time to spare."

As Sonya held out her mug for a refill, something about the words "fund-raiser" cut into Perry. He said slowly, thinking aloud: "That's very good of you, Sonya, I'm sure, but, presumably, now that you've got all the names stored in the memory, anyone could send out those letters. Dilys could do it herself, for example?"

"Anyone could who knew how to use the computer, how to mail merge. I don't really like other people using it when I'm not here. It tends to get broken if you get people using it who don't really know what they're doing." She laughed.

Perry wasn't really up to date with all this technology and mail merge stuff. He asked Sonya to show him what she meant. It was really very simple: a chosen letter could be sent to any number of names from the mailing list by placing both the names and the letter in the computer files, with special codes to instruct, for example, the recipients' names and addresses to be typed in places ready for the envelope windows and for the recipients' names to be included in the letter. All that was then necessary was to instruct the computer to merge the list of names with the chosen letter, so that any number of individual letters could be produced. Sonya obliged Perry by running off a few examples. He was duly impressed. If only he'd used that sort of thing when he'd been in business; it was an advertising godsend. Sonya, he decided, was an altogether superior type.

Perry then asked the obvious question: "So for this mail merge to work, the letter asking for funds, or whatever, has to be stored on disc?"

"Yes, that's right." She pressed a couple of keys, and a list came up on the screen. Sonya then pointed out some of the file names and dates. "They're some of the letters. You can find one you like by calling them up and just glancing through them, or you can put a new letter in a file if you need to."

Perry was becoming horribly interested in the possibilities of Sonya's technology. "Tell me another thing, Sonya. If I wanted to mail shot our donors' list, would it take me long, once I'd got a suitable letter on disc?"

"To mail shot the whole list? Yes, it takes hours, because we have to print them off and check them."

Perry made a decision. He quickly went over to Sonya's outer office door and slid the catch down so they were locked in. "Sonya, I want you to go through the files on your disc, call them up, and see if there are any soliciting donations that you don't recognize."

She boggled: "You're not asking much, are you? Do you know how many there are on this disc alone? And I've got others in here." She flipped open a desk drawer to reveal two boxes of discs. "And why the secrecy?" She nodded in the direction of the locked door.

Perry thought it was an endearing part of her personality that he didn't consider the locked door might mean anything else. No one could ever say Sonya was dirty minded. She was almost as wholesome as Dilys. Perry was sure he could be honest with her. "Well, I'll tell you, Sonya, but you must absolutely keep it to yourself." She nodded bewildered assent, Perry produced the copy of the newspaper cutting from his wallet, where he had put it for safe keeping. "Recognize anyone?"

Sonya stared at the crumpled piece of paper. "It looks like Miss Owen."

"It is."

"Oh no!" she gasped. "It can't be."

"It is. Mr Cielo recognized her when she put her head round the door yesterday, after our little bit of excitement with Mr Peters."

"I can't believe it."

"Believe it," he said firmly. "I'm going to go over to see Palmer later."

She looked puzzled. "But I don't see what all this has to do with my mailing lists, Mr Barrett."

"It occurs to me, Sonya, that someone else really may be responsible for the trouble you've been having with your computer. Someone who doesn't quite know what they're doing may have been using it. You said yourself that you didn't remember doing what Mr Barber said you must have done."

"You mean someone, Dilys, has been sending out their own mail shots asking for money?" she asked, following his thoughts.

"I do."

"Oh, but that would be terrible, awful. For us, I mean. It wouldn't just be the money, although that would be bad enough, but everyone would know, if it came out. All the donors would know they'd been conned; they'd never give us another penny."

"That's why I want you to go through your discs. Do it now and keep at it until you've checked them all. I'll get you paid overtime, if necessary."

"No, there's no need for that. I'll have to think for a minute or two. There must be some way of narrowing it down." Sonya sat in silent repose for several minutes, then she reasoned: "If what you think is true, it can only have been done since she came here, and all the files are dated, see?" She pointed so some numbers adjacent to the file names on the screen. "The computer does it automatically."

"If we are correct in our thinking, our friend knows less about this equipment than you do, hence all the problems, so it's unlikely she'd falsify the dates, so you can start with the files which have been put on since she came. If you don't get any joy, go on to the older ones afterwards, just to be on the safe side."

"Right-o. That should cut down on a lot of work, with any luck. Now, if it were me trying to do that sort of thing, which disc would I be most likely to put the letter on?"

"The best place to hide a needle is in a haystack," said Perry, somewhat confusedly.

"You mean she'd put it on the disc with the other fund-raising letters?"

"Yes, why not?"

"It's as good a place to start as any."

Sonya then began the lengthy task of reading through the letters on her discs. Half an hour later, they had discovered that the letter, if it existed, was not in the obvious place. She ploughed on doggedly. Perry was amazed by the sheer volume of verbiage she typed in a month. It appeared to be never ending.

The door handle rattled. Someone was trying the door. "Quick, turn it off," instructed Perry. "We don't want anyone to see." Sonya did as he asked, and he went over and unlocked the door.

On the other side was a bemused Dilys. "Oh, Mr Barrett, did you know you'd locked yourselves in now?" She smiled and peered at him through her gold rimmed spectacles.

Perry swallowed hard. His heart was thumping. "Er... Yes..."

Sonya chipped in: "We were trying out a new arrangement for the office, so I could get more light, but it didn't fit very well, so we moved it back again."

"And you didn't want people to come in and fall over the furniture. Very sensible now." Sonya's peculiar excuse seemed perfectly logical to Dilys. She continued: "Look, I won't keep you, I've brought over some first copies of the colour prints from the photographs. You look a real treat, Mr Barrett. Doesn't he, Sonya?" She beamed at them both while showing the photographs.

"They're great," said Sonya sincerely.

Perry managed to say: "They've made me look almost young again. They're very good; you could use any one of these. That one of Ben is particularly good, don't you think?"

"Yes, I'm sure they'll all be pleased. I thought I'd go and show them after I'd let you have a look, so I'll be off now. Don't work too hard." Dilys laughed her happy Welsh laugh and was gone.

Perry felt as if he'd just survived an extended interrogation by the KGB. He thought: I'd never make a spy, or a crook, come to that. I'd give myself away in five minutes, but not so Sonya. What was it Mark Twain had said? 'An experienced, industrious, ambitious and often quite picturesque liar.' But only in a good cause.

He didn't lock the door again. "She won't be back, now she's gone off to chat to the others about the prints."

Sonya meanwhile had begun to tap away on her computer. It took only a few more minutes for her to find the letter they had both hoped would not be there. "Look, Mr Barrett, here it is. I didn't type this one."

121

He peered over her shoulder. "Are you sure?"

"Yes, I'm sure. Even if I can't remember them from the file names, I always remember them when I put them up, and besides, this one isn't laid out properly. Look at the ends of the lines. They're all uneven. I would have set the letters out properly. I didn't type this."

Perry read the letter carefully: it was a nicely judged appeal for funds to help the PVB celebrate its anniversary by expanding its services. Replies and cheques were to be sent to Miss Dilys Owen at a post office box number. The letter was signed, "Dilys Owen. Chief Fund-Raising Officer".

"Clever," remarked Perry. "Very clever. With cheques addressed to her personally, she could just pay them into an account in that name. They wouldn't have to go through our bank accounts because they wouldn't be made out to the PVB. At the same time, it's clear that people would be sending the cheques to her in her capacity as chief fund-raiser, or so they would think."

Sonya added: "I saw something like that once or twice when I worked in the bank. Some of these financial advisers, often the small ones, acting independently, not tied to any one insurance company, and having their own offices, where only they would check their mail, would get gullible clients to make out cheques for investment schemes to them personally instead of to the company direct. They used to tell the clients the money would be put in various different schemes, so it would make things difficult if they made out their cheques to individual companies. Of course, the cheques never went further than the adviser's back pocket, and the clients would lose their money. Sometimes they came in to us to try and stop the cheques being honoured, if they'd heard a rumour or seen something on the telly. It was usually too late. There was nothing we could do to help them."

"This is still a very clever idea, all the same," remarked Perry. "Even if one or two of the respondents made their cheques out in such a way that she had to put them through the PVB's account, it wouldn't really matter. She could afford to be generous."

"What are we going to do now?" asked Sonya.

In truth, Perry didn't really know. He said: "A lot depends on whether she's already sent out some of these letters and received the cheques. If she has, it's a criminal matter, and we're going to be faced with an uphill struggle to get the money back. If she hasn't, we should be able to stop her doing so and just fire her without calling in the police." Thinking about Mr Cielo's instructions, he asked, "Have you any way of finding out whether she's printed any of the letters?"

"We should be able to check if both files have been used together, but we wouldn't know if she was sending out letters or just checking that the system worked. Even if she's printed a stack of letters, we've no way of finding out if she's actually sent them. She might send them out a few at a time as she prints them, or she might save up a whole lot and send them out all at once."

Perry considered the problem. "She obviously couldn't print the whole lot in one go, especially if she's having to do the work piecemeal in the evenings and at weekends, but even if she has sent some letters and we can get evidence of that, we wouldn't stand any chance of recovering the money unless we could find out where she's hidden it." He looked hopefully at Sonya.

"We know the name of the account holder, but we have no idea which bank she's using. It wouldn't be the same one she's paying her salary into. You can bet she's got a second account well hidden away, probably in some obscure foreign bank. It might even be in the Channel Islands or the Isle of Man. If I was going to do something like this, that's what I would do."

Perry interrupted: "Even if we could somehow find out where the account is, we've no way of knowing how much is in it, how much she would have stolen from the PVB."

"You don't get your cheques returned with your bank statements these days, like you used to, so even the donors would have no idea where their cheques had ended up. The only chance we have, if she has sent out the letters and received cheques, is to contact the donors and get the police to trace known cheques through the banking system. They could do it, but it would mean informing the donors they'd been ripped off."

Perry groaned. "One thing I don't understand though: sooner or later this would be bound to come to light. One way or another, a donor would talk about it with a local fund-raiser or one of us, and then we'd query the whole thing."

"With whom?" Sonya asked quietly.

"Mm. Well, I suppose with Dilys herself, more like than not, at least in the first instance."

"And the minute that happened, she'd be off. She'd present herself in person at the bank holding the second account, withdraw as much as she could, and disappear. She could easily gain a day or two's time by promising to write to the local fund-raiser or donor with full details or to investigate the whole thing, and she'd simply run for it. For all we know, she may already be transferring funds out of the second account on a regular basis, so that there's never a very large balance left vulnerable in case she's caught out."

"I can see you would have made a master criminal, Sonya. If you'd put your mind to it, you could have put even dear Joan in the shade." Sonya seemed quite pleased at the compliment. Perry continued: "But that doesn't help us now. As far as I can see, she's got us. The only way we could find out if, and by how much, we've been robbed would be by asking the donors, and she knows we could never do that." They sat silently bent over the computer, looking on glumly as the letter burned itself into the screen.

Eventually, Perry said: "I don't think we've any alternative but to call in the police. We have a reasonable suspicion that we're being robbed. We know Dilys has done a similar kind of thing before, that she's stolen from a charity. We don't know how she did it in that case, but, at the very least, she got her job here under false pretences, and now we've found this suspicious letter with her name attached. If we just fire here on the basis of her past history, we may lose money and the donors might find out about her past anyway. It would look even worse then, if we hadn't called in the police. As far as I can see, I have a clear duty to stop her sending any more letters or even starting to send them. We've got to prevent her from having further access to your letter files, and we've no way of doing that without showing our hand, so I think we should show it decisively, and call the police before she gets wind of what's going on and does a runner." Perry had liked the sound of that speech, but when he stopped, the room was very quiet. "What do you think" he asked.

"I think you're right, Mr Barrett." Sonya was emboldened by this unusual plea for advice and went further. "I think that, given how late it's getting, you should call the chairman over here instead of going to his offices, and show him what we've found, and then call the police straight away, if he agrees.

Perry looked at the clock; it was well past five. He'd have to be going soon, if he wanted to make it across town by six. Instead, he did as Sonya had suggested. He phoned Eric Palmer and explained that he simply wouldn't be able to make it to his office because something had cropped up unexpectedly, but that he really needed to talk to him.

The chairman sounded worried: "Nothing wrong, I hope?"

"Oh no," lied Perry, "but I do need to see you today. It's nothing to worry about though." Mark Twain came back to mind.

Sonya busied herself tidying her office and brewed yet another coffee as they waited impatiently for the chairman's arrival. Looking out over the drive, they saw Dilys Owen leave work, for what was possibly the last time, at a quarter to six. Her little turquoise car sped blissfully away along the road into town.

"She's gone," remarked Perry. "Just as well. It might make her suspicious if she saw he chairman driving in." Around them the life of the PVB began to wind down for the day. The administration block became strangely quiet. The paid officers went home for the evening, and the residents went to their

125

accommodations. The switchboard closed down, leaving a single direct external line from Perry's office.

At about a quarter past six Eric Palmer drew up in his Rover. He looked harassed and was in something of a huff about being called out. As he listened to Perry's recapitulation of his findings, his face changed from red huffiness to purple. He sat staring at the photocopy cutting and repeating: "Oh my God. Oh no. Oh my God." Sonya offered him one of her coffees. "I can't believe it. She seemed such a lovely woman, just perfect for the job."

"I'm afraid it's true," said Perry. "At the very least she's got a criminal record for theft from a charity. At the worst…" he shrugged.

"Oh God."

"But you agree with me, we must call the police," Perry pressed the chairman.

He wavered. "Well, I agree with you, with what you've discovered, of course. Well done. Both of you." He nodded in Sonya's direction. "But well, I don't think we want to go that far, do we? We can't even prove she's stolen anything from the PVB. We've no way of knowing. You said so yourself. I think the best things is if we deal with this in-house. Just give her the push. After due consultation, of course," he added hastily.

Once again, Perry found himself up against Eric's almost wilful obtuseness. "We can't prove she's stolen anything from us, I admit, but we have a very strong presumption. If she has, and it all comes out and we've done nothing to get our money back, the consequences would be unthinkable. We'd never get another penny from the public. Never. When Mr Cielo told me about his suspicions, he suggested very strongly that we ought to protect our backs. If there is the slightest chance she's already set to work on us, we must call the police. Mr Cielo was most emphatic that we should not try to cover it up; he has more experience in this area than we do and I agree with him."

The chairman vacillated. "She might be trying to turn over a new leaf, make amends, put things right somehow. We don't know."

Sonya snorted. "A new leaf. A gold leaf, more like." Eric shot her a warning glance.

Perry supported Sonya. "Trying to start again and do the decent thing. Under a false name? I don't think so, Eric."

"I was just trying to be practical and humane. What could we tell the police if we called them in? We've no proof."

Perry replied: "We tell them what I've told you. Getting proof is their job. We should let them do it."

CHAPTER NINETEEN

Sonya started to tap idly on her computer. The chairman cast her an irritated glance and said: "Miss Owen had excellent references."

Perry asked: "Did we check them?"

"Oh yes, they would have been checked, not by me personally, but I'm sure they would have been checked before we offered her the job."

"By whom?"

"Jack usually does that; he's very conscientious, you know."

"Yes, I do know," agreed Perry, "but it doesn't make any difference, We've saddled ourselves with a crook; it's as simple as that."

Eric started to defend Dilys again, but Sonya interrupted him. "Hang on. Sorry to butt in, but I've just had an idea. If I were going to send those letters out, I'd probably just work my way through the donor list in manageable stages. The names are in alphabetical order, so it's more likely than not, if she has sent out any of the letters, they would have been received by people whose surnames are at the beginning of the list, right?"

"Sound reasoning," agreed Perry, "But where does it get us?"

"It gets us Mrs Bernice Adams, my Auntie Bernie. She's not a gossip and she knows I work here. We're quite close."

"So?" queried the chairman.

"So why don't I phone her and see if I can find out if she's received a letter?"

"If she's reliable, why not?" asked Perry.

Eric was against the idea. "I don't think so. No, we couldn't risk it."

Perry was tiring of Eric's equivocations; he sighed loudly. "Eric, I think it's a good idea. It's the only way forward that I can see. Thank you, Sonya. At least we could make reasonably sure whether she's up to her old tricks again, with the minimum of exposure of the problem to the public."

"With any luck I may not have to tell her anything at all, but if I do, I'm sure she'd be trustworthy. After all, I do work here and I am her niece."

The chairman was clearly well out of his depth by now, as he had been over twenty years before when Joan Mayflower got him in her clutches. At least now, however, he was honest enough to admit the problem was beyond him and that something needed to be done quickly. "All right, go ahead," he said. "I suppose it's the only thing we can do."

The two men waited in tense silence as Sonya dialled her aunt's number. "I only hope she's in," she joked. Then her face lightened. "Hello, Auntie Bernie, it's Sonya." They could only hear Sonya's side of the conversation, as she poured out her spate of domestic news and listened in turn to her aunt's weekly details. "Well, then it's telepathy," she said, sitting upright in her chair. "Me phoning you just when you were thinking of the Princess Victoria's. ...Oh, you have, well, there's a thing." Sonya looked directly at Perry. "Yes, I'm sure it was a very nice letter. No, I didn't type it, it's not one of mine," she said, trying to keep her voice light. "You were just wondering whether you should send in a few pounds?"

This was something they hadn't been prepared for. Sonya's aunt had obviously received a letter and, judging by Sonya's end of the conversation, it was the one letter she hadn't typed. Unfortunately, her aunt was also clearly considering sending a donation. This put Sonya in a very difficult position. Eric looked blank. Perry thought quickly and grabbed a piece of paper and a pen. He scribbled: "Tell her. Get her to send a cheque. We will reimburse, if necessary." He pushed the paper in front of Sonya. She nodded. He could hear the sound of a voice at the other end of the line.

Sonya spoke again: "Yes, I'm still here, auntie, but to tell you the truth, there's something I need your help with, that's why I'm calling." Briefly, and as tactfully as possible, she outlined the problem to her aunt: they might have a problem in their fund-raising department, with cheques going astray. They couldn't be sure, so it would help them enormously if they could trace one cheque through the system. Naturally, they would need a friendly and discreet donor to help them, and Sonya had recommended her aunt. They would refund her money, of course, but it would be a great help. Did she mind? Apparently Auntie Bernie didn't mind at all; the idea of playing Sherlock Holmes appealed to her.

"A little excitement, Sonya, a little colour in the grey tapestry of life. Do you think someone's got their hand in the till?" she asked, conspiratorially.

"I'm afraid it may come to that, auntie. I hope not, but we can't be certain."

Perry was as amazed by Sonya's tact as by her aunt's relish for coming to grips with the criminal underworld.

At the end of their conversation, Sonya wrote some numbers on her pad and, after profusely thanking her aunt and promising to keep her fully abreast of developments, she turned to Perry. "She'll put a cheque in the post, first class, tomorrow. £10 made out to Dilys Owen. She found her cheque book and told me her account number and the number of the next cheque. She banks at the Westchester."

"Thanks a lot, Sonya, that was a great job you did there, really great," said Perry.

"Yes, indeed, I must congratulate you. Many thanks," added Eric.

Perry asked: "I suppose there's no doubt now? We've got to call in the police. She's obviously started the swindle already. We've got to put a stop to it and salvage whatever donations we can."

"Agreed," said Eric. Inwardly, he was cursing Jack for landing them with this mess.

Perry called the police there and then, before Eric had a chance to change his mind. It was almost an hour before the youthful Sergeant Twomey turned up and listened, with great seriousness, to their story. He examined the newspaper article with careful concentration and made a note of Mr Cielo's address and telephone number. He stood and gazed at Sonya's computer screen bearing the bogus fund-raising letter. Perry explained that it was contrary to the PVB's usual procedures for the fund-raising officer to receive cheques in her own name or to use a post office box. The sergeant appreciated these points and asked Sonya to print out a few copies of the letter for him to take away. He then asked about their normal procedures for dealing with cheque donations, Perry informed him that every donation, whether in cash or by cheque, was recorded in a daily ledger by the fund-raiser, and a standard acknowledgement sent out. Cheques were banked at the end of each day. The sergeant was pleased with the arrangements the trio had made with Sonya's agreeable aunt and considered that this was as good a way of obtaining evidence of a crime as any he could think of, given the PVB's wish to avoid publicity.

Perry carefully emphasized the problems that would occur if the press got hold of the story, and the need to reclaim any donations which might already have been sent as well as to prevent others from similarly going astray. The detective suggested Sonya should report a serious fault in her printer and render it inoperative by removing the fuse from the plug. "That should make it impossible for her to send out any more than she's already prepared, unless she has access to another printer."

"Not here she hasn't," replied Sonya, "and presumably she hasn't got one anywhere else, or she wouldn't have put her letter on my disc."

The sergeant shook his head, like a wine-taster faced with an inferior vintage. "Silly woman. If she'd put her own letter on her own disc, copied your name file on to that disc, and used her own set-up, this would never have come to light. Given her previous history, I suppose she didn't want all that at home, although the risk of it being discovered there was very slight. I'd like to search her office now."

The four of them trooped down to the small room on the floor below. It wasn't locked. "Don't you lock your offices at night, sir?"

"Oh, yes, of course we do," replied Perry "Dilys must just have forgotten. Sonya and I always make sure our offices are locked, but it wouldn't be difficult for anyone who works here to get a key. There's a spare set at the main reception desk. People forget keys, and I suppose a really determined person could just take the spare set."

The sergeant grunted. "She's probably had a duplicate key for your office made up, if your thoughts are correct, sir."

Dilys' office proved to be as well organised and wholesome as the lady herself. The desk and filing cabinets were in order and the window sill was festooned with potted plants. "Well, it was just a long shot, sir; she'd have to be really daft to keep anything incriminating in her own office. It's probably at home, what little there is to see. She doesn't need much. She probably does all the printing work here and then just drops the letters in the post box on the way home."

After his tour of inspection the sergeant said he would report to his superiors. "We'll be contacting Mrs Adams about having her cheque traced through the banking system, and we'll be keeping a discreet eye on that post office box number, to see who comes for the mail."

"One more thing, sergeant," said Perry. "So far we have concentrated on the possibility that Miss Owen has been planning to obtain money using these letters, but in the normal way she handles fairly large sums of money, from local fund-raising events and donations, some of it in cash, every day. I have no idea how she stole the money last time, but I should think it's possible that she might also simply be making off with some of the cash too. Mr Cielo advised us to get the books checked and to contact the local fund-raisers to see how much they've handed over to her, but that was before this problem came to light. What do you think we should do?"

The detective thought it over and advised against showing their hand by openly going through the accounts. "It looks more probable to me, sir, that she's planning to scoop the jackpot with these letters. We have some evidence that she's doing that already; we have no evidence that she's also stealing cash. On balance, I think you have more to gain by catching her at this and getting some of your money back than by going after the cash at this stage. We should be able to get something solid within a very few days, and then you can check your books for more evidence of theft. Let's hope you don't find it, sir."

After the sergeant had departed, Eric Palmer headed for home. On his way out, he thanked Perry and Sonya yet again for their diligence. Perry carefully locked his office and offered Sonya a lift home. She was beginning to look very worn. On their way home she remarked that the next few days were going to be very difficult. Perry thought that was putting it mildly.

CHAPTER TWENTY

In the event Perry and Sonya were spared the unpleasantness of coming face to face with the suspected Dilys. By about a quarter to eleven the following morning, it was clear she was not coming into work that day. Having disabled Sonya's system, so that no one, including Sonya, could send out any letters, she and Perry were wondering what to do with themselves all day. Sonya said she would catch up with her paperwork. Perry said he would start his rounds early. He hadn't been gone for more than five minutes when he re-entered the office, accompanied by Sergeant Twomey and an older man, whom he introduced as Superintendent Mackie. Perry informed them that Dilys hadn't reported for work, an absence attributed in her desk diary to a visit to the dentist.

"Not the dentist, sir; the nick. We arrested her twenty minutes ago."

"My God, that was quick. How did you manage that?" asked Perry.

The Superintendent informed him that between them they had netted a much bigger fish than they had at first thought. On checking with records, they had found out that, as well as the offence which had made the newspaper headlines, there had been two smaller offences where the charities had declined to prosecute for fear of the publicity. Superintendent Mackie explained that his own father-in-law, a local JP, was also a supporter of the PVB, and had responded to Dilys' bogus appeal by sending a cheque, which had already cleared his bank account. The superintendent had taken his evidence, together with that supplied by Perry and Sonya, and had applied for a search warrant first thing that morning. A search of Dilys' modest home had revealed letters waiting to be sent, some cheques, and a completed bank paying-in slip. There were also several covering letters, making it clear that the donors thought they were sending their money to the PVB, and not to Dilys personally. She had been arrested there and then.

Despite herself, Sonya had to laugh: "Poor old Dilys; all that careful scheming, and one of the first letters she sends goes to the father-in-law of the local police chief."

Perry said: "We're grateful to you, Superintendent, for having acted so rapidly. I'm sure your quick action has saved us a lot of money and unpleasantness."

"We've got her down at the station now, sir, so she's not going to have the chance to clear out her bank accounts, and we're going to see the manager at George's Bank later this morning. With any luck, you might well be able to retrieve most of the money, either from there, or from any other accounts she may be using. In any case, we've nipped her activities in the bud; judging by the letters and cheques we've already recovered, she hadn't got past the letter B in the surname file. She's a fly lady, though. At the moment, she's not even admitting to being Olwen Davies, but fingerprints will clear that up soon enough. She's even trying to claim she was intending to hand all the money over to the PVB in her own good time, but that won't wash, not now that we know she was banking the cheques into her own account."

"Well, Superintendent, I don't see that we could have done much better. In the circumstances, we've all acted as fast as we possibly could, when you consider that twenty-four hours ago we had no inkling that anything was wrong. From our point of view, prompt action may well have saved the day. If we can get most of the money back and if it transpires that she hasn't stolen any cash from us, the only thing we've got to reproach ourselves with is having hired a crook in the first place."

"You'll have to be very careful who you pick next time, sir. It wouldn't do to get yourselves landed with another lemon. Still, you know your own business better than I do. We'll be in touch when we've spoken to her bank and, in the meantime, I'd be grateful if you and Miss Bishop could both provide

Sergeant Twomey with statements outlining your parts in all this."

"Do you think she'll try and get out of it?" asked Sonya.

"If you mean, is she going to plead guilty and go down without a fight, not if the last time is anything to go by. She'll probably get herself an expensive lawyer. She should be able to afford one. Then again, she knows her appearance is all for her; she looks so honest, and there's no doubt that goes down well with juries. Last time she tried to convince them she was a female Robin Hood, stealing from the rich to give to the poor. Her mythical friend never turned up, but the jury were close to believing her."

"But she went to jail."

"For a few months, Miss Bishop. Everyone was very sympathetic and she was a model prisoner. A victim of circumstances really. It'll be interesting to see what she comes up with this time."

Perry didn't get to do his rounds that morning; he and Sonya were busy making statements and answering Sergeant Twomey's polite but direct questions. Like them, he couldn't understand how they'd managed to get themselves lumbered with a fund-raiser with a criminal record. Perry referred him to the chairman for the answer to that one. Even as he did so, he was uncomfortably aware that it was his friend, Jack, who was responsible. Poor old Jack was going to have some explaining to do and not only to the board.

After the sergeant had left them, Sonya replaced the fuse in her printer's plug and got on with some correspondence, while Perry went on his rounds. The new block was now ready for habitation, and there had been the usual amount of jockeying for privilege which was one of the less desirable aspects of institutional life. Despite Perry's insistence that some of the older, wheelchair-bound or unsuitably housed residents should be accommodated in the new block, some of the other old-timers were claiming length of residence as a priority for allocation to one of the new rooms. He was reminded of the truth of the saying that it was impossible to please all of the people all of the time. As things stood, he would have settled for fifty per cent.

Since the new arrangements had benefited both Ben and Franjo, they both smiled benevolently on him when he chatted to them. Franjo was even waxing witty: "My friend, I give many of my little buds here to our new lady. She asked me for them; always she says: 'I will pay you when I get change.' Do I get my money?"

Perry didn't know what to say. He hadn't expected the police to move so quickly. He hadn't had time to think about what he should say to either the patients or, God help him, the press. And as for the local fund-raisers, his mind boggled. He gave Franjo a watery smile and said: "Maybe." The gardener didn't look as though he believed him.

Perry beat a hasty retreat to his office, just in time to receive a happy phone call from the chairman. "Damned good piece of work that, eh, Perry? And quick too. Yes, they've been here already this morning and I've given 'em a statement; same for you two? We did rather well there, I think. We've all had a lucky escape."

There was no doubt about it: either Eric was exceptionally stupid, or he had a remarkable talent for burying his head in the sand. Perry had a number of requests. Firstly, he wanted the chairman to authorize an investigation of the accounts and to notify the local fund-raisers as tactfully as possible about the reason why. Eric's euphoria evaporated, but he reluctantly agreed. He really had enough to do with his own business, but he understood that Perry was not employed to deal with fund-raising; in the absence of a fund-raiser, the buck stopped with him. He knew there would be a lot of smoothing down to be done, and he didn't relish breaking the news to the likes of Colonel Charles. Damn Jack.

Perry volunteered to write a letter to be sent to all their clients, both residents and day workers, and the other paid officers, along the lines that Miss Owen had been removed from her post, pending the outcome of a police investigation into certain matters connected with their fund-raising

137

operation. He hoped that would do the trick temporarily; there was nothing more they could say until the police finished their investigations. He went on to suggest that if the chairman or other members of the board were troubled by the press, they should refer all enquiries to him at the PVB offices, and he would issue a press release along the same lines as his letter. Perry didn't want Eric's ideas exposed to the probing of the press any more than Eric himself did. The chairman agreed and gratefully rang off.

Perry got to work on his letter and statement straight away, and both he and Sonya braced themselves for the onslaught. It didn't come. In the middle of the afternoon the police called to inform him that, true to form, Dilys had called on the services of her expensive solicitor; she was even using the same firm as before. According to the bank, she had recently been transferring large sums of money into an offshore account in Jersey, and was now presumably gambling on being able to keep that money. She was therefore giving the police as little help as possible. Not only would her solicitor have advised her to say nothing, but every delay would allow more of her ill-gotten gains to complete their journey to the Channel Islands. Superintendent Mackie offered to contact the bank in question, but was none too sanguine about the outcome. "They're like the Swiss about banking secrecy over there, I'm afraid, sir, so it's very likely you will lose out, at least to some extent."

Perry expressed his relief and gratitude that, under those circumstances, they had stopped Dilys so quickly.

CHAPTER TWENTY-ONE

The following day was a Saturday, and Jack and Perry had their usual round of golf together. Strolling along in the warmth of the summer's morning, Jack said: "What a mess about Dilys, then. Eric was on at me yesterday, as if it was all my fault."

"I'm sorry about that, Jack; it certainly isn't all your fault. It's Dilys' fault. She's the crook, but I am afraid it's going to rebound on us all."

"I did the best I could," moaned Jack. "You know how it is when you've got a business to run. I can't spend all my time on the PVB. I just did what I do when I hire my own staff: I called the two numbers she gave me. I've never hired a crook."

"You hope," laughed Perry, "but seriously, Jack, what did these two types say?"

"If I remember correctly, the Bishop of Wensleydale was either out or engaged the whole time.

She'd given him as a character reference, but his diocesan administrator had his permission to provide the reference. The other one was the co-ordinator for the UK end of Give the Kids a Hand: she said Dilys was hard-working and conscientious, but somewhat old-fashioned in her ideas. I remember I wasn't too impressed with that particular lady, but she gave Dilys a clean bill of health."

Perry missed his putt and remarked: "It looks as though they didn't know about her past at the children's charity then; she probably got a friend to supply the other reference for her. Mr Cielo suggested she might well do that." He tried his putt again. "Got it." I must admit, though, Jack, the Bishop of Wensleydale sounds a bit dodgy. Is there such a person?"

"I don't know, I'm not interested in religion. I never have been."

"It would be interesting to phone those numbers again now and see if either the Bishop or her previous employers would still want to sing her praises."

Jack looked sheepishly at Perry. "I did that yesterday afternoon, as soon as Eric got off the line. The Bishop's number was discontinued. He must have changed his number, moved, maybe." Jack sounded defensive.

"Oh dear," sighed Perry. "I don't really think that's very likely, Jack. I wouldn't have thought bishops move around that much as a rule." He patted Jack on the shoulder. "Don't worry; it was a mistake anyone could make."

"You're just glad it wasn't you who made it, right?" asked Jack, echoing a previous conversation.

"Yes, but there's no culpability on your part. You followed accepted business procedures, and you're not a paid officer of the charity, you're doing all this in your spare time, out of the goodness of your heart. You're not getting paid for it. If the press come round hassling you, you just refer them to me; I'll make all the statements."

Jack looked at him uncertainly. "Thanks, I don't think I could face the press over this. Not now, with the business going so badly. I've got more than enough on my plate. It's this damned recession. Even when I get the work, the blighters don't pay up when they should. You've no idea."

Perry had. He had every idea. Genuinely saddened for his friend, he said: "I'm sorry, Jack. I didn't know things were that bad. Is there anything I can do to help?"

Jack smiled. "Thanks, I know you mean it, but there's nothing I can do except sit tight. I know you probably won't agree with me, especially the way things turned out with Per, but you made the right decision to get out when you did."

"There was no question of choice, Jack. We simply went bust."

"I know, but if you had managed to get out of that and struggle on, you'd probably be facing going bust now for a whole lot more."

"True, true." Perry over-shot. Jack cheered up a bit.

After they had finished their round and were strolling back to the club house, Perry broached another topic to Jack. "With Dilys' speedy and unexpected demise, we'll be on the look out for another chief fund-raiser again."

Jack groaned. "Well this time I'm not going to check their references. I'll leave that to Eric or someone else. Anyone else. As long as it isn't me."

"I've been giving the matter a bit of thought, and I think I may have come up with a solution." As he ordered two pints, Jack's face brightened. Perry continued: "What about Sonya?"

"Sonya? What, our Sonya? Your typist?"

"She's my secretary, Jack, not a typist, and she's pretty sharp, you know. It was she who helped me unravel all this business. She knows all about banking as well as office work, and she knows all about the PVB and the way we operate. She's loyal, hard working and good natured, and, above all, she has a proven clean track record. That counts for a lot in the circumstances. We can't afford to take any chances, not after the last two fiascos. We've got to get someone who's whiter than white. Sonya's popular with the local fund-raisers too; they all have a good word for her when they visit. I think she might be just the job, what do you think?"

Jack wasn't certain. He knew Sonya was a lot brighter than most people gave her credit for, but he was concerned about her lack of specific experience. "Do you really think so?"

"I do."

At least Perry's suggestion would let him off the hook. "Well then, I'll go along with that. It would save a lot of trouble all round, and we could point out to the press that our new fund-raiser is one of the two people who discovered the problem with her predecessor, the other being our astute administrator. It might get us a bit of credibility back. I'll go along with it. It'll mean you'll have to train up a new secretary though."

"I'll live with that." Perry signalled for two more beers. "Thanks, Jack, but keep it under your hat until I've squared it with Eric. And I haven't even asked her yet. She's only on secondment with us at present. She might be unwilling to leave the bank, not that I think she's got much of a future with them, and the chief fund-raiser's job would mean a considerable increase in salary."

"I wonder what sort of references the bank would give her?" joked Jack. Perry hadn't thought of that. It would be interesting to see how they managed to recommend, for a post involving handling money, someone who had literally let hundreds of pounds slip through her fingers. Not that it would matter. There could be no doubt about her honesty, and that was what mattered.

When he returned home Perry phoned the chairman and canvassed the idea of Sonya becoming their chief fund-raiser. "We do need someone quickly and we need to be sure they're honest and in sympathy with the work we're doing. We can't afford another cock-up." Eric was, at first, inclined to question whether Sonya could do the job, but he had been impressed by her understanding of the situation with Dilys Owen and the clever way she'd helped out in the emergency. He gave in without too much of a struggle, and agreed that Perry should sound her out. If Sonya agreed, he would call a quick board meeting for later in the week. Perry thought Eric sounded only too glad to have the problem off his hands. He enquired after Helen and received a non-committal reply.

On his drive into work on Monday Perry was feeling happy and confident. The summer was continuing in its beautiful, languid way, and the world looked good. He felt happy to be bringing Sonya some good news.

When he got into his office, she was tapping away, as usual. "Coffee, Mr Barrett?"

"Yes please, Sonya, and bring yours through. There's something I want to discuss with you." Sonya duly produced two coffees in the old "Sailing Ships" series mugs.

"Sit down," he invited. "You know that Dilys is no longer with us and we're going to have to find ourselves a new fund-raiser."

"Shall I get the old advertisement dusted down?"

"Well, I've been giving the matter some thought over the weekend, and I was wondering whether you wouldn't be ideal for the post. You're honest, hard working, and in sympathy with what we're doing here. I can't think of a better candidate."

Sonya smiled her little girl smile. "Oh, Mr Barrett, that's very kind of you. I never thought about it myself. Are you sure?"

"Of course I'm sure, Sonya, I wouldn't be asking you if I didn't think you were right for the job. We can't afford any more mistakes, and we have to get someone fairly quickly. We need someone in charge to help sort out the mess Dilys has left behind, someone of proven integrity, but, more importantly, someone the local fund-raisers know and trust. If we advertise, we run the risk of getting an unsuitable stranger. What do you think? I know it's a big step; you'd have to resign from Barwell's. You'd be working for us full-time, not just on secondment. What do you say?"

Sonya didn't need to think twice. "Oh, Mr Barrett, it's wonderful. I'd love to. Thank you very much. I won't let you down. I promise."

"I'm sure you won't, but be sure it's what you really want. You'd get a better salary with us, but there would be less job security, and you'd have to transfer your pension rights."

Sonya laughed. "Haven't you seen the news on the telly recently? Barwell's are chucking out their counter staff as fast as they can; the personal touch is out. They can't shed people fast enough. There's no security in banking any more; there's certainly no future for me with them. Besides, working here is much better than working at the bank. I really feel I'm doing something useful and worthwhile, not just hassling poor people about their overdrafts."

"I suppose technically the board may have to advertise the post, I don't know. It's their decision, not mine, but I expect they'll put you in in an acting capacity, with the bank's permission, and then, after a month or two, confirm you, and at that stage you'll become an employee of the PVB."

Sonya asked. "Do you think the board will go along with your suggestion, Mr Barrett? They may have someone of their own in mind."

Perry smiled: "I've talked to Jack and the chairman, and they agree with me. So, if you agree, I'll phone the chairman and get him to call a quick board meeting."

"Oh yes. Yes please. Thanks, Mr Barrett. Thank you so much."

Perry was overjoyed to see Sonya's happy face and shining eyes. "Well, get me a line then." He was laughing too.

As arranged, he called Eric at work. However, things were not as straightforward as he expected. "You've asked her, then?"

"Yes. I said I would, remember? She agreed at once. There really is no future for her at the bank." The chairman didn't reply. Perry prompted him: "So you'll call a board meeting for later this week, like we agreed?"

"Eh? Oh, yes. It's just that, well, I know you don't want to disappoint her, having asked and all that, but I was wondering if she really is the right person for the job. Perhaps we should hold our horses a bit. Other candidates may come forward."

Perry was angry. He was not going to let Sonya down. He couldn't. "What's going on? Why have you changed your mind since Saturday?"

"I haven't. I was just thinking."

"Considering I've just asked Sonya if she would like the job, you'd better tell me about any reservations you have. Sharpish."

"I haven't got any reservations about Sonya. None at all."

Sometimes Eric infuriated Perry. This was one of them. "Well then?"

"I was talking to Helen over the weekend and, you know Sonya was one of her pupils, she just didn't think she's got what it takes."

"Sonya left school years ago. She's come on a lot, even in the time she's been here. All she needs is a chance. You saw the way she handled that business with Dilys."

144

"Yes, I know all that, but Helen's at a loose end these days, and she said she'd like to have a go at it. That's all."

Perry nearly resigned on the spot. But then he remembered how much he needed the money. He'd only spoken to Helen once, on the telephone, but it had been enough to convince him the woman wasn't normal. She was not in full possession of her senses. She would be a disaster as a fund-raiser. Keeping his temper as far as possible, Perry asked: "Do you really think that is a good idea, Eric? Given her unfortunate illness and her previous association with Miss Mayflower."

"She's much better now; her doctors are very pleased with her. They suggested she should do something to occupy her time, and she thought this might be just the thing."

Perry countered: "The job of chief fund-raiser is hardly a cake-walk. It requires a lot of hard work and tact. Do you really think Helen would be up to all that? And then, there's the old objection to nepotism, especially in the present circumstances. It might look like a cover-up. We need someone who isn't personally connected with anyone here."

"I hadn't thought of that," conceded Eric quickly. "I don't want to hurt Helen, though, not now she's doing so well."

Perry thought he could quite justifiably point out that Helen never seemed to have been adverse to hurting other people, and that in itself should disbar her from working with disabled and vulnerable people. He said: "You'll have to, Eric. It just wouldn't work; you know that. She should be able to get herself another job without too much difficulty, if her doctors say she's cured, but this is not the job for her. Sorry, but I'd have to protest if you went down that road."

The chairman knew what that meant and capitulated. "All right then. I'll try to arrange a meeting for Wednesday afternoon if that would suit you." Perry indicated that it would and the conversation closed.

CHAPTER TWENTY-TWO

Perry then immediately received a call from the police: Superintendent Mackie wanted to come straight over, if it was convenient.

The Superintendent gave a concise account of their progress so far. They were doing better than expected. "Once we'd proved her former identity and leaned on her a bit, she was more forthcoming. We also got lucky over the weekend. The Jersey police informed us that they'd contacted the local bank manager there and he was only too willing to be helpful. Apparently, they'd been done over by the Watch Out consumer programme on TV last year for having received funds from bent financial advisers. They didn't want a repetition, least of all involving theft from a charity. The bank is prepared to co-operate fully, so you should eventually get all of your money back."

Perry sighed with relief. "Thank you, Superintendent. That means a lot to us. It's not just the money, though heaven knows we need it, but it means the donors can still trust us and that's important." He automatically eyed the small collection box on his desk. The Superintendent failed to follow his line of vision. Perry continued: "I'm very pleased. It will help to restore donor confidence."

Superintendent Mackie said: "Your prim and proper lady fund-raiser called the Jersey bank officials 'a load of bastards' when we told her they would be co-operating with us."

"Most picturesque."

"She says the scam with the letter was the only one she's pulled on you, but you'll be able to verify that when you've been through your own accounts."

"We're doing that now; it shouldn't take long. At this stage, I'm inclined to believe her. Why get caught with your hand in the till for the sake of a few pounds when you've got something much more profitable and difficult to detect in the pipeline?"

"I hope you're right, sir."

Superintendent Mackie then came to the main point of his visit. "As well as advising her to come clean, her expensive brief also advised her to acquaint us with the sob story. This time it's not a friend in financial difficulties, it's blackmail."

The mention of the word "blackmail" sent a shiver down Perry's spine. He felt in his pocket for his bottle of tablets, but decided to try not to take one. "Oh yes?" he asked cautiously.

"Yes, and I'm afraid there's going to be trouble in it for you people, possibly big trouble. Our Miss Davies, as she is really called, comes from a good family and is saying that, 'having made one mistake', as she puts it, she was trying to atone by working hard for charity, and it was with this in mind that she took the job with you people."

"Under a false name!" exclaimed Perry.

The Superintendent smiled. "She claims she was only doing that so that you would give her the job in the first place. It was her intention, she claims, to do a good job for you and to somehow repay the system by anonymously donating large amounts of her salary to the PVB."

Perry was angrily reminded of some of the excuses Eric had tried to make for Dilys' conduct. He found these attempts to excuse almost more shocking than the original thefts. He asked: "Her legal salary, or her unofficial overtime?"

"Quite, sir. I didn't ask her. But, it's a good story, inventive, and almost believable. She might even get a jury to fall for it; I doubt it, but she evidently thinks it's worth a try."

"So what went wrong with her plans, Superintendent?"

"Your previous fund-raiser, a woman called Joan Mayflower, I believe."

He got no further before Perry put one hand up to his face while the other scrabbled for his tablets. "That woman will be the death of me, Superintendent. You've no idea of the trouble she's caused. No idea."

The Superintendent looked round for a glass of water, as Perry struggled to swallow a tablet. "Inspector Henderson has liaised with me, sir. Apparently there was some feeling she may have been mixed up in the death of Barry Kemp. There was an idea, correct me if I'm wrong, that, blaming you for her dismissal she was out to implicate you in some way."

"From what I know of her, it would have been in character for her to try, but I can't see how she knew I would be seeing him that afternoon. I've subsequently received a visit from Mr Peters, the husband of the woman who shoved Barry down the fire escape. He and his wife were under the impression I was going to whitewash Barry when he came to trial. Their anonymous female informant had put that idea into their heads, so I got the impression they were not adverse to dropping me in it, although he wasn't going to admit anything."

"According to you, sir, that informant would be this Miss Mayflower?"

"Yes."

"Our Miss Davies had some interesting information for us in that respect. According to her, Miss Mayflower was a great deal cuter than the rest of you. She found out, don't ask me how, that Dilys Owen was Olwen Davies, and that she had a criminal record. Being short of funds herself and unable to find another job, she then proceeded to blackmail the reformed and repentant Miss Davies. And it wasn't only money she wanted. It was revenge. Revenge on the PVB in general and on you in particular. She got Miss Davies to spy on you and pass on interesting bits of information. When the news came up that you were about to visit that young man, the chance must have seemed too good to miss."

Perry asked eagerly: "Dilys definitely remembers passing on that piece of information? She would swear to it?"

"She definitely remembers and she would swear to anything which would get her a lighter sentence. The problem is that neither she nor we can prove anything. I've seen the Mayflower woman. She flatly denied knowing Dilys Owen or

148

receiving money or information from her. Miss Davies says she always had to pass the money over in cash; no cheques, nothing traceable. She claims the only reason she resorted to theft this time was that the demands became too heavy."

"And the Peters won't come forward?"

"I'm afraid not, sir. They've decided to keep faith with their informant; they still regard her as the friend who helped them to justice. I doubt now that we'll ever get anything more out of them. Even if they did change their minds, all they could identify is a once heard voice. A clever defence counsel would tear them to shreds. Mrs Peters has apparently decided to take the whole thing on her shoulders; she's refusing to answer any more questions and has said she will plead guilty at the trial. I got the impression she doesn't care what happens to her. From your point of view, sir, all that is past history. There's nothing you can do about it. The important thing is that we've got Miss Davies out of your way. You can go forward now. If you get any more trouble from the same source, call me, and we'll see what we can do. In the meantime, just be careful."

Perry didn't like the sound of that advice at all.

CHAPTER TWENTY-THREE

The rest of the next two days was occupied with fielding anxious enquiries from local fund-raisers and residents and paid officers at the PVB complex. At first, no one could believe that their Dilys was a crook. The later view was that she was just too good to be true and, on reflection, that they should have known they couldn't be that lucky; there was bound to be a fly in the ointment. As yet, no news of Sonya's proposed promotion had leaked out, and there was therefore much general anxiety about finding a suitable replacement for Dilys.

Perry received a phone call from Colonel Charles. "What the hell's going on up there, Barrett? Have you all gone mad?"

Perry explained, as tactfully as possible, that the delightful Miss Owen was not Miss Owen at all and that she had a criminal record. She had just begun to rip off the PVB by means of bogus fund-raising letters, when he and Sonya had found out and called the police. Perry emphasized that he didn't think there was any cause for alarm concerning cash handed over by the local fund-raisers, but they had to check to make sure. Discreetly.

The colonel was somewhat mollified: "Prompt action there. Very good. May have saved the day. But if there has been any hanky-panky, it's going to be damned difficult to rally the troops. Nobody likes being made a fool of, you know, especially when it comes to money."

Perry couldn't disagree with that argument, but explained that in his press release he had managed to play up the positive aspects of the whole episode by emphasizing the speed with which the theft had been discovered and with which he had acted to stop the rot, resulting in the anticipated complete recovery of the stolen funds. No one was safe from a really determined crook, but the PVB were being completely open and above board about it all; there was no hint of a cover-up, nothing unsavoury.

The colonel agreed with him as far as that went and then raised the problem of choosing a successor for Miss Owen. "You'll need to get someone above reproach, and to get them in a hurry; that won't be easy."

"Well—" began Perry. He got no further.

"Look here, Barrett, I've talked this over with Maggie and we've agreed that, if necessary, I could step into the breach. I could travel across for a few weeks, until you get yourselves sorted out. Only in an acting capacity, you understand, but if I can help out in an emergency, I think I should."

He sounded rather hopeful, and Perry wondered if he wasn't finding retirement a little boring. With the board meeting less than a day away, and the promised support of Jack and Eric, Perry though he could risk it. The thought of Colonel Charles helping out in an emergency was only marginally more pleasant than the thought of Helen Robertson-Palmer. "That's very kind of you, colonel, really very kind, but I think we've already found a suitable candidate. We're going to have a board meeting here tomorrow but, subject to agreement, that problem may have solved itself. But I won't forget your offer, just in case we need it."

"That's all right then. Just don't get yourselves lumbered with another non-starter, for God's sake." With that, he abruptly rang off.

Following Miss Davies' brief appearance in the magistrate's court, it was only to be expected that the PVB would be the centre of press attention, and Perry's prepared statement had been handed out or read over the telephone to interested parties. However, Perry hadn't expected that the other paid officers and patients would be hunted down at the PVB complex. He thought there was something rather unkind about the sight of two hopefuls from the local rag pursuing Freddie up the drive. He had no hope of getting away from them, particularly as one of them had run ahead to stand in front of him on the path. Perry ran out to encounter them and firmly directed the journalists to his own office, where they would receive the press release. Freddie looked relieved. He couldn't cope with that kind of pressure. Perry realized there were quite a few others at the PVB in the same boat.

The two journalists retreated reluctantly under Perry's firm guidance. When they arrived in his office, they immediately turned their attention to Sonya. Perry pointed out that he alone was authorized to speak for the PVB, and that all he had to say was contained in the press statement, which he handed to them. He was unable to answer further questions at the present time.

The older, more experienced reporter looked contemptuously at the single sheet of paper. "This it, then? Well, don't blame us if we have to go elsewhere for information. We're giving you your chance to put your side of the story." He waited for a response from either Perry or Sonya. He didn't get one. Neither of them so much as pointed out that there was no "side" to put; it wasn't a dispute, it was a criminal matter.

The younger journalist piped up hopefully: "You rely on us for publicity, you're glad enough to talk to us then." The older hack nodded sagely, but the remark had been a mistake.

Sonya had been leafing through some of the fund-raiser's files, and she conspicuously retrieved a copy of the full page paid newspaper advertisement the PVB had placed the previous December to announce their Christmas Bazaar. She inserted her thumb under the word "Advertisement" and looked guilelessly towards the two hacks. They knew they couldn't afford to antagonize their advertisers. Gracelessly, they picked up the press release and disappeared down the drive in the direction of the main gate.

"Well done, Sonya, very well done," said Perry. "I can see you're going to be a great asset. What we didn't say, they can't mis-report to their own advantage, but they got the message all right. I've no doubt they'll be back, or, if not them, someone else. We can't have the residents and workers here pursued all over the complex, so I think we'll have to call in Nite-Safe to man the main gates for a few days. That should stop them getting in. And I'll have to write a quick memo reminding people to refer all enquiries to me."

CHAPTER TWENTY-FOUR

By the time Wednesday afternoon arrived, Perry was beginning to think the worst might well be over until the trial. Surely there couldn't be a TV station, radio station or newspaper in the country which hadn't received a copy of his press release. As members of the board began to file in, they appeared to be relatively cheerful. Jack looked pretty sick, but then he knew he was in for some stick. The others had evidently taken the events of the past few days in their stride. In view of the single item on the agenda, it was agreed that Perry should take the minutes instead of Sonya, who used the opportunity to catch up on her letters.

The chairman was in brisk mood, and started by depreciating the activities of Miss Owen and congratulating Perry and Sonya for having saved the day. Perry chipped in with the news that most of their money had been located in the now frozen bank account in Jersey.

"I should bloody-well think so." Councillor Fairbrother was off to a flying start. "What the hell were we thinking of, taking on a known criminal? We're going to be a laughing stock, taking on a con-artist to raise funds for us. Jack, you checked her out, or didn't you?" he asked belligerently.

Jack looked profoundly miserable. "Yes, I checked her out. The UK coordinator of Give the Kids a Hand recommended her without reservation. Her other referee was a bishop, who was always unavailable when I called. What more could I do?"

"What more? You should have bloody-well asked her to provide another referee, one who would answer his telephone, that's what you should have done."

Perry noticed that Jack hadn't mentioned the possibility that one had not been genuine: he probably didn't want to admit that Dilys had conned him rotten. In between taking notes, which Perry found much more difficult than he had expected, he tried to pour oil on the troubled waters. "I think we should try to put all that behind us, learn from the experience, so that we don't get caught out again, and go on from there. Our objective today is to get a new fund-raiser in post, to help us sort things out and restore public confidence."

"Agreed," said Eric. "I've been in touch with you all during the week and, informally speaking, I think the feeling is that we should offer the post to Miss Bishop on three months' trial. If she can do the job, she can keep it; we're not obliged to advertise the vacancy. I know Miss Bishop has no fund-raising experience, but Perry says she is a quick learner and I agree with him." He paused.

There were satisfying murmurs of assent round the table. Even Councillor Fairbrother didn't have anything to object to. "Pleasant enough young woman, and she seems to be very efficient around the office, at least from what I've seen of her, and we can be sure she's honest."

The chairman looked round. Jack proposed they offer Sonya the post on a three months' trial, to be made permanent subject to satisfactory performance. Mr Patel seconded the motion, and it was passed unanimously and with suspiciously little discussion. Perry thought that either Eric or Jack must have leaned very heavily on some of the other board members or, more probably, they could see no other way of extricating themselves from a very difficult position. Eric said that he would write to Barwell's Bank, asking them to continue Sonya's secondment while she temporarily stood in for their absent fund-raiser. He remarked that he did not propose to mention the possibility of a permanent promotion at this time, "Just in case things don't work out, and it affects Miss Bishop's position with the bank." What he really meant, thought Perry, was that he didn't think Barwell's would pay her salary for the next three months if they knew the PVB was grooming her to leave them.

"We'd better wheel her in then, tell her the good news," said Eric.

When she entered, Sonya was bearing her usual tray of coffee and biscuits.

"Congratulations," said Perry warmly.

"Indeed," echoed Eric. "We are pleased to offer you the appointment of chief fund-raising officer on a three months' acting basis, to be made a permanent appointment at the end of that time, subject to satisfactory performance."

"Thank you. Thank you very much." Sonya was beaming at everyone.

As there was no other business on the agenda, most of the board members stayed just long enough to enjoy their refreshments, and then began to disperse.

"Thank goodness that's over," muttered Jack to Perry.

"Anyway, you didn't come out of it too badly; there's no reason why you should, of course, but I realize no one enjoys unpleasantness."

"Except Fairbrother. Next time they appoint a new member of staff here, he can do the checking, and we'll see what kind of a job he makes of it."

The councillor had obviously heard his name mentioned, and looked very directly at Perry and Jack, but didn't say anything. The chairman looked at his watch. "Are you in a hurry to be off?" asked Perry.

"No, Helen is picking me up, and she said she'd be here about now."

"Didn't know she was still driving," said Fairbrother tactlessly.

Judging by Eric's discomfiture, Perry wondered if she was legally allowed to drive. A few minutes later the chairman's Rover was observed creeping up the driveway, and in due course Helen made her way up to the boardroom. It was the first time she had been back to the PVB since her time as a patient.

The chairman asked her if she had had a good afternoon round the shops and introduced her all round, ending with Sonya, "our new chief fund-raiser."

It was difficult for anyone present to later recall everything that then happened, but it began with Helen declining the introduction. "Oh yes, I know Miss Bishop of old, don't I Sonya?" Sonya began to explain that Mrs Robertson-Palmer had been her old headmistress, but she was interrupted by an angry Helen. "Still up to our little tricks, I see. Who is it this time? Mr Barrett?" She had turned to face Perry. "That's right, isn't it? I suppose now it's this stupid girl."

There were gasps of astonishment from the remaining board members Eric shouted: "Helen. Helen. Stop it. You know that's not true."

"Isn't it?" she yelled. "Isn't that why this little bitch has got the job?"

Perry said firmly: "Mrs Palmer…"

"Robertson-Palmer."

Perry ignored her correction. "If you are trying to imply the existence of a relationship between Miss Bishop and myself, I can only say…"

"Of course I am; why else would anyone employ a stupid little trollop like that instead of me? She's stupid now and she always was." Helen started to hit Sonya around the head with both hands.

Sonya tried to fend off the blows, but no one else moved. The other board members obviously thought it was up to Eric to control his wife. He didn't. He just stood crying in the middle of the room. Tears coursed down his puffy red cheeks and several times he repeated: "Helen. Oh no. Helen dear."

Perry moved over to Sonya and Councillor Fairbrother, who was nearest to Helen, grabbed hold of her and pulled her away from Sonya.

Eric was by now in full flood, sitting on one of the board room chairs. His head was lowered into his hands. Mr Patel went over to comfort him.

Helen, meanwhile, showed no signs of abating her rage. "Oh don't think I don't know. You're all at it. None of you is any good."

Mr Patel was unwise enough to try to protest. "Mrs Robertson-Palmer, I, for one, am most certainly not 'at it'."

"There's no need for you to look holier than thou, either, Jack. I could tell them a few things about you and yours, and don't you forget it."

Jack looked as though he had been struck by lightning. He turned purple and then white. He was almost as angry as Helen.

Councillor Fairbrother asked loudly: "What does she mean, 'got the job instead of me'? Surely no one in their right mind would consider her for this job or any other." It wasn't the happiest choice of words, but no one seemed to notice, except Helen, who rewarded him with a filthy look.

Helen had got her second wind by now and was off again: "You've got yourselves more than you bargained for there, so don't come running to me when she louses it up. I won't be held responsible. I won't. I won't."

Sonya had recovered her poise a little by now, and was wise enough not to try to remonstrate with Helen. The chairman was meanwhile also recovering under Mr Patel's ministrations. Old Patel was a kindly soul and looked to be saddened beyond words by the awful Helen. While they all drew breath, Perry looked at Helen. He made an effort to pull himself together. Taking up Sonya's phone, he dialled the clinic number. Dr Anderson was usually in attendance on Wednesday afternoons. He could only hope he was still there and was much relieved when the doctor's calm, flat voice answered his ring. While Perry asked him to come to his office urgently, Helen was still standing in the middle of the room, looking around her.

Sonya's experience had taught the others to stay out of range, so Helen stood alone, spewing out her rage.

Five minutes later, the sound of Dr Anderson's soft footfalls made them all sigh with relief. Helen's flood of bile had slowed a little by now, but she was still very red in the face and was still accusing Sonya of unspecified acts of criminality, sexuality and incompetence. The chairman had walked over to her and was clearly trying a practised routine for calming her. Dr Anderson had some general idea of Helen's history and quietly asked Eric what medication she was taking. By way of a reply, Eric slipped a bottle out of his jacket pocket. "Three a day. I give them to her, to make sure she gets the right dose," he explained.

The doctor nodded and observed Helen for a few minutes, while the excited board members all tried to tell him what she'd been up to. He looked sympathetically in the direction of a very flushed Sonya, before filling a syringe from the contents of his case. "Just a mild tranquillizer," he explained gently.

Helen heard him: "I don't want your bloody tranquillizer. What I want is that stupid little bitch fired; that's what I want." Even the doctor looked shocked. "But there's no chance of that is there, Mr Hand-in-the-till Barrett?" The board members and the doctor gasped. "Don't think I don't know about that business with Paul Russell. In it together weren't you? Bastards." She had barely got the last word out before the doctor deftly managed to take her arm and inject her. She stood for a few minutes, like a child stung by a wasp, waiting for the effect, and then she slid gracefully into the doctor's waiting arms.

Dr Anderson spoke to Eric: "She'll have to be hospitalized again, I'm afraid. I'm very sorry; for both of you. I'll call the ambulance from here if I may." Perry nodded assent.

Eric went over to Sonya. "I'm very sorry about that, my dear, and you too, Perry," he said, half turning towards him. "You must understand, though, that she's ill. She's not responsible for what she says or does when she gets like this. Are you all right? Did she hurt you?" She clearly had; Sonya's face was showing angry red patches where she had been struck, but she bravely said she was OK. "It goes without saying that none of what she said is true. No one would believe there was anything between you and Perry, not for one minute." The other board members murmured sympathetically. "I can't understand it," muttered Eric to himself. "She was doing so well; her doctors were so pleased with her. I just don't understand it. When she left Marshwood they said she would be fine."

He was close to tears again, when Dr Anderson announced that the ambulance was on its way. He picked up the bottle of tablets Eric had shown him and said: "I'd better take care of these now and I'll go with you both." The doctor then turned his attentions to Sonya; she was more shocked than injured, although he warned her to expect a few nasty bruises later.

When the ungainly process of manoeuvring the now recumbent Helen down the stairs and out of the PVB complex was over, the others speculated on the scene they had just witnessed. Mr Patel shook his head and said: "I don't suppose she will ever come home again; not now. She is a public danger. It is most sad. I understand she used to be a professional woman of some standing. It is most sad." Having enquired after Sonya's well-being, he departed, still shaking his head.

Perry said: "I'm so sorry, Sonya. I had no idea it would all turn out like that. I bet you're sorry you took the job now."

"Not at all. I really want this job and you can't live your life according to the dictates of others."

"True. There's nothing more any of us can do here, so I suggest we just lock up and call it a day. Tomorrow's a new start. Can I give you a lift, Sonya?"

Still nursing her sore places, Sonya was glad of a lift, and Perry was glad to see her safely home, but she was very quiet during the journey and barely said goodbye to him when they reached the house.

During the drive to his own home Perry thought about some of the bizarre things Helen had said. Why on earth did she have such a down on Sonya? She was the most inoffensive of people. Was it because Sonya had got a job Helen had wanted, or had someone put her up to it? Eric had obviously been talking to Helen about the PVB's business; there was no reason why he shouldn't. Even so, he couldn't understand why she had linked him with Paul Russell's thefts. Apart from Joan, no one else ever had. He concluded that as Helen had freely distributed her venom amongst those present, it was probably a piece of spite on her behalf, as ludicrous as the suggestion that he was having an affair with Sonya. Helen's illness obviously predisposed her to think the worst of everyone, including the highly respectable Mr Patel.

CHAPTER TWENTY-FIVE

That evening over dinner Perry gave Pam an account of the afternoon's entertainment. Fortunately, they'd always had a very happy marriage. Neither of them had ever been tempted by pastures new. Even when Perry had lost the business and their home had been repossessed, Pam had stuck by him. It was therefore possible for Perry to tell her about Helen's accusations without the faintest touch of anxiety that they might be believed. Forking out the apple crumble, Pam didn't react as he had expected. "After all, I'm a good twenty years older than she is. Why on earth would she want an old buffer like me?" Pam managed a smile. Perry sensed this wasn't going as well as he'd hoped. He'd always been honest with Pam and he thought she had always been honest with him in return. Looking at her now, he was beginning to wonder. She was clearly working herself up to something. He wondered what. His heart began to churn again. It was strange, he thought, that he had been all right this afternoon, coping with a lunatic, but the anxiety he was feeling now had started it off in a big way. It was easier to resolve to stop worrying about things than it was to do it. He felt awful and reached for his tablets.

"Are you all right, dear?" asked Pam.

"Yes, love, just the aftermath from this afternoon, I expect. Wretched woman."

Pam looked kindly at him and said: "I don't know where she got her stupid ideas from, but she's got no right to make accusations like that. I don't care whether she's ill or not."

"But Pam, she didn't know what she was saying. It was just words. She might as well have been reciting *Hamlet*. She really had no idea what she was saying. At one point she accused Mr Patel, the newsagent, of being at it as well. She was completely mad. You should have seen her."

"No thanks, darling. I think I've heard her, and that was enough."

"What do you mean?"

"I didn't want to bother you, love. It was so stupid and I didn't believe it for a minute. You had enough on your hands with the job and I didn't want to worry you."

"I don't understand, Pam. What are you on about?"

Her last words had come in a welcome rush of explanation but, in fact, they had explained nothing at all. Pam realized that now, and began: "It was just a few weeks ago, after you had all that trouble with Miss Mayflower. I got three phone calls: the first two were while you were at work, and the last one was on a Saturday morning when you were golfing with Jack. The woman said much the same thing on all three occasions. It was very simple, very straightforward. She said she thought it was her duty to let me know what was going on at the office between you and Sonya Bishop."

"Oh love, love, why didn't you tell me?" Perry was upset and showed it. His heart was working overtime and his face was suffused with colour.

"I knew it wasn't true, dear," she replied simply. "I trust you. I always have." She took his hand across the table. "And I really didn't want to upset you. I thought it was just a crank, a malicious patient or someone like that. After all, you do get a pretty mixed bunch up there."

"What did you do?"

"I always thought the best way to deal with a crank caller would be to blow a loud whistle down the phone at them."

"We haven't got a whistle, Pam."

"I know, dear, so I just put the receiver down the third time she called and let her waste her money. I suppose she realized there was no one listening and didn't bother again."

"You did the right thing, Pam. Absolutely the right thing, and she's never called again?"

"No, it stopped after the third call."

"It was a foul thing to do," said Perry with feeling. "I was almost beginning to feel sorry for her, but not now. It seems to

163

me, what with one thing and another, she's more sinning than sinned against. One thing's for certain, though. She won't be making any more phone calls from Marshwood."

"Is that where she's gone?"

"It's where she was last time, I believe." Perry was silent for a few minutes and then said: "You know, Pam, I'm really upset about this. It's so unfair on you. You're right: even if she is ill, she shouldn't be allowed to ruin other people's lives with her lies. I've a good mind to call Palmer and tell him what his wife has been up to."

"I think that might be a good idea, love. Why don't you call him after dinner? It can't do any harm and, at the very least, it will let him know how sick she really is. More crumble?"

Having polished off the crumble and two cups of coffee, Perry repaired to the phone. Eric had returned home from the hospital, and immediately launched into a stream of apologies for Helen, mixed with a few hopeful excuses. "Apparently, it's not unusual for patients to have a bit of a relapse now and then. It's nothing serious to worry about, but nonetheless, I'm sorry it should have been you and Sonya she turned on. It's usually me," he added sadly.

"I'm sorry too," replied Perry with some warmth. In a way, he was sorry for Eric: he obviously loved Helen and, after her outburst, Perry better understood the hell of a life lived with someone who was as mentally ill as Helen. But he loved Pam and he wasn't going to allow Helen to turn their lives into a hell as well. He briefly outlined what Pam had told him.

"Oh no, I can't believe that. She wouldn't. She couldn't. She's such a kind person, underneath it all, you know."

Perry had been up against this particular brick wall before and by now he knew how to deal with it. "Oh come on, Eric. I'm sorry she's ill, but you saw what she was like this afternoon, what she said. There was no kindness in any of that. Helen is, in my opinion, more than capable of making malicious calls when her trouble is on her, and I'm sure you know that as well as I do. I only wish dear Pam had told me sooner, but she didn't want to trouble me." He smiled at her across the lounge. "It's a good job Pam is such a sensible person, but understand, Eric, that neither she nor I will stand for a repetition. Next time Helen makes accusations of that kind, we shall go straight to our solicitors, so it's up to you to keep her in line when she comes home."

Eric asked if Pam could be absolutely sure it was Helen who had made the calls. She couldn't, because she had never heard Helen's voice before, but Perry forcibly pointed out that Helen was the only person ever to have made such outlandish and unjustifiable accusations against him and Miss Bishop. As he was speaking, he wondered why she'd made them but, bearing in mind the influence of a certain ex-fund-raiser over Helen, and the timing of the calls, just after her dismissal, it was not too difficult to deduce the source of Helen's inspiration.

Eric apologised to Pam through Perry and promised to let the doctors at Marshwood know about the calls, in case they thought them relevant.

Perry thought he probably wouldn't. He hadn't missed the hopeful tone of Eric's voice. He would be angling to get Helen home as soon as possible; he wouldn't want to add to her list of misdemeanours. Perry finished his call by repeating his previous warning, and thought how disappointed Joan must have been when Pam hadn't reacted to the calls.

CHAPTER TWENTY-SIX

"Well let's hope that's the last we hear of that," said Pam decisively, as Perry replaced the receiver. Before he could reply, the phone rang. It was Jack; after a brief enquiry about Perry and Sonya, he asked if he could visit Perry: there were a couple of things he wanted to talk over. Perry's heart had not settled down, and he had a nagging feeling of tiredness, but he couldn't ignore the pleading tone of his friend's voice.

In answer to Pam's raised interrogative eyebrow, he said: "Jack wants to come over; he seems worried about something." Pam sighed and went to unearth a pizza from the freezer. Jack always liked a bit of pizza and a glass of vino.

It didn't take Jack long to drive over from the estate where Perry and Pam had also once lived. In the darkness of the summer evening he looked haggard and upset. As usual, he was alone; Angela very seldom visited with him. Without ceremony, Jack made himself comfortable in the small lounge. Pam discreetly repaired to her kitchen, calling: "Hi, Jack; pizza coming up in about ten minutes."

"Hi, Pam," he called out. He looked meaningfully at Perry and asked quietly: "Everything OK, then?"

"Yes, everything is fine, thanks. Pam and I had a long talk about this afternoon's exhibition and I called Eric at home. I don't suppose we'll get any more trouble out of Helen for a while."

"Good; I'm glad." Jack's voice was genuine, but Perry sensed that his heart wasn't behind his words. He poured them two small white wines. Jack sat in silence for several minutes, as if working himself up to some revelation. "You know, Perry, I think Helen Robertson-Palmer is responsible for a great deal more trouble than we've given her credit for."

"I know," replied Perry shortly. Then, seeing that Jack was puzzled, he added: "We think she's been making malicious calls to Pam, suggesting an affair between me and Sonya."

Jack looked surprised. "How horrid. You poor souls. Look, I know that's bad enough, but it's not what I meant. You know I'm a local man, and I've known Eric Palmer nearly all my life, but I've not spoken to Helen in years. Most of the time she's been in and out of hospital or stuck at home. It wasn't until I heard her speak this afternoon that I thought I recognised her voice. I'd forgotten, after all these years, what she sounded like. She has a peculiar, flat, precise diction. You must have noticed it."

Perry thought about it and, yes, Jack was right. It had been even more noticeable in the one telephone conversation he had had with her, but even this afternoon, when she had been raving, it had still been discernible.

"You know, Perry, I have an awful idea that she was the woman I spoke to when I got that reference for Dilys Owen. I couldn't swear to it, but I'm pretty sure."

Perry was taken aback. Assuming Dilys had not provided her own glowing reference, which would have been an unwise thing to do, considering her marked Welsh accent, Perry had never thought she would have used local help. However, if, as Dilys claimed, she had been manipulated by Joan Mayflower, the use of Helen Robertson-Palmer would make sense. Helen had been manipulated by Joan for years and, notwithstanding a good dose of stiffening from himself and Eric, was it really reasonable to suppose her hold had been broken that easily? This afternoon's display had shown that Helen was still mentally unstable, and, therefore, very vulnerable. Her outburst had held all the spite and malice of Joan at her worst.

Jack was asking what he should do: "What do you think, Perry?"

"I don't know. Unless you could swear to the identification, it might not help the police much to know. They've made a pretty solid case against Dilys. If we feed them more information about a possible entanglement with Helen, and hence with Joan, she might be able to use it to her advantage; she's already claiming she was forced into crime this time because Joan was blackmailing her for excessive amounts of money. If the press got hold of that, it wouldn't reflect too well on the PVB. One crooked fund-raiser is one thing, but two… is unthinkable. As it is, I don't think Dilys can prove anything unless we help her and I don't feel inclined to do that, so I would forget it, if I were you, Jack."

Jack looked relieved. Pam entered with the pizzas. "There you go, boys." She disappeared into the kitchen again as Jack attacked his pizza with relish.

"I didn't get any tea," he explained. "Angela was too upset, and that's another reason why I've come round tonight. Angela can't bring herself to think about it, but I think we need some help."

Perry lifted a small slice of pizza and nibbled; unlike Jack, he'd eaten a big meal and was beginning to feel uncomfortably full. "I'll do anything I can to help you."

"You know Angela and I have got the two boys, Jackie and Pete?"

"Yes." Perry wondered if one of them was in trouble. "Problems?"

"Not with the boys or Angela. But you know Angela was already married when she met me?" Perry nodded. Jack had told him a long time ago. "And you remember she had a daughter, Amy, by Gary?"

"He was an army sergeant, wasn't he?" asked Perry. He remembered Jack talking about Gary, and he knew there had been a step-daughter in the background.

"That's right. And he was an RC, so he was dead set against a divorce, and things got very ugly before Angela finally managed to get rid of him. It affected Amy; she was about seven at the time, and she took after her father, even then. Angela and I were more than willing to make a home for her, but she didn't want to leave her grandparents. She and Angela had been living with them while Angela was waiting for her divorce, and Amy had become settled."

Jack gulped down his wine in one go. His voice became harder and sadder as he continued: "Even in primary school, she started to get in trouble. It was a mistake, allowing her to live with Harold and Naomi. They had no control over her; they just let her do what she liked. Angela and I always kept in touch with her, and tried to treat her just like the boys, but it was no good; she couldn't come to terms with her parents' divorce.

"Then she passed her eleven-plus and went to that bloody awful school. It wasn't until her second year that she really started to get in trouble; and then there were small sums of money and silly bits of equipment going missing from a few of the girls in her class, and Amy got blamed for it. Angela's parents had to go up to the school. They were her legal guardians by then, and Helen graciously offered not to call the police provided Amy apologized to all the girls she'd stolen stuff from and paid them all back for what she'd stolen. Amy swore she hadn't taken anything, but Miss Robertson was adamant. She'd got it into her head that just because her parents were divorced and she was living with her grandparents, she was automatically a thief. She wouldn't hear any views to the contrary."

Perry said dryly: "That sounds about right for her. Even the guilty are entitled to a fair hearing in this country; but, judging by what you've said, Helen doesn't even seem to have made the pretence of hearing both sides of the story. What happened?"

"Amy hanged herself. We found her dead in the shed on her grandfather's allotment."

Perry was horrified. He'd had no idea of what was coming. Jack had never talked about Amy before tonight. He was totally unprepared. He couldn't find the right words; probably there were none. He spoke rapidly and with embarrassment, out of shock. "Oh Jack, that's terrible. I'm so sorry. I had no idea. The poor child."

Jack was subdued. "It was a long time ago now, but you never forget. It was worse for Angela, Amy was her daughter.

She's kept all her old photographs and toys. It's with her every day, like a lead weight around her neck. She can't get rid of them, not without losing all the good memories she had of Amy. I admit Amy was a handful; she was a difficult child, but she had her reasons. I could understand that, but I couldn't understand why Helen had it in for her like that; she just took an unreasoning dislike to her." Jack looked ten years older as he came to the end of his speech.

Perry tried to comfort his friend. He felt very inadequate for the task. "Jack, you and Angela have nothing to feel guilty about in all this; you know that, don't you? You were in love and you got married; judging from what you've told me, you tried to do your best for Amy. And you weren't to know that one day she would go to a school with a loony for a headmistress; no one could foresee that. If Helen didn't like divorce, she should have taken it out on you and Angela, not on the child. But surely there was some official investigation after Amy hanged herself?"

Jack shook his head sadly. "The police investigated, but they found out she'd been in trouble at school, and that before she'd gone out that day she'd had a row with Harold and Naomi about some boy she was seeing. That was the worst thing about it. She didn't leave a note, you see, so the police drew the obvious conclusion, and it was easy for other people to assume she'd done it because she was unhappy at home and had been caught out thieving at school. Angela's parents were heartbroken; they died within a short time of one another not long afterwards. They thought they were to blame. They weren't. Helen Robertson was to blame."

Perry's mind ranged back to Wendy Jackson's history. He wondered if perhaps he was seeing two sides of the same coin, but the picture didn't fit together. For one thing, Wendy had told him no one had helped her when she had been bullied; no one had been punished for stealing from her. As far as he could tell, Helen had been employing a double standard: one law for her favourites and another for the unbeloved. But even if Amy had bullied Wendy, she hadn't deserved to die. Looking at Jack's crumpled face, Perry couldn't bring himself to ask if Amy had been one of Wendy's tormentors.

"It's tragic, Jack, just tragic. I can't understand how Helen kept her job after that."

Jack sounded bitter: "But it was so easy, Perry. We all complained to the Local Education Authority, but Miss Robertson countered that Amy had been caught stealing, and that she had done the only reasonable thing she could in the circumstances. After all, she couldn't allow theft to go unchecked. We understood that, but we didn't agree that Amy was a thief. But, of course, she had had her ups and downs, and that didn't help her case, and then, she had hanged herself. It looked very much as though she'd just taken the cowardly way out. The Local Education Authority concluded that Helen had acted with what they called "compassionate firmness", and that she could not be held responsible for the subsequent actions of a very unhappy young teenager. Angela's parents were no help at the time: her father had just suffered his first heart attack, and her mother was nearly out of her mind with worry. We couldn't win. We just had to let it drop. You know, I've always blamed Miss Robertson for Harold's heart attack, so, in a way, she was responsible for his death as well as Amy's. That's a lot to have on your conscience," he finished.

"Assuming she has one, which seems to me to be pretty doubtful. The old adage about the school days being the happiest of your life certainly doesn't apply to anyone unfortunate enough to have gone to Miss Robertson's school."

"You can say that again, and it's not only the pupils. Angela and I are still affected by it, and being in business here just made it worse. For a while, after Helen married Eric and got herself a social life, you couldn't go anywhere without bumping into her, and that was certainly something neither Angela nor I wanted to do."

Perry refilled their glasses and mused: "I can't understand why he married her. He must have been an eligible bachelor, his own home, own business doing well. Why did he saddle himself with someone like that?"

"I don't know, but she was quite a good-looker in those days. She was cultured, with a good job, and she wasn't showing signs of her illness, at least, not outside the school. I suppose he loved her." Jack shrugged.

"And, as far as I can see, he still does. God knows why."

The two friends sat quietly over the remains of their supper, as the sound of percolating coffee issued from the kitchen. Perry thought he should have a word with Sonya in the morning to see if she could throw any more light on Jack's story. He asked: "Why are you telling me all this now, Jack?"

"It was this afternoon's bash that brought it all back. When I told Angela what Helen had shouted at me, she got upset, and said Helen shouldn't be allowed to go round hurting innocent people. I said, as you'd had more dealings with Eric recently than I had, I'd come round and ask your advice, see what we could come up with to keep her quiet."

Perry shook his head. "I'm sorry, Jack, but I can't see what you can do. The damage is done now. Poor Amy is dead. Helen hurt you and Angela and me and Pam and, of course, poor Sonya this afternoon, and none of us has ever done a thing to her. When I phoned Palmer this evening, I said that any repetition on Helen's part would result in us going straight to our solicitor. I think that shot went home. If someone with Helen's history starts persecuting folk, they run the risk of being compulsorily admitted to a mental hospital; that would be the last thing she would want. But I don't know what you and Angela can do. She didn't accuse either of you of anything, and she didn't mention Amy. Even if she starts spreading stories about her in the future, I'm not sure there would be anything you could do about it; I seem to remember you can't slander the dead. I'm sorry, Jack, but I don't see what you can do unless she turns her persecutions to you and Angela."

"I suppose you're right," said Jack heavily. He was silent for a few minutes and then said: "Given Helen's connection with Joan Mayflower, didn't you get the feeling this afternoon that she was emulating her? She knew she'd lost that round, but she went on, making threats, and it occurred to me that she was letting us all know she had something on us, so that when, in the future, she wants something, we'll oblige."

"Including poor old Patel." Perry couldn't keep the amusement out of his voice. Even Jack managed a smile. "If she's thinking of getting into blackmail, she should have taken a few lessons from Joan first. She would seem to have forgotten that anything she does against the PVB will rebound on Eric and, let's face it, without him she'd be in a right hole. Even she can't be daft enough not to realize that."

Jack wasn't so sure, but he said: "It certainly makes you wonder if it's all worthwhile, doesn't it? She was a patient at the PVB for a short while after her accident, you know. The PVB helped to rehabilitate her and look what she's done to us already." Perry had no answer for that and, after finishing another glass of wine, Jack said: "I'd better be off now, old son. Thanks for giving me a shoulder to cry on. You're good mates, you and Pam both."

In the kitchen Pam smiled up from behind her magazine. She hadn't heard much of the conversation, but after Jack had left, Perry recounted it to her. Like Perry, she was rapidly coming to the conclusion that it was a toss up between who was the most dangerous: Joan or Helen.

CHAPTER TWENTY-SEVEN

The following morning Perry helped Sonya reorganise herself into the chief fund-raiser's office and made his enquiry about Jack's step-daughter. To his surprise, she didn't seem to know anything about it. "She would have been a bit older than you, I suppose," he said, trying to jog her memory.

She shook her head and replied: "It's possible, I suppose, that it had something to do with Wendy's problems, but I don't remember hearing about anyone hanging themselves. What did you say her name was?"

"Amy." Perry stopped short and thought for a moment. "But I don't know her surname; it wouldn't be the same as Jack's; he was only her step-father, and she was living with her grandparents, so I don't suppose she ever changed it."

"Sorry, I still can't remember."

"It doesn't really matter."

As they were sorting through fund-raising paperwork, Sonya suddenly exclaimed: "I remember. It was before I went to the grammar, but people still talked about it. There was a story going round that one of the girls had killed herself, but I heard she'd taken a load of pills because she was pregnant or something. I never knew her. I had no idea she was Mr Fisher's step-daughter."

"It doesn't sound like it was the same girl. Amy hanged herself and she wasn't pregnant."

Sonya gave one of her snorts. "It was a rotten school, I admit, but even we didn't have more than one suicide. At least, not that I know of. Auntie Bernie might know, she was on the LEA about that time. I said I'd meet her for lunch today; do you want to come along?"

Perry wasn't sure how far he wanted to delve into his friend's past and he began to demur, when Sonya said brightly: "She's dying to meet you and get all the gen on Dilys."

Accordingly, half past twelve found Perry and Sonya sitting opposite an amazingly plain woman in her late sixties in a small English-menu restaurant off Market Square. Auntie Bernie confided that the roast pork was very good, and so they all ordered roast pork. Sonya enjoyed it, and Perry was relieved when he cut into the well cooked lean meat. It could have been much worse. Perry thought it wasn't only that Auntie Bernie was extremely plain, it was that she dressed in an old-maidish fashion. He was aware that tweeds and long skirts and sensible shoes were now considered the height of fashion, if the Sunday supplements were to be believed, but Auntie Bernie clearly didn't aspire to that kind of price bracket. She was rather badly dressed in a grey skirt and home-made cardigan. But hers was by no means a negligible personality, and Perry thought he could detect a family resemblance in Sonya's intelligence: quiet and restrained, but always working.

"So tell me all about it, Mr Barrett, all about our crime. I'm dying to hear all the gory details."

Perry appreciated the "our". Here, at least, was one donor who wasn't running a mile from the PVB. Aided by Sonya, he plunged into a spirited account of the unmasking of the arch swindler.

Auntie Bernie was almost gurgling with delight behind her steel-rimmed spectacles. "You know I had the police round, all very polite and all that, but they didn't do anything about the cheque. I suppose they'd got her before she had a chance to bank it." She sounded disappointed. "Still, you won't get any trouble like that with Sonya. I can vouch for her myself." She laughed and then added, more seriously: "It will give you all a chance to settle down a bit."

Sonya looked enquiringly at Perry and launched into the tale of Helen Robertson-Palmer's histrionics. Auntie Bernie's face became, at first, studied with seriousness, and then, almost open mouthed. "That wretched woman!" she exclaimed. "I suppose it's not a very charitable thing to say, but I would have thought she'd learned her lesson by now. Mentally ill or not, she cannot expect to be allowed to go round assaulting people. You should have called the police, my girl, there and then. She's s been allowed to get away with too much for too long."

Before Sonya could explain that the last thing the PVB needed was to have the wife of the chairman of the board of trustees arrested for assault in the PVB's premises, Perry nipped in quickly: "You mean all that sad business with Anne Baker and Wendy Lalovic, Mrs Adams?" She nodded, but said nothing.

Sensing his discomfort, Sonya took the plunge for Perry. "It wasn't only Mr Barrett and me. It was one of the other board members too, Mr Fisher, Jack Fisher. She started on about how she could tell the world a thing or two about him and his family."

Auntie Bernie looked keenly at her niece, and still said nothing, but she had obviously recognized the name. Having finished her main course, she toyed with her cup of coffee and finally said: "Oh dear. I didn't know Mr Fisher was involved with the PVB."

Perry explained that Jack had been a member of the board of trustees for some years, and that it was thanks to him that he had got the job of administrator after his business had gone bust. He was amazed at how easy it was to talk to this elderly, plain woman, with her curious personal reserve hidden underneath a spinsterish charm. Usually, he was very loath to admit that he'd been a failed businessman, but with her he didn't mind. He had the feeling she probably knew anyway.

Sonya was used to dealing with her aunt and knew how best to draw her out. Auntie Bernie had to be allowed a good deal of thinking time before she spoke. Eventually Sonya prompted: "Mr Fisher thinks Miss Robertson was responsible for his step-daughter, Amy, hanging herself, and he was very upset by what she said yesterday."

"Naturally. The whole thing caused a terrible stink at the time and I remember the family writing to the LEA about it."

"Wasn't there anything they could do to help them?" asked Perry. "I know Amy was dead by then and nothing cold bring her back, but at least her memory wouldn't have been sullied with unproven allegations of theft and goodness knows what else."

Mrs Adams toyed with a slice of cheesecake and said: "Well, you know, Mr Barrett, it wasn't really up to us. The police were in charge of the investigation into the circumstances of Amy's death, and we couldn't do anything against Miss Robertson unless their investigation supported the family's allegations."

"But surely they would have done, if they'd done their job properly." Perry was aware that his voice had become uncomfortably loud; he moderated his tone. "Why should she have killed herself, unless it was because she was upset by the unjust allegations of theft coming from Miss Robertson?"

Auntie Bernie spoke very slowly, choosing her words with care: "It was a sad thing to happen, Mr Barrett, but the evidence, for once, supported Helen Robertson's version of events. There was more to the case than was ever aired in public, I'm afraid."

Perry thought she was giving him a clear hint to stay away from Jack's tragedy and he respected her opinion. Even on such a short acquaintanceship, he thought of her as a woman of integrity. After all, she had been willing to help the PVB and to be discreet about it and, in some respects, she was right. He had no real justification for prying into his friend's past, other than an uneasy feeling that it might be about to affect all their futures. He thought back to the time when he'd lost the business and he and Pam had had to move. Several of his old neighbours had made unkind comments implying that there had been financial chicanery and tax evasion, which had only seemed to multiply after Per had killed himself, working on the principle of "no smoke without fire". Life had been very unpleasant for him and Pam for a while; how much worse must it have been for a young school girl?

He tried to explain to Bernie: "I realize, Mrs Adams, that I have no right to dig into Jack's past or the deliberations of the LEA on the subject, and I don't ask out of idle curiosity, but I feel that I can understand the injustice of her position. I know nothing can help her now, she's beyond that, but at least we can stop her parents having to suffer any more than they have already. Jack was also concerned that, given the continuing connection between Helen and Joan Mayflower, Helen might be thinking of trying a bit of blackmail on her own account."

Bernie gave him a shrewd look and asked: "Anything else?"

Perry once again found himself disclosing information, rather than receiving it. "Jack did just think that he might have recognized Helen's voice as that of the woman who provided Dilys Owen with a reference when she applied for the fund-raising job at the PVB." Sonya dropped her fork into her cheesecake.

"How interesting. How very interesting. So what it comes to, is that you're worried Joan Mayflower may still be using Helen Robertson-Palmer in her campaign against the PVB?"

"Yes, that and the injustice of her treatment of Amy."

"Oh dear," replied Bernie, in a rather schoolmarmish way. "You were right, Sonya, he really is a bit of a knight errant, isn't he?" Sonya blushed, but much less than Perry. "In this case, Mr Barrett, I'm afraid you're more erring than errant. Your friend Jack has left you with a bit of a false impression. I'm sorry."

Perry rather stupidly said: "It's not your fault."

Bernie continued: "In the strictest confidence, Mr Barrett, I can tell you that while young Amy certainly did kill herself, in all probability, it wasn't because Helen Robertson accused her of theft. The autopsy revealed she had been having sexual relations, young as he was."

Sonya kept her eyes firmly fixed on her dessert. Perry gasped: "You're not serious."

"I'm afraid I am. The police looked into her background and found out that she'd got in with rather a fast set. Like many children from unhappy homes, she found her solace elsewhere. There had been a row between her and her grandparents on this very subject before she went out on the day she died. They threatened to have her sent to a children's home, apparently. They just couldn't cope with her any more: she'd got into the habit of doing exactly as she pleased, and her grandparents realized they couldn't control her."

"I'm beginning to wish I'd never asked. Jack admitted she was a bit of a handful, but he never mentioned a sex life."

Bernie sadly shook her head. "There was a family history of some length with the social services department. Before she went to the grammar school, there had been reports of petty thefts and abusive behaviour from neighbours. Apparently, she was a delightful looking child, pretty and demure, but she was in trouble even at her primary school. At one time we considered a residential placement for her. I think she felt her situation more than Mr Fisher realized, but I'm sorry to say she was by no means an angel. It is a sad fact, but true, that unhappiness at home often makes for an unbalanced and unkind child. We used to see it all the time, trying to find placements for children beyond their parents' control. There was no doubt about it, a lot of the other girls at that school would have been glad to see the back of young Amy."

"What did she do, then?" asked Perry.

"She did, in fact, bully and steal, exactly as Miss Robertson said she did. She'd been at it for over a year by the time she finally got caught out."

"How did it happen?"

"She was stupid enough to steal a pair of gold earrings one of the girls had worn to school in defiance of regulations. The PE teacher had told her to take them out, and she'd left them with her clothes when she'd changed for gym. They weren't there when she came back, and Amy was brazen enough to wear them to school herself on the following Friday. Her grandparents admitted they weren't hers, but she thought she could get away with it. The girl herself spotted them and reported it to Miss Robertson. Amy tried to claim one of the other girls had given them to her, and that she didn't know they were stolen, but there really was no doubt she took them herself."

Perry considered this information for several minutes before asking: "All this wouldn't have anything to do with Wendy Lalovic, would it?"

Auntie Bernie smiled: "Not really, Mr Barrett, except in so far as it is part of the same, sad pattern. Amy was dead by the time Wendy's crisis came to a head."

"I know Amy doesn't seem to have been a very nice character but, considering what was allowed to happen to Wendy, Miss Robertson seems to have been operating the double standard on a grand scale."

"I agree, Mr Barrett, and it was this inability to operate a consistent policy that told against her in the end, together with her unreasoning likes and dislikes and her losses of temper."

Their meal had been over for several minutes, and the waitress was hastily clearing away, while Sonya gallantly paid the bill for them all. Perry invited Mrs Adams to his office at the PVB to continue their conversation in private. She expressed herself delighted at the prospect of seeing where Sonya worked.

CHAPTER TWENTY-EIGHT

When they were all comfortably seated around Perry's coffee table, he opened the conversation again. "It seems to me, Mrs Adams——."

"Please call me Bernie," she interrupted, with a beaming smile, which Perry took to be a sign of approval of both himself and his office.

"As I was saying, Bernie, we must do something about Joan Mayflower; I've come to the conclusion that if we don't, we'll never have any peace here again, we'll always be waiting for the next blow, and eventually she'll destroy us and everything we've built up here."

"I agree, Perry." Following her aunt's example, Sonya was now on first name terms. "And it's not only the PVB she'll destroy, it's us too, you and me, and probably poor Wendy too, if she can manage it."

Bernie said: "I agree with you both. You must take positive action, and the sooner the better. You have no hope of reaching an arrangement with her or of dealing with her in a civilized way, so I'm afraid it's got to be war."

Taking up the war metaphor, Perry remarked: "She's never been a one for taking prisoners, and she treats her allies almost as badly as she does her enemies. Just look what happened to Barry and Helen when she had no further use for them or thought they had failed her."

Sonya said thoughtfully: "I wonder if we couldn't we use that in some way. Barry's dead and Helen is too unreliable, but what about that Peters woman, the one who killed Barry? I wonder if she and her husband know what has happened to Joan's other pawns?"

"I doubt it," replied Perry. "They know Barry's dead, of course, but I bet they didn't know he was Joan's little spy before she got him killed. The trouble is, I don't see how they could help us; even if they were prepared to swear she was their informant, it wouldn't get us far. According to the police, they only heard her voice once on the phone."

Bernie asked: "What about the dreadful Dilys? If your information is correct, it was Joan who engineered her appointment here. I understand she's not local, so she probably doesn't know about Joan's antics when she was a teacher, and she may not even know about the tricks she tried to pull at the PVB. Might it not be instructive for her to learn?"

"Possibly," agreed Perry. "She's already claiming that Joan was blackmailing her to keep the wolf from her own door, so I don't suppose she is too well disposed to her at present. However, our difficulty is that anything we tell her about Joan might be used to excuse her conduct even further; for example, if we tell her about the unpleasant fates suffered by Joan's cast-off friends, she might start to claim she was frightened by her. I don't want to help Dilys if I can avoid it."

Bernie had been thinking: "If it's true that Joan wangled Dilys into her old job, it means she must have known all about her before she came here. I wonder if there is anything in that. After all, she couldn't just have picked up the information from the news media, she had to have some way of contacting Dilys. That suggests some form of personal relationship to me."

"I wonder if she was that friend Dilys claimed she was trying to help the last time she got into trouble? The one who the police couldn't trace?" asked Sonya.

"That would be just like her, to take the money and leave her friend in the lurch," remarked Perry.

They fell silent for several minutes and Sonya offered to brew coffee. Eventually Perry began to muse on the origins of all their troubles. "What I don't understand in all this is why Joan hated Wendy so much in the first place. If she hadn't treated her so badly while she was at school, she herself would have had a much better and fuller life, and so would a lot of other people. It is almost as if she's obsessed by Wendy in some way; even now she was willing to jeopardize her position here in order to be cruel to Wendy. If we could find out why she behaves like that, we may find her Achilles' Heel."

Sonya said: "The obvious answer is that it's got something to do with the Yugoslav connection. But don't ask me what, or how we'd ever find out."

Perry knew that Franjo would have all the information they needed on that score, but he was reluctant to publicize a relationship the man himself was clearly determined not to admit to. He resolved to have a quiet word with Franjo as soon as possible.

Sonya spoke again, almost breaking in on his thoughts: "Even if we were to find out why she hates Wendy, I'm not sure how we could turn it to account."

Forthright and to the point as always, Bernie remarked: "Considering the effect Joan has on those who come in contact with her, it's a miracle Wendy has stayed alive as long as she has."

Sonya pointed out that if Barry hadn't been on drugs, if he'd been capable of thinking out his plan of action more carefully, Wendy might, indeed, have been killed. "It was good luck for Wendy that Joan couldn't recruit a more reliable thug. It's a pity we never found out what he wanted to tell you that day he died."

Perry speculated: "Perhaps that was it: that he'd only tried to assault Wendy when Joan had instructed him to kill her. He might have thought if he could convince me of that, it would stand him in good stead when he came to trial."

"Why didn't he go straight to the police, if that was his mitigation?" asked Bernie.

"They would never have believed him, Auntie; the word of a drug addict who'd already killed three people would count for nothing against that of a respected charity worker, unless he could get you to support him."

The phone rang. Sonya picked up the receiver, as if by reflex action, and listened to the voice at the other end. At last, she managed to get a word in: "I'm afraid Mr Barrett is in conference at present, and I'm not sure when he will be free. Perhaps you would care to call back later this afternoon." She carefully replaced the receiver and said: "It's started. That was Mr Edwards, the crime reporter for the *Echo*. Apparently, someone has sent him an anonymous letter detailing allegedly continuing financial irregularities and sexual misconduct by officers of the PVB."

"I wonder who?" asked Perry bitterly. "If the press choose to have a field day with allegations like those, it'll be the end of us, coming on top of the assault and the fire, and this recent business with Dilys. The donors must already feel bad enough about giving money to support criminals living in a foundation which employs a con artist for a fund-raiser, but if they get to hear that, far from cleaning up our act, we've still got people with their hands in the till, who indulge in extra-marital relationships at the same time, it'll finish us off good and proper."

Sonya looked crushed. Her new job was dissolving before her very eyes. It was a job she wanted to do, and now it was being snatched from her grasp, like a child's chocolate bar. The spectre of the dole queue swam into view; there was no long-term future for her at the bank, she was sure of that. And what about poor Perry? He'd never work again: a failed businessman, who'd be branded as a marital cheat and dishonest in his job. She looked at him, as he reached for his tablets. Loss of the PVB would kill him.

"I thought we'd managed to deal with the local rag when Dilys appeared before the magistrates by gently emphasizing," he smiled at Sonya, "how dependent they were on our paid advertising. It's disturbing to think they're contemplating printing news as well as adverts."

Bernie was at her practical best when faced with a crisis. It didn't seem at all strange to Perry that this woman, whom he'd known for less than half a day, should now be taking the reins. "To be exact, Perry, they would be printing unsubstantiated and actionable gossip. I'm surprised that, considering how much the PVB must spend with them, they're willing to alienate you by pursuing the matter. But then, the press are a law unto themselves; we had no end of trouble with them when I was on the LEA."

Perry couldn't believe that Bernie would ever have found the press difficult to deal with.

"The trouble is," said Sonya, "we know who's behind it, but we can't prove anything. Mr Edwards certainly won't help us. You know what the press are like about protecting their sources."

Bernie had been thinking: "Assuming your friend is behind this, it might also be safe to assume she has persuaded Mr Edwards to his course of action by unethical means, especially if he's jeopardizing his newspaper's advertising revenue in the process."

"Now, that's an interesting thought," said Perry. "If we could only find out what she's got on him, maybe we could turn the tables on him. Maybe this time she's overreached herself."

"Perry, may I suggest you invite Mr Edwards round tomorrow afternoon. You can't leave it too long, in case he goes off and takes the risk of going into print before you've had a chance to set him straight. In the meantime, I'll try to dig out whatever dirt there is on him. I've lived here a long time and I know quite a few people through my work on the LEA."

"That's a good idea, Bernie. Why don't you call Mr Cielo at Nite-Safe? He also knows a lot of people; he used to be in the police, and he was very good to us when he unmasked Dilys. You can use the phone in Sonya's old office. Tell him you're my new secretary," laughed Perry.

"Well, why not?" she asked. "I dare say you could do with a bit of help now that you've no longer got Sonya, and surely your board couldn't object to a volunteer, until such times as they get round to advertising the vacancy."

Perry couldn't understand why, but he found himself falling in with Bernie's suggestions. As if propelled forward by the strength of her personality, he raised the receiver and dialled the number of the *Echo*. Having waited several minutes before being transferred to Mr Edwards in person, he found himself inviting the man over for a chat. Mr Edwards was unwilling to wait until the following afternoon and, by way of compensation, attempted to interview Perry over the telephone. Perry firmly resisted the pressure and Mr Edwards had to be content with an appointment for three o'clock.

During his telephone conversation Perry had been thinking about Bernie's offer. "You know, it might be some time before the board gets round to advertising for a new secretary, especially since Sonya is still technically on secondment from Barwell's, and I really could use some secretarial assistance to tide me over. Now is not a good time to be without someone to answer the telephone and I'm sure Sonya can't do both jobs, wonderful as she is, so I think I'm justified in asking the board for a salary for you."

Bernie beamed: "Well thank you, Perry, that's very kind of you I'm sure. I wouldn't want to do it permanently, mind, but I can type and Sonya can show me the basic computer stuff."

"If you would care to apply for the post, Mrs Adams."

"I'd always give you a good reference, Auntie."

They all laughed as Perry called Eric to settle the question of a salary. He was cagey at first; he had been hoping that Sonya could have carried on coping with the most urgent things, leaving the rest until her future was settled. Although this arrangement would have saved the PVB money, in the end Eric had to agree with Perry that it was impracticable, and agreed to propose the allocation of a minute salary to Mrs Adams.

"Good, that's settled then," said Bernie crisply. "But there is one other thing about this gossip about you and Sonya. Your wife could be in for an unpleasant time if the press come bothering her, so it might be a good idea to forewarn her. Why don't you both come round to dinner at my place tonight? It will give us a chance to get acquainted, and she can meet Sonya and be reassured there's nothing going on that she should know about."

"That might be a good idea, thank you, Bernie." Perry called Pam there and then. She was delighted, if a little surprised, to be invited out for dinner at such short notice, and cheerfully accepted the invitation.

As he was packing up for the evening Perry reflected that he was going to be glad of a secretary; the work was beginning to pile up, and he wasn't going to get much done tomorrow. He wasn't looking forward to his appointment with Mr Edwards, and it would take a large chunk out of his afternoon, but he was determined to fight tooth and nail to save both the PVB and Pam and Sonya from harm. He was not going to allow that rat-bag to take the best job he had ever had. He'd never admitted it to himself before, but he really did love this job with the PVB. It was by far the best thing he'd ever done: he enjoyed helping and looking after the residents and workers. They were like a family to him. It was much better than being in business. All he'd done then was struggle to make money. He'd provided the customers with a good product for their money, but mostly they had been buying home improvements they didn't really need, just finding a way to blow their surplus funds. He and Pam had done the same: they'd kept up appearances and wasted his high earnings. Perry knew that was how the system worked, but it all seemed so trivial now. As he drove home, he thought how strange it was that you never knew what you'd got until you were about to lose it. It had been the same with the business.

Pam and Perry were due to arrive at Bernie's around eight o'clock, and it was only a few minutes past when they rang the bell of the small terraced cottage. They noticed beautiful stone walls and tubs of geraniums on the pavement on either side of the door.

When Perry told Pam about the amazing Bernie and the threat posed by Mr Edwards, she had said: "I bet when you went to work for a charity, you never expected to be leading such an exciting life." She had immediately seen the sense of

Bernie's suggestion and was looking forward to meeting both her and Sonya.

When she was introduced to Sonya, Pam thought how unkind people could be. She might well be a clever young lady and a loyal friend, but she was certainly no beauty. Not Perry's type at all, she decided.

It wasn't until the meal was over that Bernie made her confession: "I've got you here under false pretences, I'm afraid. Sonya cooked the meal tonight. I can't boil an egg without breaking it."

Their conversation inevitably turned to the PVB, and Pam remarked that it was a bad day for them when they had first set eyes on Joan Mayflower. "In future, darling, they're going to have to be a great deal more careful about whom they employ. Jack will have to tighten up on taking references; Helen Robertson-Palmer has done the dirty on him twice now."

At this point, Pam told Bernie and Sonya about her mysterious telephone calls. "I suppose because Joan didn't get the reaction she wanted, she's going public with it all."

"Not if we can help it," said Bernie firmly. "Whatever her grudge with the PVB she has absolutely no right to try and drag you into it."

"Did you manage to find out anything useful about Mr Edwards yet?" asked Perry.

"I'm afraid not, Perry. From what I can gather, he hasn't been here that long, but Mr Cielo said he would do a bit of digging, so you never know."

Sonya said: "It's like a nightmare. We no sooner scotch one of her schemes than she hatches another. Why us? I mean, why did she ever have to come to the PVB in the first place? There must have been plenty of other charities she could have worked for. Why did she have to come here?"

"We're just lucky, I guess," quipped Pam.

Perry thought he knew of a more definite, and certainly more interesting, answer to that question. He said: "One thing we can count on: as long as that woman lives and breathes, she'll have it in for us. The only way we can stop her is by making her more afraid of us than we are of her."

CHAPTER TWENTY-NINE

In compliance with her role as a dutiful secretary, Bernie was in the office at nine o'clock sharp the following morning, receiving instructions from her niece about the filing system and computer.

"I'll be around the office anyway, so I'll be able to help you out."

Perry arrived later and plunged straight into his morning rounds of the complex. He thought physical action was the best antidote to the nervousness he was feeling. He stopped by Ben's workshop and admired his designs for a new plate to be sold in a local gift shop. They were beautiful: local landscapes and sites of historical interest cleverly interwoven. In the greenhouses Perry came across Franjo, in the company of his fellow gardeners. He would have liked a serious talk with him about his sister, but it was the wrong time. Perry could see Franjo was studiously bent over his cuttings, and anyway he was too nervous to be tactful. He slipped one of his tablets in his mouth as a precaution; the last thing he wanted was to face Mr Edwards with a bad feeling in his heart.

By common consent, Perry, Sonya and Bernie lunched together in the self-service cafeteria. Perry felt rather like a prisoner under escort, as if the two women were afraid he would run away if they left him alone.

When Mr Edwards eventually did arrive, over twenty minutes late, Perry thought he looked even less reputable than the other two journalists had been. It wasn't just that his suit was dirty and food-stained, it was that it had clearly been tailored to fit a much thinner man. When Mr Edwards eased himself into one of the armchairs in Perry's office, Perry fully expected the seat of the trousers to give way. He also noticed that Mr Edwards smelled strongly of alcohol.

Bernie remained in the seat she had taken up in Perry's office, and continued to read over the file of specimen fund-raising letters. She had suggested to Perry that it might be a good idea to have a witness to this conversation. Mr Edwards was obviously uneasy in her company, and for this Perry was also grateful. Over the obligatory cup of coffee, served in the "Flowers" series mugs, Mr Edwards launched into his spiel. He deplored the sending of anonymous letters, but pointed out that a journalist had a duty to discover the truth, no matter how "unfortunate" the source of his information.

Without waiting for him to ask his question, Perry asked: "And exactly what information has your anonymous source imparted to you?"

"Concerning financial irregularities and... er... misconduct on the part of senior members of staff at the PVB. There was something about the presence of Bernie which inhibited Mr Edwards from using the word "sexual" in connection with the misconduct. And that, thought Perry, was probably what Bernie intended.

"Exactly what do you mean by 'financial irregularities' and 'misconduct', Mr Edwards?"

"I understand that sums of money given by local donors have gone missing."

"You are aware, of course, of the arrest of Miss Dilys Owen. I remember handing representatives of the *Echo* a copy of the press statement, which is the only statement I can make on the matter at this time."

"That isn't quite what I meant, Mr Barrett. I'm sure you know what I mean."

Perry played dumb. "Please explain yourself more clearly, Mr Edwards. If you have any evidence of financial wrong-doing, you should lay it before me without delay." Bernie smiled approvingly.

Mr Edwards frowned; he'd hoped to cajole Perry into disclosing the story on the basis of a generalized accusation. He was usually quite good at that but, somehow, he felt inhibited by the old biddy sitting behind him. "It's rather a delicate subject, Mr Barrett, I'm not sure if…" He nodded in the direction of Bernie.

"Please feel free to discuss the matter in front of my secretary. She is here at my request."

"Don't mind me," she chimed.

Mr Edwards noisily cleared his throat. "I understand that certain sums of money, cash, given to a local fund-raiser in… er… Kent, wasn't it?" He paused, hoping for a reply. Perry tried to look blank. Bernie was still beaming encouragement. Silence reigned. Eventually Mr Edwards had to give in and continue: "I understand there was a series of thefts."

"And do you have any evidence to put before me to support your allegations?"

"My source informed me that the fund-raiser in question, a Mr Russell, had to quit. Can you confirm this to be the case, Mr Barrett?"

Perry knew they were edging towards the tricky bit. "Have you discussed these allegations with Mr Russell?"

Mr Edwards smiled knowingly. It was the smile that always got them. The "I know everything" smile. "We have naturally examined all the possible leads, Mr Barrett, this is, after all, a very serious matter."

"Indeed it is Mr Edwards and I would therefore suggest that unless you can prove your allegations, you would be wise to be very careful about what you say and what you print."

That was the problem and Mr Edwards knew it. Technically, Mr Russell had been allowed to resign. He hadn't been dismissed and, thanks to some nifty footwork, the thefts had been covered up and, with the quick repayment of the cash, written off as a mistake. He was sure that Barrett and, probably, the old biddy, knew what had gone on, but he wasn't going to get much change out of them, that much was obvious.

They heard a voice in Sonya's office call out: "Hello, anybody home?" Bernie quickly left the room, shutting the door behind her.

Mr Edwards changed tack. "That lady," he nodded in the direction of the door, "would be Miss Bishop, I take it?" He sounded as though he couldn't believe it.

"No, Mr Edwards, that is Mrs Adams. Miss Bishop is presently filling in for the fund-raiser." The lady herself re-entered the room, looking extraordinarily pleased with herself.

"Quite a promotion that, eh, Mr Barrett? I understand Miss Bishop has no previous experience of fund-raising, that she was, in fact, a bank clerk before she came here?"

"Miss Bishop is presently on secondment from Barwell's Bank and, in her time with us, has proved to be hard-working, scrupulously honest, and in sympathy with the aims and activities of the PVB. She was asked by the board of trustees to take over the fund-raising post on a temporary basis until the future is more clear."

Barwell's Bank might have swallowed this confection, but not so Mr Edwards. "But she was given the job at your suggestion?"

"She was appointed by a unanimous decision of the board of trustees and I fully concur with that decision."

Mr Edwards had the unwelcome feeling he was losing this one. After over thirty years in the business, it was not a good feeling. There was nothing for it but to try the frontal attack. "So, you can categorically deny that you and Miss Bishop are having an affair?" he asked aggressively.

"Absolutely."

Again Mr Edwards waited in silence, again he lost the peace. "Perhaps I'll confirm that with your wife, Mr Barrett?"

Unbeknown to Mr Edwards, this was the one Perry had been waiting for. "By all means, Mr Edwards. I am sure she would be only too glad to support Miss Bishop and myself in any action necessary to prevent the spread of this malicious fiction."

However undistinguished Mr Edwards might have looked, he was not a man to be lightly intimidated. "Mr Barrett, you must be aware that no reputable newspaper prints unsubstantiated hearsay; we print news." Perry coughed unkindly and Bernie chortled. Mr Edwards tried again: "Unfortunately for you and Miss Bishop, rumours have been spreading, and I have come along here today to give you a chance to put your side of the story. You and Miss Bishop both," he added nastily.

"I have answered your questions as fully as I can, and I have no intention of prolonging this interview, Mr Edwards, unless you tell me exactly when and where you heard the rumours you refer to."

"Well, people are bound to talk, Mr Barrett; it's bound to get around, it always does." Mr Edwards thought he was regaining some of his lost ground; if only the old bat would shove off, he could really get into this guy.

"There is nothing for people to talk about, Mr Edwards, so you should tell me where you heard these rumours, or are they just figments of your imagination?"

"It's a case of 'no smoke without fire' isn't it, Mr Barrett?"

Perry was angry now. "No smoke and no fire, Mr Edwards. I'm beginning to be persuaded to the view that all this is pure invention on your part, and I'm not disposed to waste any more time with you." He rose, to indicate the interview was at an end. All in all, it hadn't gone too badly. He looked across at Bernie: she was still smiling.

It was then that Mr Edwards dropped his equivalent of a bomb. "So I can tell my readers that you absolutely deny getting Miss Bishop the fund-raising post because she's having an affair with you or that you have been involved in any financial wrong-doing, Mr Barrett?" he looked as though he were framing headlines in his mind. Perry's heart almost leapt into his mouth. Bernie frowned. Mr Edwards was going to attempt to use the old journalists' trap: smear by denial. Heads, I win; tails you lose.

CHAPTER THIRTY

It was then that Bernie spoke for the first time: "Sit down, Mr Edwards." Perplexed, both men sat again. Bernie spoke slowly and evenly: "Mr Edwards, I do believe you've been drinking: I can smell it on your breath."

It was true, he had had a couple of scotches in the pub at lunchtime, but so what?

"I'm sure your newspaper's owners would be dismayed to learn that you turned up to an interview in a state of inebriation, the more so when it is remembered how much our annual advertising budget with your paper amounts to. And for how much longer could you continue with your work if we informed the police?"

Mr Edwards was struck dumb.

"Do we understand one another, Mr Edwards?"

He muttered something that sounded like "Bitch". More clearly, he replied: "Yes."

"So then you understand that we cannot allow unfounded allegations contained in anonymous letters to remain in circulation. So hand over."

"No." The journalist in Mr Edwards came bravely to the fore. But not too far. "I don't have it with me," he added defensively.

Bernie looked speculatively at him, as if weighing up what she should do next. Both men were certain she knew. "Then Mr Barrett and I will accompany you while you fetch it."

"All right, all right. There was no letter." I got a phone call, but it comes to the same thing; you've got no way of tracing her, she never gave her name, so there's nothing you can get hold of." He sounded rather satisfied about that.

"Or, to put it another way, you can't prove you're not just spinning a yarn to get a story," countered Perry.

"In the circumstances, I wonder how your editor would view this kind of activity against a well-respected local charity. I'm sure your drunken arrival here today would provide him with a much better story, if he's short of something for the front page."

Mr Edwards looked as though he could quite cheerfully have killed Bernie on the spot. Perry wished he was able to be so verbally manipulative. It would have saved him a great deal of trouble with the Revenue.

"OK. OK. It was a woman called Mayflower. She said she used to work here. She arranged to meet in the Wheatsheaf one evening, and told me about you and Miss Bishop and about the missing money."

Perry and Bernie considered this information for a few minutes, while Mr Edwards pointedly kept looking at his watch. Bernie suggested: "I think it's about time we gave dear Joan a taste of her own medicine. I want you to arrange to meet her again tomorrow evening. Tell her you want to talk your findings over with her. Do it now."

Reluctantly, Mr Edwards called the familiar number. She didn't answer at once, but eventually, he heard her voice. "I thought I'd let you know I've been to the PVB, but we should talk again before I write it up. Yep. Same place. Cheerio then, till tomorrow."

He had replaced the receiver before Bernie spoke: "Thank you, Mr Edwards. You can go now. Come back here at five tomorrow for your instructions."

Mr Edwards was only too glad to get away from Dracula's mother. He didn't even protest about the inconvenience of a return trip. On his way out of Sonya's old office, he saw a woman of about thirty sitting behind the desk and wondered if she was the fabled Miss Bishop. Surely not. She was almost as ugly as the other one. As he climbed into his car, he only hoped he could get back to the office without being stopped by the police.

CHAPTER THIRTY-ONE

Sonya entered Perry's office, and the three of them watched Mr Edwards manoeuvre his car out of the drive and on to the main road. He appeared to be driving at about twenty miles an hour and hugging the edge of the road. "What a little rat," said Perry.

"How did it go?" asked Sonya.

"Very well, dear. Perry fenced with him like a real diplomat, and I was lucky enough to get hold of some information which enabled us to turn the tables on him. We got him to admit it was Joan Mayflower who had put the idea into his head; he is due to report his findings to her tomorrow night. In the meantime, we can think out a plan of campaign."

"Do you think we can trust him not to run straight off to her and spill the beans?" asked Perry.

"I think so; right now we are his immediate problem, not Joan. You see, some years ago he ran over and killed a little schoolgirl while drunk-driving."

"How horrible."

"Disgusting man. But how did you find out about the accident with the child?"

"That marvellous Mr Cielo checked with his old friends in police records. It was he who called on us during your interview."

"I saw him coming up the drive, and I wondered if he'd got anything for us," remarked Sonya. "Do tell, I'm dying to know."

Bernie found the slip of paper on which Mr Cielo had written a brief account of the case. "It was in Hampton Fields in Swale Vale. The local primary school was just finishing for the day and the children were being collected by their parents. According to an eyewitness account provided by a trainee teacher, he just came from nowhere and ran over a seven year-old girl. The headmistress, who was in the playground at the time, ran in and phoned the ambulance, while the trainee teacher went across to see if she could do anything to help the child. She is reported as saying: "The car had come to a crash stop, hitting a lamp post. The driver came staggering out of the car and stood over us. He smelt very much of alcohol, even though it was only three-thirty in the afternoon. It was terrible; the other children and some of their mothers were crying. There was nothing to be done. The ambulance took the child to hospital, but already she was dead. The driver stood swaying about on the pavement, saying: 'I didn't see her.' over and over again."

"When the police arrived, he actually tried to run away. Apparently, he realized that his car wasn't going to get him anywhere, wrapped around the lamp post as it was, so he tried to run in the opposite direction to the approaching police. After a few yards he fell over, and was actually crawling along the pavement on all fours when they caught up with him. The trainee teacher said: 'It was a disgusting exhibition; I shall never forget it.' And, of course, she never did. It's interesting, don't you think, that her level of English, as shown in that statement I read, was by no means perfect at that time?"

"Oh ho!" Perry had only just caught on. "Serves him damn well right, of course, but how unlucky can you get? To have her as a witness to your crime and then to wind up working in the same town after all these years."

"It's a miracle he ever got his licence back," said Sonya.

Bernie shook her head. "My dear, he was banned for life. That's why he's so afraid now. It isn't only the shame of the past he's trying to hide, it's the fact that he's driving illegally now. If he gets caught, he won't be able to keep his job and I suppose he might well go to jail."

Perry said: "I feel guilty about letting him drive off like that."

"We can shop him to the police when we've finished with him," replied Bernie. "With any luck, he might even blame Joan."

CHAPTER THIRTY-TWO

Sonya absently began to brew more coffee and asked: "What are we going to do now?"

Perry considered the situation for a few minutes, while sipping his coffee. He noticed they had run out of milk. Auntie Bernie wasn't much of a housekeeper. "Now that we have Edwards in our power, I suggest we use him to turn the tables on Joan. I think it would be a good idea for Pam, who neither Joan nor Edwards knows, to be at the Wheatsheaf tomorrow night to witness that meeting and to overhear as much of it as she can. That way, we will have our own observer to back up whatever information Edwards gives us later. And for good measure, perhaps we could prevail on Mr Cielo to be there as well. He would be a completely independent party. In that way we would have three witnesses to Joan's machinations." Perry was feeling very proud of his idea: using Edwards to get rid of Joan would ensure the discretion of the local press. His was one story they would never want to publish.

"I know," Sonya piped up brightly. "We could ask Mr Cielo if he could get one of those listening devices for Mr Edwards to wear, like they do in the spy films."

"Even better," Bernie was brimming with delight. "That way there could be no way she could get out of it. I'll see if I can't come up with some suggestions for the way Edwards should lead the conversation, to get the most incriminating material."

Perry thought about Franjo and Wendy; surely they both had a right to know what he was planning. In particular, he wanted to inform Franjo. He was, after all, Joan's brother. He didn't finish his coffee, but explained where he was going.

The sun was shining for the first time that day as he walked briskly in the direction of the greenhouses. He took it as a good omen. Franjo was raking an empty flower bed.

"Good afternoon, my friend. And a very beautiful one it is now. You bring the sun with you."

Perry was relieved to find him in a good mood and on his own. The other gardeners were presumably in the greenhouses; none of them was in sight. "I wonder if I could have a serious chat with you, Franjo. Have you got a few minutes to spare?"

Franjo looked up at him shrewdly. "Naturally, for you always some minutes. But first, how is my little rose? He is happy in your home?"

"Yes, he's, it's fine. So far we've resisted the temptation to over-feed it and it's doing fine in the front room."

Franjo seemed satisfied with that answer, and asked: "What is it you want?"

"Well, it's rather confidential. Could we perhaps go to your room? I wouldn't like anyone to overhear us." Franjo acquiesced with a shrug and allowed Perry to wheel him in the direction of the new block. "How have you settled into your new room?"

"Is fine. Is good. My needs are simple, but is fine. I like also having my friend Ben next door. We play chess in the evenings."

This was news to Perry; he didn't know either Ben or Franjo played. He had been quite good himself when he was younger, but he hadn't played since he was married: "I'll have to give you a game one day. I haven't played for years, so I'll be a bit rusty, but I'd enjoy a game."

By now they had reached Franjo's room on the ground floor and, as he was unlocking the door, he replied: "Sure. It is a good game. Good for life. Everyone should play."

Inside, the room was spotlessly tidy and sparsely furnished with the furniture and soft furnishings provided by the PVB. Apart from a large transistor radio and an old record player with a small collection of LPs, Franjo had very few personal possessions. Perry thought sadly that a lifetime of living in

201

institutions, many of them probably a great deal less pleasant than the PVB, did not allow the acquisition of much personal wealth.

One thing that Franjo did have, however, was an old framed photograph of a family group. It was a faded print showing an abstracted teenage girl standing between a smiling mother and a suited, stern-looking father of massive build and, in front of them, a young school boy, who had been looking away from the camera when the photograph was taken. They were all standing in front of what appeared to be a rather dilapidated house. Perry looked at the photograph for several minutes; a memento of happier times, it made his task easier.

Before he could speak, Franjo said: "My family: mama, papa, little Franjo and his sister. It was taken when we were living at home, when we had the farm. I am here now, but can you guess where my sister is, friend Perry?"

Perry turned round and looked down, as his face creased into a smile. "I don't need to guess, Franjo. Colonel Charles told me last time he came to visit with the other local fund-raisers. He recognized you."

Franjo nodded sagely. "When I see you together, I think that old colonel is telling my friend Perry all my little secrets. He is bringing all the little shadows into the light."

It was a picturesque way of putting it, but Perry knew what he meant. "He didn't tell me very much really, and I don't want to know all your secrets. I haven't told anyone else, and I won't."

"Not even my flower Wendy?"

"No, not even Wendy. It's no one's business but yours. If you don't choose to have it generally known that Joan Mayflower is your sister, I can understand that."

Franjo laughed. "I tell you. You are my friend, so I tell you. She was always the same." He looked at the photograph, as if willing the scene back to life. He shook his head. "She looks so beautiful there, but inside, she was like she is now. What she wants, she must have, you understand?" Perry nodded. "Just like mama. She is well-to-do English lady, and she wants to marry a Yugoslav poet. So she does. Her family disapprove, but she does it all the same. Then comes the feud, and she is stuck there with little Franjo and his sister. It is not a good time. Papa dies fighting. After, it is even worse time. The men go round settling old scores on those who did not support them. They cannot forget, they cannot leave the past behind them, and they are jealous of those who have a little more than they. We have the farm and an English mama. It is enough. I get beaten up; they break my back." He reached down and touched the sides of his wheelchair. "And so here I am.

"My mama still had good connections in England; she knew the colonel and his lady. They are old friends, and the fine Margaret she now helps the Red Cross, so she brings me here for a hospital. All too late."

Franjo paused and picked up the old photograph. "Later, mama and sister come to England; they never go back. You must thank our good colonel for that; without him they never could be here. Me, I go to a place for children, and my sister remains with mama. That is all."

Perry was sure it wasn't all. As tactfully as possible, he asked why Franjo didn't get on with his sister.

Franjo spun round in his wheelchair. "At home my sister had everything, but always she wanted more. She wanted all for herself. She saw what happened to me. And does she call mama? Does she call help? No, she does not. It is the next day before they find me. Oh, you can think she is young; she is too frightened; she does not know what she has seen. But she knew. I know that when they bring me home and I see the way she looks at me. She did not want me to be alive, of that I am sure."

Perry shuddered. "Franjo, I'm so sorry. I had no idea. To think... even as a young woman. Horrible."

Franjo nodded. "So I tell you to be careful of her, friend Perry. It is why I look to our Wendy. You do not know all, even now."

"Yes, tell me, Franjo, Why does she hate Wendy so much?"

"The Lalovich are our cousins back in the old village. They come before us here as refugee. Lalovich was the only son of that family. When our grandfather dies he gets all the money; mama says always that he cheated us." Franjo shrugged. "I do not know. What was Yugoslavian money ever worth? But me, I liked Lalovich. When he had to come here, he had to leave it all behind; he could not bring it with him. So, he worked hard and trained to be an optician. He became an educated man. Wendy is one of our family; she should be our little flower, but when she comes into the power of Joan, she torments her."

"To settle an old score that was not of Wendy's making?"

Franjo smiled. "No doubt Wendy's mama and papa hoped Joan would be kind to her at school; they too did not understand my sister. Perhaps she wanted Lalovich to be forced to pay her to look after his little one. She did not understand him." Franjo chuckled. "He found a better way to spend his money: he sent his child to an expensive school. And now he is dead. I miss him. He was amusing, charming. When he was alive he used to visit me. But why did you never ask me about all of this before, friend Perry?"

"Because it was simply none of my business. Your relationship with your sister was entirely your own affair."

"But now that has changed, yes?"

"I'm afraid so, nodded Perry. "You see, now your sister no longer works here, she is trying to discredit the PVB and get me dismissed; she's putting it about that I've been involved in thefts of donated funds and that I'm having an affair with Sonya. I also believe she was behind Dilys Owen's thefts."

Franjo laughed. "Oh my friend. The Sonya, she is a very nice lady. I like her very much. But La Gioconda she is not. And no one would ever believe you would have an affair." He waved his hand, as if to clear away the laughter. "You may be sure, though, my sister will make you pay if she thinks you have hurt her. She always does. Look at the poor Wendy. That stupid boy, he tried to hurt Wendy because my sister tells him to. Is it not so?"

"I can't prove anything, but I certainly believe so," agreed Perry. He thought it might be a good idea to ask Sonya's question at this point. "Franjo, do you know why Joan came to work at the PVB in the first place? Was it just coincidence that you were living here and Wendy is one of our therapists?"

"It is just coincidence that Wendy works here," replied Franjo. "As far as I know she does not come here just to look after me. But my dear sister did. It was good news for her when she found also young Wendy again."

Perry looked puzzled. "I've said this before, but it seems so strange to me that Joan should still be persecuting Wendy after all these years. I don't pretend to understand it. She could have had a much better life if she had learned to take the rough with the smooth, and just let bygones be bygones."

Franjo was laughing again. "Ah, but you do not know all yet, my friend. Why does she start again to hurt Wendy? Joan does not like disabled people, not even her own brother, why, of all the places, therefore, does she come to work here? Why does she hate our Princess Victoria so much? I will tell you. One year ago mama dies. She is from a good family; they are all dead."

Perry suppressed a laugh. Franjo was making it sound like the only good thing about his mother's family was that they were dead. He was sure he didn't mean it.

"It is very traditional family. All capital goes to the male grandson."

"Ah." The light was beginning to dawn on Perry.

"So after many years of being poor, Franjo is now very rich. His sister is not. Naturally, she comes to care for him."

Without thinking, Perry whistled and said: "You're very lucky to still be alive, Franjo. Oh I'm sorry, I shouldn't have said that."

"Not at all, my friend. I agree. I understand my sister better even than you. Therefore I tell her: 'It will do you no good. If I die, you still don't get rich; I have left all to Princess Victoria and flower Wendy.'"

"That would explain a lot," said Perry.

"It was a mistake that I tell her. It saves me, but it puts Wendy in danger. Therefore do I look after her. It puts also your PVB in danger. She cannot kill a charity, but she tries to do the next best: to discredit it, so it will cease to exist. And when it is gone, what could be more natural than that she will take her brother to live with her?"

"God, what a ghastly thought."

"Indeed it is so. This is a very good place. I like it very much. I have friends here. I can pay my way by the work that I do. It is a good place for us all." Perry nodded. He understood that Franjo realized he and Sonya were as dependent on the PVB as he himself was. "So, now you will tell me how I can help you to stop my sister. I will do all that I can."

Perry thanked Franjo and explained: "Your sister has been in touch with Mr Edwards, a reporter for the local paper, and he came to interview me this afternoon, with a view to tricking me into admitting to something Joan could use to ruin the PVB. He didn't get anything, and Mrs Adams, my new temporary secretary, who, by the way, is Sonya's aunt, had managed to unearth the discreditable secret Joan is holding over him. Many years ago he killed a child while drink-driving. This gave us an idea for a way in which we can use him to thwart Joan."

Franjo's face creased into a broad smile and he laughed: "I should have seen this. I look at this new lady coming into our path and I ask myself from where she gets her looks. I should have seen." He looked at his watch. "Now, I think, we have time to drink some coffee. Let us visit friend Ben. He is a good chess player, we should discuss with him."

Perry could see the sense of this. Ben was discreet as well as clever, so he agreed.

CHAPTER THIRTY-THREE

Perry followed Franjo out of his room and waited while he tapped sharply on the neighbouring door. In reply to Ben's cheery: "Come in" they both entered, Perry pushing Franjo's chair. "Well, hi there, Perry. Not often we see you round here. Coffee?"

Ben's room was altogether different from Franjo's. Ben had held good jobs until his confidence had deserted him, and he had acquired a good bank balance and a large number of consumer durables, some of which now adorned his room. There was a coffee percolator, a stacking CD and tape unit, a portable TV, and any number of paintings and wall hangings. Perry had never been in Ben's room before, and he gazed in frank admiration at some of the paintings.

As Ben handed them their drinks, Franjo asked: "I may tell our friend, Ben, yes?"

"By all means."

In happily conspiratorial tones, he repeated the information Perry had given him. Ben whistled when Franjo got to the latest piece of blackmail. "The rotten cow," he said spontaneously.

Perry thought: Here's one person who doesn't know she's Franjo's sister. Ben was a mild sort and Franjo's best friend; however bad she was, he would never refer to Joan in those terms if he knew.

"But yes, friend Ben. Yes. I agree. And I should know. So much should I know. You see, she is my sister."

Perry turned round to observe the expression on Ben's face. "Oh, I'm sorry. I didn't know. I would never…" He was clearly very embarrassed.

Franjo cut him short. "But it is as you say. She is evil. My own sister and she does such things. She destroys all she knows."

"I must say, on the few occasions she and I have had dealings together he's almost finished me, and I was only doing her artwork."

"But our friend here has a way to stop her."

"Good for you," said Ben with spirit. "If there's anything I can do to help you, I will. I owe that lady one."

Perry recounted his proposition and added: "Before we go ahead, I would be happier if we were all in agreement. Why don't you both dine with Pam and me at home tonight? I'll ask Sonya and Bernie too, as well as Wendy. I feel in the mood to celebrate, and we can thrash out the details then."

Ben and Franjo both assented and Perry said he would pick them up at about seven.

"Thank you, friend Perry, but please do not tell our little flower her good fortune."

Ben was puzzled, but Perry understood. He said a temporary goodbye to his fellow conspirators and went off in search of Wendy. He found her walking down the flower-scented drive on her way home. She was in no hurry, so he briefly explained about the relationship between her family and Joan, and about the threat Joan currently posed to the PVB and his proposal for dealing with her, before asking her to dinner.

"So she's hated me all these years because of some old family feud that happened before I was born?"

Perry was a little economical with the truth at this stage: "That was certainly the start of it, but I've no doubt she enjoyed the power she had over you."

"God, how horrible." Wendy shivered, despite the warmth of the late afternoon. "Poor Franjo. You know, I had no idea he was her brother. Mind you, he has been very kind and protective towards me ever since I had that run-in with Barry. It never occurred to me that might be the reason."

208

"That, and genuine concern. I'm sure it's not just hatred of his sister; he has a real affection for you. He told me how much he used to like your father when he was alive."

"As regards Joan, Perry, you know I'll do anything I can to help you, but she's going to take a lot of stopping. We can all talk more about that tonight. I'll see you about eight."

Perry returned to his office and made a quick call home. If Pam was dismayed by the prospect of stretching a casserole intended for two to feed seven, she didn't say so; she was only too happy to learn that at last Perry might be finding a way of permanently dealing with Joan.

When Perry returned to the residence to collect Ben and Franjo, Franjo excused himself from the evening's entertainment: "Tonight I am more tired than usual, also, it will be easier for you all to speak of my sister when I am not there. Please convey my regrets to your good wife, but I am sure she will understand. I wish you all good planning." With that, he wheeled himself to his room.

When they finally reached Perry's home, Pam had managed to prepare some more potatoes and heat up a frozen shepherd's pie, to accompany the casserole. Perry made the introductions and they all sat down to eat.

Bernie, for one, was enjoying her meal: "You know, it's one of the regrets of my life that I've never learned to cook properly, but Sonya sees to it that I don't starve."

Pam said: "It's a pity Franjo couldn't come, but it's lovely to get to meet you both, Wendy and Ben. I've heard so much about you that I feel I know you already. One good thing about Joan is that she's brought us all together. It isn't until the chips are down that you get to know who your friends really are." She smiled at Perry.

Ben agreed and added: I feel sorry for Franjo. Even after all she's done, she is his sister. He must still have some feelings for her."

Perry was not so sure. He outlined the plan once again in detail for Pam's benefit and to ensure that the others were in full agreement.

Pam thought the idea a good one, but, like Ben, was only willing to sanction it if Mr Cielo was in prior agreement.

The evening finished at about eleven, when Bernie and Sonya departed. Not long after, Wendy offered to run Ben back to the PVB complex.

CHAPTER THIRTY-FOUR

The following morning Perry decided on an early start. In all the excitement his ordinary work was getting sorely neglected but, if the plan succeeded, it would be worth all the effort. It would be worth far more to the PVB than anything else he could do. As he drove into work, he thought about what Ben had said the night before: Franjo might seem to be in a difficult position but, as far as Perry could see, he showed every sign of enjoying it. Whatever the reason that had prevented him from joining their little party, Perry thought it was unlikely to be sensitivity about the delicacy of his position. Probably he had simply been too tired. The skies had started to cloud over, and the trees and flowers in the PVB's grounds were gently rustling in expectation of a storm.

When Perry reached his office, he found Bernie earnestly engaged in conversation on the telephone: "No, I'm sorry, Mr Barber, this afternoon wouldn't be possible. If you can't come this morning, we'll have to leave it until tomorrow morning. Yes, it's not a very good start is it? Still, I'm sure I'll get used to it in time. Miss Bishop? Am I related to her? Well, it's funny you should ask that. She's my niece. Ah! She was always doing this, was she? Oh. Well. You'll try to be round about eleven, then. Thank you so much. Bye."

"Computer gone again?"

"I'm afraid so, Perry. I can't think what I did to it. I'm sure I was only doing what Sonya told me to do. I'm very sorry."

"It's not your fault, Bernie. We've had it repaired before, we can have it repaired again." Perry hadn't the heart to mention the size of the last bill.

"All ready for the big day, then?"

"As ready as I'll ever be. It's the only way. One thing I've learnt from all this, though," Bernie questioned with her eyebrows. "You women are fantastic plotters. I'll have to be much more careful of you all in future. But I must admit, I'm rather looking forward to this afternoon." It was true. Perry was well and truly happy about the prospect of getting one back on Joan Mayflower.

It was Sonya who spoiled his moment of pleasure. She came rushing into the office, closely followed by Superintendent Mackie and Sergeant Twomey. "Good morning, Mr Barrett."

"Good morning, Superintendent." Perry noticed the Superintendent was looking at Bernie, as if trying to remember if he had seen her before. "Do you know Mrs Adams, my new temporary secretary?"

"No." They shook hands. "I wonder if we could have a word with you, sir?"

"Come into my office." Sergeant Twomey managed to exclude the two women, and Perry found himself facing the two police officers alone. He suddenly began to feel very guilty.

"I'm afraid we have some rather bad news for you, sir."

"Pam?" gasped Perry.

"Your former chief fund-raiser, sir, Joan Mayflower, was found battered to death at her home late last night."

Perry stuffed his bottle of tablets back in his pocket and sighed heavily. "I thought for one minute you meant something had happened to my wife, Pam."

"Oh no, sir. Nothing like that. Indeed, bearing in mind our previous conversations, you might not even regard it as bad news." The Superintendent paused.

Perry wasn't sure whether he was trying to imply that the event might not be regarded as bad or that it might not be news. Either way, he decided caution was the order of the day. "What happened?"

Superintendent Mackie related that at about a quarter to eleven the previous evening, one of Miss Mayflower's neighbours had reported hearing a noise coming from the back of her house and had phoned the police. By the time they arrived, this Mrs Manning had also noticed a strange car being driven away at speed from the front of the house; she had made a note of the registration number.

The police had then effected an entrance into Miss Mayflower's house, and had found her dead in her sitting room. They had soon managed to apprehend the driver of the strange car. "We picked him up a few streets away. He was driving down the centre of the road on the white line. He was well over the legal limit and he didn't have a valid licence. He was lucky he hadn't been caught before."

Perry had to ask: "Who?" even though he knew the answer.

"A character called Edwards, a journalist with the local paper. I understand you know him, sir?"

Not knowing how much the Superintendent knew, Perry thought it best to stick to the truth: "Yes... um... yes. He came here for an interview yesterday afternoon. It was the first time we'd ever met."

"So he told us, sir."

Perry hoped his show of honesty had entitled him to ask a question: "How did he explain his presence at Miss Mayflower's home?"

The Superintendent, long resigned to the perfidy of mankind, replied: "He claims he found the body. His story is that there was something urgent she wanted to discuss with him, and she thought half-past ten at night was a good time to start a discussion, so he called on her. He says he got no answer to his knock on the front door and, as the lights were all on, he peered in the front room and saw what he thought was the figure of Miss Mayflower sitting in one of the armchairs. Being desperate to see her, he went round the back and found the kitchen door open. He went in and found her slumped, dead in a chair in the lounge. There was a blood-stained golf club on the floor nearby."

"How awful, Superintendent. I admit I didn't like the woman, but to die like that. Have you any idea who did it? Or shouldn't I ask?" Perry was beginning to regain his confidence. Whoever had done for Joan, it couldn't have been him; he had an alibi for the whole of the previous evening, until about eleven. And so did Pam, Sonya, Bernie, Wendy and Ben. In fact, all the people most likely to want her dead were in the clear, and for that Perry was very grateful.

"We've arrested Edwards. He admits being there at the material time, and his prints are all over the place. He'd obviously tried to search for something. He didn't find it, but we did. Miss Mayflower was a very methodical lady and she kept her important papers in a small safe. Edwards had tried to force it, but he was unable to get it open. Judging from the information you'd already given us about that lady's character, I should say she was blackmailing him. She had kept press cuttings about an accident he was involved in that she had witnessed; a child had been killed and he'd been banned for life. He was using document's in his brother's name. This time when he was tested, the meter said he had the best part of a bottle of Scotch inside him. We think he took on a bit of Dutch courage and went round to have it out with her, and they got to arguing, and then…"

"Oh, I see." Despite himself Perry had to ask: "Are you sure he did it?"

"As sure as we can be about these things, sir. As a matter of fact, he tried to drag you and Miss Bishop into it. He suggested Miss Mayflower had something on you and was planning to blackmail you over it."

"Superintendent, whatever she might have thought, Joan had no hold over either me or Miss Bishop. She tried to use this Edwards to dig up some dirt. That was why he came round here yesterday afternoon, but he was unlucky. There was nothing to dig." Perry could see no way of avoiding admitting the reason behind Edwards' visit. He had had no opportunity to consult with Bernie and Sonya, and couldn't be sure what they would say, if questioned. He went further: "As a matter of fact, Superintendent, Miss Bishop and her aunt, together with Mrs Jackson and Ben Farrell, our resident artist, spent last evening together with my wife and I at our home, discussing what we should do about our never ending problems with Joan. The party didn't break up until eleven, and Mrs Jackson volunteered to drive Ben Farrell back here."

To Perry's relief, Superintendent Mackie didn't ask him what conclusions they had reached. Instead, he said: "Well, Mr Barrett, it looks like Mr Edwards has solved your problem for you. I don't suppose many people here will be too sorry about that. She was trouble, that woman, from start to finish. When we went through her papers, we found one or two interesting items. We found an application from Dilys Owen for the position of Regional Organizer with the Martin Luther Missions. They evidently rumbled her, and she never got the job, but she did get to meet Joan Mayflower. It looks very much as though she was speaking the truth when she said Joan was blackmailing her; although we didn't find anything definite amongst her financial papers, her bank account did show several large cash receipts after her dismissal and before Miss Davies' arrest."

"So it looks as though Joan's death will help Dilys when she comes to trial. I mean it's given you access to her bank accounts."

"Unfortunately for that lady, she still can't prove the cash came from her." The Superintendent didn't look too worried by the absence of proof. "Fortunately for her though, she's still on remand, so she couldn't have murdered the good Miss Mayflower any more than you could, sir. We managed to stop her getting bail on the strength of that Channel Islands account; it gave the impression that she was well prepared for a quick getaway.

"We also found more press cuttings, no doubt donated by Mr Edwards, covering Barry Kemp's accident, and we found Mrs Peters' phone number in her private book, so it looks as if you were right about that, sir. Not that it matters now."

"It's very good of you to tell me all this, Superintendent. I know it's nothing I didn't know already in my heart of hearts, but, somehow, it's good to know for certain."

"Well, I do have one other piece of information you might not know, sir, and that's the reason I've come to have this chat with you now. From her personal papers, we fond out that she was originally a Miss Mihailovic, and that she has a brother who lives here, Franjo. We haven't told him his sister is dead yet, sir; it seemed sensible to have a word with you first, in the circumstances."

CHAPTER THIRTY-FIVE

Perry thought the situation might need careful handling as far as Franjo was concerned. Being wheelchair bound and unable to drive, he could never be suspected of killing his sister, but Perry thought it might be as well to give a brief explanation of their background to Superintendent Mackie. "As a matter of fact, Superintendent, I did know she was his sister, but I understand they've never been close, and the relationship isn't generally known. Franjo is confined to a wheelchair, and while she worked here, she never seemed to care about him, or he to care about her."

The Superintendent nodded sagely, "I see, sir. All in all she wasn't a lady to be mourned, was she? Not even by her own brother, by the sound of it. It's ironic in a way; now that she's dead, he should come into a nice little inheritance; she had some savings and her home; not that I suppose he'll think that's much of a recompense for such a lonely life. How is his health otherwise, Mr Barrett? Do we need a medical attendant before we break the news?"

"He's fine, as far as I know, Superintendent, but I can give Dr Anderson, the PVB's medical adviser, a call, if you like, just to be on the safe side."

"Perhaps that might not be a bad idea, sir, and I was wondering if you couldn't come along too when I tell him. In the circumstances, a friendly face might be all the help he needs."

Perry called Dr Anderson's surgery and left a message with his receptionist, and then he and the Superintendent set out to find Franjo. Just before they reached the greenhouses, they espied Franjo, in conversation with Ben. Perry introduced the Superintendent, and he looked up at them both, searching their faces with his piercing blue eyes. Perry said: "Franjo, there's nothing for you to worry about, but I wonder if we could all go to your room and have a chat?" He hoped Franjo got the message: he didn't want him to launch into a guilty explanation of their plans of the previous day, nor did he want to give him any needless anxiety.

"As you wish, my friend, I am at your disposal." Franjo jerked his chair away from Ben and started to wheel himself in the direction of the new block. Perry noticed that Ben looked distinctly nervous. He could only hope the Superintendent didn't decide to question him: Ben would stand no chance of keeping their deliberations secret when faced with even the mildest interrogation.

On the way to Franjo's room, the Superintendent made small talk: "I must say I admire your grounds here, they always look so tidy. I can't even keep my garden in order in the summer."

"But you are so busy man, I am sure, Superintendent. Gardening needs patience; a little work every day, a small improvement every day. It is like chess; you play?"

Superintendent Mackie had to admit that he didn't. For some reason this seemed to please Franjo. By the time he had let them in to his room, he was in a relatively chatty mood.

Franjo manoeuvred his chair so that he had his back to the window and his face was in shadow. Perry stood up and the Superintendent sat in the one comfortable chair. "How can I help you, friend Perry?" asked Franjo.

The Superintendent began: "I'm afraid I have some bad news for you, Mr Mihailovic. We found your sister, Miss Joan Mayflower, dead at her home late last night. She'd been murdered."

Without thinking, Perry said: "I'm sorry, Franjo. Whatever she was, she was still your sister." He could only hope Franjo wasn't going to be shocked into any unfortunate revelations. If they could just get over this crucial interview, they might never have to disclose their plans.

Perry needn't have worried, Franjo took the news well in his stride. "Tell me what happened. How did she die?"

218

"She was battered to death with a golf club, sir. We've got the man that did it, a journalist called Edwards. We found him drink-driving soon after he left her home."

Franjo suddenly became animated: "And he has confessed? He has admitted this?"

"He admits to visiting her at home last night, and he was seen to drive away shortly after your sister died. We think he was searching for evidence she was holding to blackmail him. He didn't find it, but we did. He hasn't admitted to the murder, but that's not surprising."

Franjo smiled. "I see. Now I understand."

"I wonder if you could come down and give a formal identification of the body, Mr Mihailovic? As far as we know, you are her only living relative. Would that be right, sir?"

"Yes, there is just me left now." Franjo sounded grimly satisfied. He added: "I will come, if you take me. My chair can fold into a car."

Perry asked: "Are you all right, Franjo? Would you like me to get Ben or Dr Anderson for you? Or should I stay with you?"

"No thank you, my friend. I am fine now. She is gone. I am just fine."

Perry thought Franjo was being very unwise to parade, in front of a police superintendent, his evident satisfaction at the demise of his sister. He wondered if he should try to intervene.

Franjo continued: "Do not look so concerned, friend Perry. I make no secret: I did not like my sister. But, I did not kill her. How could I? I cannot leave this place without help, and I am here all evening. How could I do it?"

Superintendent Mackie offered reassurance: "I think you can set your mind at rest on that score, Mr Mihailovic; we're not looking for anyone else in connection with your sister's death. Whether Mr Edwards cares to admit it or not, we have more than enough to go before a jury." If you're ready, sir, we could go now. Get it over with."

"I am ready."

Perry helped to wheel Franjo down the drive and install him into the waiting police car. He said: "Give me a call when you get back, and I'll come over. In the meantime, I'd better get on to everyone here, to let them know what's happened, if that's all right with you, Superintendent? I'd rather they heard it from me than from the radio or the local press."

"That's quite all right, sir. A short note, stating the fact that your former fund-raiser has been found dead, would be quite in order in the circumstances."

Perry watched the police car turn slowly on to the main road, and then went in search of Wendy and Ben. He found them chatting together in the leather-craft workshop, and invited them to come up to his office.

Ben asked: "Is everything all right? You know, about our plans? Is it all right?" His nerves were shot already.

Wendy said: "I saw the police car in the drive as I came in. What's up?"

Perry replied: "Joan Mayflower has been murdered, but it's all right; we're all in the clear. She was battered to death with a golf club sometime just before eleven last night, when we were all together. The police are convinced that Edwards did it. They found him drunk-in-charge a few streets away, and he'd been there yesterday evening."

"Thank God we've all got alibis," said Wendy.

By this time they had reached the administration block, and on their way up to Perry's office they called in on Sonya to invite her to join the discussion.

"I saw the police car driving away with Franjo in the back," said Sonya. "They haven't arrested him or anything, have they?"

"No; he's just gone to identify her. The Superintendent wasn't looking for anyone else in connection with the death, but I thought I should have a quick word with you all about what we discussed last night. Apparently, Edwards told the Superintendent about his interview here with me yesterday afternoon, and he also tried to suggest that Joan was blackmailing Sonya and me, He was, of course, trying to suggest that others, apart from himself, had a motive for wanting her dead. Fortunately, I was able to reassure Superintendent Mackie that Joan was only using Edwards to dig dirt where there was none to be dug. In view of the fact that, at the relevant time, both Sonya and I were engaged in a meeting at my home to discuss our mutual problems, together with some highly respectable witnesses, the Superintendent was disinclined to believe Mr Edwards."

"So, if anyone asks, it's probably better if we neglect to tell them about our plans concerning Joan?" asked Bernie crisply.

"I think so," agreed Wendy. "We should steer well clear of the whole thing, if we can."

Sonya also agreed: "If we tell him it might look as if we'd got something to hide, and we don't want Edwards to suggest he was acting under instructions from us."

Ben had said nothing since he'd heard the news. Perry asked: "Is that all right with you, Ben?" His voice echoed his obvious concern.

"Oh yes. I think you're right not to say anything. If anyone comes round asking me, I'm just going to refuse to say anything until I've got a lawyer or a doctor present. My nerves are bad enough as it is, so I think that would be the best line for me to take."

Perry was grateful Ben was being so sensible. Perhaps he would get Dr Anderson to look in on him later in the day. He said: "If we're all agreed, I'll phone Pam and let her know. From what I can tell, I don't think it's very likely the police will ask any of us, except, perhaps, to confirm our alibis."

Sonya remarked: "It's not as if we're perverting the course of justice or anything like that by keeping quiet. It's obvious Edwards did it. In a way, we should be grateful to him: he's saved us the trouble of dealing with Joan ourselves, and he chose an excellent time to do it, when we were all together."

Bernie said: "It's a good job we don't have to put our little plan into action. If he went round to see Joan last night, it can only have been because he was going to betray us. I'm afraid it looks as though we were much less formidable adversaries then we thought. Still, at least we shouldn't have any difficulty with the local press over this: I wonder how they'll write it up, without their star reporter?"

Sonya remarked: "He may not have been very distinguished as a writer, but he'll certainly make headlines in the papers over this, and serve him right too."

As there was nothing more to discuss, they all went back to their duties, and Perry phoned Pam. She was surprised and very relieved Perry had been at home at the relevant time. "What a good thing we didn't need to put your scheme into action, darling; with a little worm like that, who knows how it would have turned out."

By the time Perry had finished his call, Dr Anderson had arrived. He knew nothing about Joan Mayflower's death and, when Perry tactfully explained their ex-fund-raiser had been found dead, with her head bashed in, he remarked: "I'm sorry to hear that. I understand she wasn't the easiest of colleagues to get on with, but no one deserves that. Do the police have any ideas?"

Perry said cautiously hat he believed an arrest had been made. He thought it better, in line with the Superintendent's indication, not to broadcast the identity of the culprit beyond the necessary circle. "Unfortunately, Joan had a somewhat tangled personal history, and that's why I've called you. You see, her brother is a resident here; Franjo Mihailovic. He's gone with the police now to identify the body, but when he gets back, the shock will really have sunk in, I should think, so I thought it prudent to call you, just in case."

"Well, that's a turn up for the book. I never had anything to do with her, but I've seen him a few times, and he never said anything about her being his sister."

"They didn't get on and the relationship wasn't widely known," replied Perry mildly.

"You were right to call me. Even if they didn't get on, she was his sister and shock can be a funny thing. While I'm waiting, I'll get over to the clinic; there's always plenty to do there. Give me a call when he gets back." With a wave of his hand, the doctor turned and headed for the stairs. As he passed Bernie's desk, he accidentally dislodged a pile of unopened letters. In all the excitement she had forgotten to sort the morning's post.

"Oh dear," she exclaimed, as she scrabbled on the floor, picking up the letters. "I'm afraid I'd forgotten all about the post. I'll never make a secretary."

"You have other compensating qualities," remarked Perry, as he and Dr Anderson gallantly bent down to help her. The task completed, the doctor went on his way. Reaching the exit, he called out: "It looks like Franjo's being driven back. I'll go up to him now."

With the computer still out of action and the post unsorted, Perry had nothing to do, and his mind ranged back over the events of the past few days. He felt as if a cloud had drifted away, as if, for the first time since he had met Joan, he could look up and see the sun in its heaven. Suddenly, he knew he had to see Franjo. He called out: "I'm just going over to see if Franjo is OK. I'll be back soon."

When he reached Franjo's room, Dr Anderson was just concluding his visit. Franjo was bearing up remarkably well, and had declined a sedative: "But no, doctor; today is a beautiful day. I wish to enjoy it. Do not worry, all is well with me." The doctor left his telephone number and said he would call later in the day.

"How are you now?" asked Perry.

"Me, I am fine. How are you?"

Perry carefully seated himself in the easy chair, so as to be on the same eye level as Franjo. "Tell me, how did you manage to get Edwards to do it?"

Franjo laughed: "My clever friend. Last night, when you have all gone to your home, I am sitting just outside my little window, by the roses which climb, and I think. Chess, friend Perry. You have captured her pawn, but you will not win the game. Only death will stop her. She would destroy my home here, the best I ever have. She would destroy my Wendy. She

223

would destroy you. Then I think a little more, and I see I have a chance to make it all come well. In life, there is only one chance, so I take it. This is the only way and the only time: when all those she would harm have alibis together."

"No one would ever think that any of us would resort to murder."

Franjo shrugged. "Perhaps not, but you have had so many troubles with her, and many murders are made for less."

Perry regained some of his composure. "What did you do?"

"I telephone to my dear sister and I tell her that this Edwards has betrayed her, that he has told you, friend Perry, all, to save himself. She was not surprised I telephoned to gloat. I know her so well, you see; it was exactly what she would do. And also I know what she will do then: she will call him to say she knows what he has done and she will tell him her use for him is ended. He knows what this will mean."

Franjo gazed up at Perry and smiled. "From there I can only guess how it happened. But I knew it would. Edwards had the hopeless position. He is afraid and can see only one way to save himself. He drives to my sister's house, obtains entry, and kills her. He has silenced the eyewitness to his great crime, but still he is not completely secure, so he searches for papers and tries to break in the safe, so he can remove evidence she has kept about him, but also, perhaps, to seek documents which he can use to keep you and your friends quiet. In this he is unlucky. Also, he has taken too much courage on board before setting out, and the police stop him near to my sister's house."

"So, now you know, friend Perry. What will you do?" Franjo was transfixing Perry with his sharp eyes, those eyes which had reminded him so much of Joan.

He knew what he should do: he should hasten away to Superintendent Mackie. And if he did? Franjo would deny everything. He stood up, and patted Franjo on the shoulder. "Nothing," he replied with a sigh.

Slowly, Perry walked away from the new residences. As he passed the leather-craft workshop, he could hear the sounds of happy chattering coming through the open window. Ben waved to him as he passed the design room. The birds were singing and the flowers were in full bloom. Back in the administration block Sonya would be busily raising funds and Bernie would be awaiting the arrival of Mr Barber.

Lightning Source UK Ltd.
Milton Keynes UK
UKHW02f2343091117
312414UK00005B/278/P